**Praise for the Novels
of LuAnn McLane**

A Little Less Talk and a Lot More Action

"McLane has a knack for rollicking Southern romances, and her newest is no exception."
—*The Cincinnati Enquirer*

"[A] fun and flirty contemporary romance about grabbing that second chance." —*Fresh Fiction*

"Macy and Luke are fabulous lead protagonists. They make this tale work as a deep yet humorous character study with a strong support cast."
—*Midwest Book Review*

Trick My Truck but Don't Mess with My Heart

"There's . . . an infectious quality to the writing, and some great humor." —*Publishers Weekly*

"This sweet, funny story of family, friends, and stepping out of the roles expected by others is a real Southern-fried treat." —*Booklist*

"[A] quick-paced, action-packed romantic romp."
—Romance Designs

"With her honest and comical writing, McLane brings us a spunky new heroine. Readers will enjoy quirky Southern characters." —*Romantic Times* (4 stars)

continued . . .

Dancing Shoes and Honky-Tonk Blues

"[A] comical and poignant modern-day rags-to-riches romance."
—*Booklist*

"Abby shines as the sweet and lovable duckling-turned-swan. Lighthearted comedy and steamy romance combine to make this a delightful tale of a small town that takes Hollywood by storm."
—Romance Junkies

"A hoot a minute . . . LuAnn McLane shows her talent for tongue-in-cheek prose. . . . [A] winning tale not to be missed."
—Romance Reviews Today

"A fun story filled with plenty of laughter, tears, and all-out reading enjoyment."
—Fallen Angel Reviews

"A fabulous story. . . . Get ready for a deliriously funny, passion-filled rumba in this book."
—The Romance Readers Connection

"A fun small-town drama starring a delightful . . . lead couple and an eccentric but likable supporting cast."
—The Best Reviews

"LuAnn McLane makes the pages sizzle. . . . *Dancing Shoes and Honky-Tonk Blues* is one of the better romances out there this month."
—Roundtable Reviews

Dark Roots and Cowboy Boots

"An endearing, sexy, romantic romp that sparkles with Southern charm!"
—Julia London

"This kudzu-covered love story is as hot as Texas Pete, and more fun than a county fair."
—Karin Gillespie, author of *Dollar Daze*

"A hoot! The pages fly in this sexy, hilarious romp."
—Romance Reviews Today

"Charmingly entertaining . . . a truly pleasurable read."
—*Romantic Times*

Also by LuAnn McLane

Contemporary Romances

Redneck Cinderella
A Little Less Talk and a Lot More Action
Trick My Truck but Don't Mess with My Heart
Dancing Shoes and Honky-Tonk Blues
Dark Roots and Cowboy Boots

Erotic Romances

Driven By Desire
Love, Lust, and Pixie Dust
Hot Summer Nights
Wild Ride
Taking Care of Business

HE'S NO PRINCE CHARMING

LuAnn McLane

A SIGNET ECLIPSE BOOK

SIGNET ECLIPSE
Published by New American Library, a division of
Penguin Group (USA) Inc., 375 Hudson Street,
New York, New York 10014, USA
Penguin Group (Canada), 90 Eglinton Avenue East, Suite 700, Toronto,
Ontario M4P 2Y3, Canada (a division of Pearson Penguin Canada Inc.)
Penguin Books Ltd., 80 Strand, London WC2R 0RL, England
Penguin Ireland, 25 St. Stephen's Green, Dublin 2,
Ireland (a division of Penguin Books Ltd.)
Penguin Group (Australia), 250 Camberwell Road, Camberwell, Victoria 3124,
Australia (a division of Pearson Australia Group Pty. Ltd.)
Penguin Books India Pvt. Ltd., 11 Community Centre, Panchsheel Park,
New Delhi - 110 017, India
Penguin Group (NZ), 67 Apollo Drive, Rosedale, North Shore 0632,
New Zealand (a division of Pearson New Zealand Ltd.)
Penguin Books (South Africa) (Pty.) Ltd., 24 Sturdee Avenue,
Rosebank, Johannesburg 2196, South Africa

Penguin Books Ltd., Registered Offices:
80 Strand, London WC2R 0RL, England

First published by Signet Eclipse, an imprint of New American Library,
a division of Penguin Group (USA) Inc.

First Printing, October 2009
10 9 8 7 6 5 4 3 2 1

This book is dedicated to singer/songwriters
everywhere, especially my son Tim.
Thanks for the music!

ACKNOWLEDGMENTS

I would like to thank my son Tim for sharing his knowledge of songwriting and the music industry. You helped me understand the mind of a musician.

I would like to extend a special thanks to editors Lindsay Nouis and Laura Cifelli for taking extra pains to make this book special. We worked right down to the wire but the end result was worth it!

As always, thanks to my agent, Jenny Bent. Your belief in my ability to tackle new and exciting challenges keeps me growing as a writer.

1

Of Mice and Men

"Eeeeeee!" Dropping her purse with a thud, Dakota screamed, and then shouted, "Get off, get off, *get off!*" While dancing in a circle, she slapped at the spiderweb she had walked into upon entering the musty cabin. With another squeal, she tugged at the cobwebs sticking to her hair, and then frantically brushed at her arms. "Oh! Oh!" Feeling itchy, she wriggled and squiggled, imagining there were baby spiders crawling all over her body.

"Okay, okay, settle down," Dakota scolded herself while taking shallow breaths. "Okaaaay . . ." After a moment, her rapid heartbeat calmed a bit, but then she felt a tickling sensation as if something was crawling between her shoulder blades. "Oh! God!" Wincing, she reached behind her back and slid her hand up her shirt, but the tiny tickling persisted just out of her reach.

She grumbled, arched her spine and tilted back her shoulders in a move that would have made Cirque du Soleil proud, but then in desperation tugged her T-shirt over her head. She slapped at her back with the sleeve and, sure enough, flung a big black spider into the air. "I knew it! Okay, now where did you go?" With a shudder, she squinted down at the hardwood floor.

With the curtains drawn, the room was in semidarkness, with the only real light slicing in through the open front door. "Aha—there you are!" Nervously twisting the T-shirt in her fists, Dakota crept forward with the intention of smashing the spider beneath her flip-flop. She even went as far as to raise her foot, but then stood there balanced on one leg, looking as if she were doing a karate pose. She swallowed hard and glared at the spider, but imagined the imminent pop and squish, and her foot remained poised in midair. "You can do this," she whispered fiercely, but could not bring herself to perform the deed.

Dakota concentrated hard, dug deep for her killer instinct. "Okay, here goes nothing," she murmured, gritted her teeth, and prepared herself to end the life of the spider.

"Are you okay?" a deep voice from out of nowhere questioned.

Jarred from her task, Dakota's head whipped up and around. She dropped her shirt, lost her balance, and took a step back, squishing the spider with an audible crunch. Her eyes widened at the tall figure standing in the doorway, blocking out most of the waning sunlight. "Oh, God—ew!"

She kicked off the flip-flop she had soiled with spider guts and blinked up at the giant man standing in the shadows. Well, he wasn't a giant—maybe six-two or -three, but to Dakota's five feet four, and that was on a big-hair day, he seemed huge and looming. His dark hair reached nearly to his shoulders, and equally dark stubble shaded his square, unyielding jaw. A black T-shirt stretched across a well-defined chest and seemed to test the limits of short sleeves that revealed bulging biceps. Faded jeans ripped at the knees hugged muscled thighs. *Day-um.*

"What made you scream?"

"Um . . ." Dakota inhaled a calming breath and was beginning to think she was in overreactive fight-or-flight mode when she noticed—*Oh, dear Lord*—that he had an ax by his side! With a gasp, she started backing away, thinking it had been a while since she had come home to Pine Hollow Lake, and perhaps things had changed.

"Hey, I'm not going to hurt you," he promised in a deep voice that sounded a little bit insulted.

I'll just bet that's what all the ax murderers say, Dakota thought while wondering whether she could scurry past him and run for the hills. She suddenly felt as if she had stumbled into a bad horror flick and she was Sarah Michelle Gellar. "I know karate," she bluffed, hoping he had mistaken her one-legged pose and screams for some martial arts moves. Fat chance, but it was worth a try. "So just back off!" Dakota quickly removed her other flip-flop and held it up over her head as if it were a samurai sword.

Yeah, right. Even though it did kill the spider rather handily, the flimsy rubber wouldn't do much damage to the man in the doorway. Still, knowing it was all in the attitude, Dakota wielded her weapon with all the fearlessness she could muster, which, unfortunately, wasn't much, so she narrowed her eyes and added in a low and lethal tone, "I'm serious."

"Are you, now?"

"Yes," she said in a whisper of warning, and waved the flip-flop so hard that the fake daisy adornment fluttered to the floor and landed near his feet, as if she had just thrown down the gauntlet. Not good.

After a brief moment of silence, he shook his head, making Dakota feel as silly as she must've looked. Well, at least his demeanor suddenly didn't seem so sinister, and that somehow eased Dakota's fear, but then she became a little miffed at his uninvited intrusion.

She was trying to come up with something haughty to say when she suddenly remembered that she was standing there in her skimpy lace demi bra with the little lock-and-key charm dangling between the pink cups. With her low-rise jeans hugging her hips, she realized she was giving him quite an eyeful. Exuding as much dignity as she could muster, which was none at all, she scrambled over to her T-shirt and hastily tugged it over her head.

"Okay," Dakota said with her hands on her hips, "just who do you think you are, busting into this cabin without so much as a knock?" She asked this in a snooty tone, since now that she had come to her senses, she was pretty much convinced that he wasn't a crazy backwoods killer. When her shirt felt funny, she realized she had put it on backward, and hoped he didn't notice.

He scratched the side of his chin. "Well, the fact that you screamed several times had something to do with it. Pardon me for asking, but just why did you scream, and why were you half dressed?"

Dakota lifted her chin a notch. "If you must know, I was attacked by a spider."

"Attacked?" he asked dryly.

She narrowed her eyes at the amused inflection in his voice. "Yes," she answered primly, and then further explained, "I walked straight into a huge cobweb, and the spider"—she paused to demonstrate the hugeness by opening her arms in a circle—"crawled beneath my shirt."

"So that's why you were half naked?" He leaned one shoulder against the doorframe and crossed his arms over his wide chest.

"I wasn't half naked!" she sputtered, but felt heat creep into her cheeks. Despite nine years in L.A., her Southern drawl suddenly returned with a vengeance. "And I have, you know"—she widened her eyes and put a hand to her chest—"aracnaphelia."

"You mean arachnophobia?"

"Whichever one means that spiders scare the ever-living daylights out of you." She waved a hand in the air, wishing he would come out of the shadows so she could get a better look at his face. Maybe it was because she was so used to metrosexual men, but for some reason his rough-around-the-edges appearance was making her female hormones kick into high gear. Feeling a little self-conscious at her wayward thoughts, she averted her gaze and looked around. "This place needs a good scrubbing."

"Well, this isn't a Holiday Inn. Look, I'm not sure where you were heading, but you must have made a wrong turn. You're at Willow Creek Marina and Fishing Camp. This particular cabin belongs to Charley Dunn, the owner's father. The owner lives in L.A. and hasn't been here in years," he explained, but then suddenly stood up straight. "Wait, who are you?" he asked bluntly, even though Dakota could tell he had just put two and two together.

"Dakota Dunn, Charley and Rita Mae Dunn's daughter." While angling her head to the side, she peered at him more closely, still wishing the lighting in the room were brighter. "Are you Trace Coleman?" She had seen pictures of the ex-bull-riding star, and the man standing before her did not look like the former hotshot Professional Bull Riding champion. But then she remembered her father telling her Trace had been forced from the dangerous sport due to serious injuries.

"Yes," he answered tightly.

Embarrassed at her incredulous tone, Dakota gave him a smile. "Well, it's nice to meet you. My father tells me you do a bang-up job running the marina." She moved a couple of steps closer to him and was about to offer her hand, but to her amazement he didn't make any move to enter the room or to welcome her there.

"So, are you just checking up on things? Passing through?" Any hint of friendliness was suddenly gone, replaced with a distinct you-don't-belong-here attitude.

"No, I'm moving in," Dakota answered a bit stiffly. "I need some peace and quiet for a change," she added, leaving out the fact that this marina was the only thing left in the world that she owned and she had nowhere else to go unless she headed to Florida and lived with her parents. *No, thank you.*

"Oh." He seemed annoyed. "But it *is* temporary, right?"

Dakota shrugged, since she didn't really know the answer to his question. She certainly hoped so; living in a fishing camp cabin was a far cry from her house in L.A. But she didn't think it was necessary to explain to Trace Coleman that her bubblegum pop days were long gone, or that her record label had released her several years ago.

"So you're not sure?" he persisted.

"I'm reevaluating my career choices," she responded vaguely. "I thought Daddy's cabin would be a good place to—"

"Reevaluate?" He pinned her with a sharp look and waited.

"Yes." She knew what this marina meant to the community, and she wanted to assure him that she wasn't there to sell the property. But unless she got her act together, she might have to, so she refrained from making promises she couldn't keep. Her manager had advised her that if she wanted to salvage her music career, she must ditch her wholesome, squeaky-clean image. She had been instructed to sex up her brand and return to her redneck roots, with the hope of breaking into the hot country music scene.

There was only one problem: Her upbringing was Southern middle class, and her demeanor more genteel than redneck. Her manager wanted a kick-ass Gretchen Wilson or Miranda Lambert, but Dakota was more sugar and spice than gunpowder and lead. Although L.A. had broadened her horizons, she was still more at home at a potluck social than in a honkytonk bar. "Plus, I have some serious songwriting to accomplish."

"And you think this fishing camp will inspire you?"

"Yes," she repeated softly, more to herself than to Trace. She suddenly felt a bit lost and alone as she gazed around the sparsely furnished cabin. Her career had skyrocketed her to the top, but she had quickly fizzled, and then landed with a resounding thud, not unlike many teen stars. But hard work and determination had always been her strong suit, so Dakota planned to dig deep for her inner redneck and give it her best shot. Perhaps big, bad, and broody over there could lend her a helping hand in that direction. She angled her head at the rough-and-tumble cowboy. "That's my plan anyway."

"Yeah?" he said in an irritated tone. "Well, good luck with that one."

You'd better hope so was on the tip of her tongue, but he folded his arms across his chest, causing a ripple of muscle that chased her train of thought right out the window.

Trace swallowed hard. It had been a long time since a gorgeous woman had looked at him with such unbridled interest. And after just having seen her breasts all but spilling out of her lacy bra like a Victoria's Secret model's, he was suddenly breaking into a sweat despite the cool evening breeze blowing at his back.

I do not need this, he thought.

"So you're sticking around for a while, then?" He knew his tone was chock-full of disapproval, but he couldn't help it. She might own the place, but she was clearly out of her element.

"I'm just going to lie low, write songs, and reassess things."

Trace jammed his hands into his pockets and gave her a look that said he wasn't buying what she was selling. He could feel it in his bones that she was holding something back, and he sure hoped she wasn't thinking about selling the property. Willow Creek Marina was his reason for getting up in the morning, and he couldn't even let his brain consider that possibility.

"I do expect regular business updates, though."

"Not a problem," he said. She probably had no earthly idea how hard he and his crew worked or what this place meant to the locals who fished here. Plus, a fishing camp was no place for a woman, especially one who looked like her. Even with her T-shirt on backward and her sloppy blond ponytail sliding sideways, she was still sexy enough to make his mouth water. "But listen, we're real busy right about now, and things can get pretty rowdy at night when the guys come back from fishin'."

"I'll be fine—trust me."

"I'm serious, Dakota." Trace told himself that it was because she was Charley Dunn's daughter that he felt a sudden surge of protectiveness where she was concerned. If Charley hadn't rescued him from what could have been a permanent perch on a barstool and thrown him into this job, he might still be sitting there, pissed off at the world.

"Really, you won't even know I'm around. I'll be as quiet as a church mouse."

"Right," Trace said with a deadpan look meant to remind her of her recent screams.

She put her hands on her hips and gave him a comical put-out expression that almost wrangled a rare smile from him. "Look, the spider thing was a fluke. I grew up around these parts. My daddy was a fishing guide, for pity's sake. I'm hardly a shrinking violet, Trace."

Oh, wow. The silky sound of his name on her lips awoke something in Trace that he thought he had buried in a deep, dark place never to be reached. But within a few short moments of meeting her, Dakota Dunn had managed to reach inside him and yank unwanted emotion to the surface.

And he didn't like it.

"Oh, really," Trace scoffed in a hard tone that was meant to tick her off.

"Yes, really." When she did a sassy little head bop he knew he had to get tougher.

"Well, let me explain something to you." Trace remained in the shadows but stood up straighter, even though it hurt to put his full weight on his bad leg. "This is a fishing camp. Full of men out to have a good time."

"I know that. I own this good ole boys' club, remember?"

Ignoring that pesky little fact, Trace continued. "Yeah, well, at night these guys come back in from the lake and party it up. They play pool and poker and try to drink one another under the table. It's no place for a woman like you."

"Like me?" She jammed her thumb at her chest. Of course, Trace's gaze traveled there, reminding him of what was beneath her backward T-shirt—a skimpy pink bra and lush curves.

"Yeah, like you," he ground out, becoming more and more annoyed at his unwanted attraction to her. After his career-ending accident, the buckle bunnies who had banged down his door for attention disappeared in a flash. Not one of them had come to his bedside while he lay there in the hospital, bruised and broken in more places than he could count. Nor had any of them showed up during his painful rehabilitation. Since then, he had sworn off women for life, and he wasn't about to let Dakota Dunn change that fact.

She had to go.

Trace decided he would have to scare her away, and, judging from recent experience, it shouldn't be too difficult.

"Just what do you mean by a woman like me?" she persisted, interrupting his thoughts.

Another wave of sexual awareness washed over him, pissing him off even further.

"Well?" She demanded sharply, but when she tilted her head to the side, her sloppy ponytail slipped sideways. Someone needed to tell her she really sucked at being a badass.

But Trace had to stifle a groan. Dakota Dunn was a heady combination of sex and innocence, making him want to grab her and kiss her crazy, rip that shirt off, and bury his head between . . .

Oh, damn it all to hell. She really has to go. Inhaling deeply, he knew he had to be a jackass, which was luckily something he excelled at. "A pampered, spineless, high-maintenance city chick who does not belong here."

Her golden eyebrows shot upward and she gasped. "Sp-sp-spineless?" Her eyes narrowed and she fisted her hands at her sides. "How dare you!"

Knowing he had hit a nerve, Trace decided to go for the kill. "You were afraid of a damned spider! These woods are filled with much worse."

"Need I remind you that I have a condition where spiders are concerned? I'm not afraid of anything else." She folded her arms over her chest and arched one eyebrow.

"Not coyotes, raccoons, or snakes?"

"No, no, and *no*!" she insisted.

"Or mice?"

"No!" she said, but her eyes widened just a fraction and she swallowed hard.

"Well, that's good."

"Why?"

"Because one just scurried across the floor right behind you. This cabin has been closed up for a while. It's probably infested with them."

She blinked rapidly but shook her head. "You're just messin' with me."

Trace raked his fingers through his shaggy hair, and then shrugged. "Whatever you think," he casually replied, but then made a show of looking over her shoulder and raising his eyebrows.

"Oh, come on—I'm not stupid. You don't want me here at this camp so you're trying to frighten me away. Well, Trace Coleman, I'm not afraid of a little ole mouse or"—she took a step closer, giving Trace a whiff of her delicate perfume—"big, bad you!"

"Is that right?"

"Yes!"

"Okay, then." Deciding it was time Dakota got a good look at him, Trace reached over on the wall and flicked the light switch.

Then he limped into the room.

2

Who's the Boss?

Dakota blinked in the sudden bright light burning directly overhead, but couldn't keep her eyes from widening when Trace came into the cabin. His limp was a pronounced, almost angry gait, and she would have backed up a step but instinct told her he was still trying to intimidate her, so she held her ground. But barely.

When she didn't budge, he turned his head to the side in a sharp movement meant to draw her attention to a thin pink scar that started at the outer corner of his left eye, bisected his cheekbone, and then disappeared into the dark stubble shading his jaw. Vivid images of a fierce bull tossing him to the ground and stomping on him came to life in her head, causing her to shudder. "Ohmigod," she said softly. The pain reflected in his light blue eyes told Dakota he had mistaken her shudder for horror at the sight of his scar. "Trace—"

"Not pretty, huh?" Trace took a step closer, towering over her, and even though her heart was thudding, Dakota looked up at him with what she hoped was a you-don't-scare-me expression. But it wasn't entirely genuine. While she didn't find the scar offensive, it did give him a dangerous edge that made her heart pound harder. There was an angry-at-the-world aura about him, and yet something vulnerable flickered in his eyes, making Dakota want to reach out to him. For a moment his expression softened, but then he seemed to catch himself and glared down at her.

"Trace, you misunderstood, I—"

"Save it," he interrupted curtly.

"No, listen," Dakota began, but in her peripheral vision she spotted something small and furry scurry across the floor. The mouse! So Trace hadn't been lying, but she had been when she had said she wasn't afraid of them. A scream gurgled up in her throat. Not wanting to show her fear, Dakota put a curled fist to her lips and tried to disguise it as a cough, but it came out a high-pitched "Urrrrhhhh."

Trace gave her a funny look, as if he couldn't quite make sense of her odd noise, but he also looked a bit smug, undoubtedly thinking his scare tactics were working. "Are you okay?"

"Fine and dandy." Dakota stood up a little straighter and placed her hands on her hips while trying not to think about the probability of mice hidden in the shadows. Although Dakota knew she didn't look it, she was made of sterner stuff than what most people imagined. Leaving her home and family at sixteen had taken guts, and not everyone could get up in front of thousands of people and sing. Regular domestic animals didn't bother her in the least. In fact, she was an animal lover, but rodents and spiders were on her short list of things that made her shiver.

Dakota saw the mouse dart back across the floor, this time toward the door. *Yes, leave*, Dakota prayed.

Head for the woods and never come back! She made a mental note to get a cat, but just when she thought the coast was clear, the little critter did an about-face and sat on his haunches behind Trace, as if mocking her.

"I'm not afraid of you," Dakota muttered while eyeing the mouse.

"You sure about that?" Trace asked, obviously thinking she was referring to him.

"Yes!" she answered, but when the mouse inched forward in her general direction, she imagined it climbing up her leg, which was silly, she knew, but still . . . "Urrrrhhhh!" She did the cough/scream noise again, telling herself it was only a stupid little mouse and she could crush it beneath her flip-flop. But when that nasty image entered her head, she covered her mouth with her hand.

"Are you sure you're okay?" Trace asked.

His concern had a bit of a bite to it, since it ticked him off that his appearance was so disgusting to her. He knew the scar was ugly and he was trying to frighten her off, but *damn*, she was all but gagging. Her amber eyes rounded in fear, even though she had the decency to try to disguise her scream again with a ridiculous-sounding cough. If he still possessed a sense of humor, he supposed he might find the situation somewhat darkly amusing. But he didn't. Now all he wanted to do was to get the hell away from her, because in spite of it all, he was feeling a pull of attraction that he just couldn't shake.

"I, uh . . ." She caught her bottom lip between her teeth and took a step backward.

"Dakota," Trace began, deciding he had taken this a bit too far. "Do you need to sit down or something?" After all, she did own the place, and if he wasn't careful his job might be in jeopardy. "Look, I'll send some-one up to help clean up and set some mouse traps."

Her eyes widened. "And kill it?"

Trace gave her a deadpan look. "No, take it into pro-tective custody," he answered dryly, but then frowned. "Wait, what do you mean *it*?" Trace asked, but then saw his furry little bluff scurry past him.

Dakota started to backpedal.

"Dakota! Stop!" Trace warned when he spotted shards of brown broken glass scattered on the floor be-hind her, no doubt from kids sneaking into the vacant cabin to party. If she took one more step, her bare foot would likely get cut. "Don't move!" he shouted, but she was fixated on the stupid mouse and ignored his plea.

"Damn it, Dakota!" Trace rushed forward, cursing his lame leg. Reaching out, he snaked his arm around her waist and they stumbled backward, smacking into the wall with a thud. In the confusion, he had unin-tentionally grabbed her ass, and she was pressed in-timately against him. Her breasts pushed against his chest, and when he inhaled a quick breath, her light, alluring scent filled his head. Her cheek rested against his thin cotton shirt, and he was sure she could feel the rapid beat of his heart.

Trace supposed she was in shock, because for a moment she didn't move, and when he tilted his head down to explain to her why he grabbed her, she lifted her head up at the same exact moment. Their lips brushed ever so lightly, but Trace's body reacted instantly.

Her amber-colored eyes widened and then dark-ened to the color of barrel-aged bourbon. "What are you doing?" she asked in a husky, velvet tone that washed over Trace like warm, gentle rain. It took everything in his power not to kiss her.

"Saving your ass."

"So that's why you're squeezing it?"

"Oh, uh . . ." Trace dropped his hand and would have backed away, but he was up against the wall. "I didn't mean to," he ground out.

She gave him a sure-you-didn't look. "I guess you didn't mean to kiss me either?"

"I didn't kiss you." He didn't embarrass easily, and yet he felt heat travel up his neck. Dakota was somehow managing to wrestle emotion from him that he didn't know he was still capable of feeling, and he had been in her presence for only a few minutes.

And he didn't like it. Or did he? Frustrated, he said, "I wasn't putting the moves on you." But he suddenly felt the heat creep from his neck to his face. *Putting the moves on you? God, I sound like such an idiot*, Trace thought to himself. "There was glass on the floor and you were about to cut yourself," he explained tightly.

Dakota backed away a step and looked over at her daisy-topped flip-flop. "Everybody wears these. They are very popular right now," she added, as if she had to defend her choice of shoes.

"I grabbed you for your own good," he added firmly, "not to cop a feel. In case you didn't notice, you're not in Hollywood anymore, *Princess*. No paparazzi here." He leaned in close and said low in her ear, "And believe me, if I had meant to kiss you, you would have known it." He knew his behavior was bordering on flirting, and for just a moment Trace felt like his old confident self. It had been a long time since he had a woman in his arms, and damned if he didn't like it.

"Don't you think you're protesting a little too much,

cowboy?" Dakota leaned forward and put her hand on his chest, giving him a little shove for good measure. When she swallowed hard, Trace had to give her credit for standing her ground.

"You think so, huh?"

Trace looked down at her with those intense light blue eyes, but she left her hand on his chest even though her heart was beating like a jackhammer. The warmth of his skin seeped through his shirt, and despite his dark and dangerous demeanor, Dakota felt like running her hands over the soft cotton and pulling his head down for a long, hot kiss. Crazy. And yet for a heated moment, she could have sworn he wanted to do the same thing.

"Yeah, I think so." Dakota knew she was playing with fire, but she suddenly didn't care and stubbornly left her hand right in the middle of his chest. She knew she was coming off like a brazen Hollywood hotshot, but so be it. After being on top of the world, she was reduced to living in this old cabin in a fishing camp. She was tired. She felt lost, but she was far from defeated.

Mice or no mice, she wasn't about to let Trace Coleman run her off. The past year had been filled with worry and stress, and Dakota had been knocked around enough. Besides, she was supposed to discover her sexy, sassy side, and so she dug deep, arched one eyebrow, and tapped his chest with her pink-tipped fingernail. "Don't forget that I'm your boss."

He wrapped his big, warm, calloused hand around hers and stopped her tapping finger. "Not if I quit."

Her heart thudded and her pulse raced. "You're joking, right?"

He tilted his head to the side. "Are you?"

She licked her bottom lip, not quite sure how to respond, but took a step back. He still held her hand, and something she couldn't quite define shook her to the core when she felt her fingers slip through his.

Their gazes held, locked.

"Okay, look," she said, trying to keep the tremor out of her voice. She cleared her throat and attempted to sound matter-of-fact. "Like I said, I'll keep to myself and let you do your job. But you still have to keep me informed. Deal?"

When Dakota looked up at him with anxious, hopeful eyes, Trace felt another unwanted surge of protectiveness. Once again he had a suspicion there was more going on than she was revealing.

She extended her small hand, and even though she attempted to appear businesslike in spite of her backward shirt and sloppy, sideways ponytail, it was hard to take her seriously.

"I'll hold you to that," he said in a firm tone, and shook her hand. Her fingers felt delicate and feminine in his firm grasp, reminding Trace that like it or not, he was going to have to keep an eye on her.

"Listen, I live in that cabin right across the gravel road," he said, and jammed his thumb over his shoulder. He reached in his pocket and gave her a card. "My phone number is on there, but cell phones don't always get good reception and we only have a land line down at the camp offices."

"Thanks." She took the card from him and smiled.

"Don't call unless it's an emergency," he warned.

"I won't," she answered stiffly, and her smile faded.

"I'll send Sierra up to help you get this place cleaned up."

"Sierra? I thought she was the camp cook."

"I'm surprised you know her name," Trace responded.

"I know more than you might think."

"Oh, really?"

"Yes, really." She had a determined set to her mouth that took Trace by surprise, but he endeavored to maintain his bored expression. If she knew the measures he had taken to keep the camp and marina afloat, she might lose the attitude. "Sierra Miller is the camp cook, but she also cleans the cabins. She's around your age, but she's like one of the guys," he added, letting Dakota know in no uncertain terms that she was not going to fit in.

"Oh." She suddenly looked a bit lost again, but he steeled himself against giving her any friendly encouragement.

"Well, I have work to do down at the dock now," he said, then turned and headed out the door.

"Trace?"

He wanted to keep going, but her soft yet husky voice had him stopping in his tracks. He slowly turned around. "Yeah?"

"I'm sorry to have burst upon the scene without giving you any notice. My parents don't know I'm here yet, and for personal reasons, at least for the time being, I'd like to keep it that way."

"It's your marina and your cabin, Princess. I'm just the hired help." Trace shrugged. He really wished she would go back inside and not watch his halting progress down the fieldstone steps, but she came out onto the porch.

"Oh, and Trace, I might have been queen of bubblegum pop, but I'm hardly a princess. Believe me, I'm capable of cleaning up on my own. I'll head into Tall Rock later for some supplies."

She gave him a small smile, and damn it, she had a vulnerable, almost lost look in her eyes that made him want to gather her in his arms. No one, especially now, would accuse him of being a tender kind of guy, and he had to wonder where these unwanted feelings were coming from. He had just met the woman, and for some reason she had the ability to turn him inside out. *Well, enough of this crap*, he thought while absently rubbing his thigh muscle, which was beginning to tense up.

"Suit yourself. Just do like you said and keep out of the way," he answered tersely, and quickly turned away, but not before he saw the hurt look on her face. *Good*, he thought, and wished he could hurry down the path. But by this time of day, his leg ached and stiffened up and would stay that way until he could relax on his back deck in his hot tub. He'd be there already if it weren't for her interruption into his orderly day and simple life.

Still, as he walked down the gravel road, all he could think about was her pretty face and husky voice that was as silky and sweet as honey on a hot biscuit. A sudden image of her standing there in that sexy little bra had him wiping beads of sweat from his brow.

With a shake of his head, Trace wondered what the hell was happening to him. She was reeling him in just like the eager, hungry fish that were biting today, but he'd be damned if he'd let her. He reminded himself that women were shallow, callous creatures who loved you when you were up and kicked you when you were down. And in more ways than one, Dakota Dunn had the power to turn his safe little world at the marina upside down.

Maybe that's what you need slid into his brain, but he shoved it right back out.

Stay away from her, he told himself, but as he walked up on the dock toward his office, he couldn't resist casting a glance up the hill to her cabin. Sure enough, Dakota was standing there on the steps, but turned away quickly as if she didn't want him to know she was watching, and lost her balance. With a little squeal, she grabbed the banister to keep from falling. Trace shook his head and felt an odd sensation, and then realized it was because he was actually smiling. He rubbed a hand down his face and groaned. "As quiet as a church mouse," he mumbled. "*Right.*" Dakota Dunn was going to be trouble in spades; he just damned well knew it.

3

Talk Soup

Dakota barely refrained from looking over her shoulder to see whether Trace witnessed her nearly falling over her own two feet. "What in the world has gotten in to me? Can I please stay on my feet for two seconds in front of him?" she mumbled with a shake of her head.

Based on her recent klutziness, no one would ever believe she had been a part of the hip L.A. scene, even rubbing elbows with some pretty famous people in her bubblegum glory days. But then again, no one had ever thrown her for a loop like Trace Coleman did. *Must be stress or maybe PMS*, she told herself. Or perhaps her love life, or lack thereof, could have something to do with her reaction to a hard-bodied male sporting a wicked bad-boy attitude. Of course, she had other, more pressing things on her mind lately, like her shrinking finances and her failed career, and she reminded herself she had to keep focused.

After placing a steadying hand on her chest and the other on the banister, she made her way up the steps to the porch. Dakota paused, imagining some colorful potted plants, a couple of rocking chairs, and perhaps a grapevine wreath on the front door. She assured herself that with a little bit of sprucing up, the cabin could be clean and comfortable while providing the serenity she needed to compose her songs.

Dakota smiled softly when she remembered that she had written her very first lyrics while sitting on this porch way back when she was still in pigtails. She used to wander around the property with a pen and tattered journal, writing poetry and often falling asleep in the oddest of places, frightening her poor mother half to death. While smiling at the memory, she suddenly longed to grab her guitar and start strumming away, but she needed to get the cabin in order first. With that in mind, she took a deep breath and turned back toward the entrance.

"Time to get started," she said with determination. But when the door opened with an eerie creak, she caught her bottom lip between her teeth and cautiously crept into the room, careful to avoid another cobweb incident. "Don't even think about the mice," she mumbled, and then of course thought about them. Having the lights on helped, but the musty smell of loneliness clung to the air. With a wince, Dakota hurried over and opened the windows in the living room, and then stood in the center of the cabin and took a good look around.

"So much in my life has changed since the last time I was here," she whispered, but then swallowed the sudden lump stuck in her throat when memories of past visits filtered into her brain like a slide show. She closed her eyes and could almost hear the soft tinkle of her mother's laughter and her father's booming voice.

Although she had lived in a modest home in town with her parents, her father had spent a great deal of time up here at Pine Hollow Lake as a fishing guide, and as often as they could, she and her mother would join him. It had been one of her proudest moments when she had been able to purchase the marina and camp, saving it from being torn down and turned into a housing development with expensive lots overlooking the lake, unlike the small cabins that were tucked into the hillside, preserving the landscape.

Dakota walked over and gazed out of the front window. A gentle breeze filtered through the screen, bringing the scents of pine, earth, and water. Inhaling deeply, she looked out over the pristine lake that served as a haven for the hardworking folks of Tall Rock and the surrounding farming community. Dakota was well aware of the fact that she could have sold the marina and kept her home in L.A., but as she soaked in the beauty of the blue water shimmering in the late-day sun, she smiled, knowing she had made the right decision.

Her smile faded, though, when she reminded herself that she couldn't continue to fund her father's retirement and live off of revenue from the marina for much longer. Trace might think she was clueless, but she was well aware that gas prices and a slow economy were taking its toll on the profit margin. In fact, Dakota wondered just how he had managed to keep the marina in the black during these tough times. After a long sigh, Dakota turned away from the window.

She knew she should start cleaning, but the lure of a long walk along the lake suddenly seemed too enticing to pass up, and so she decided to go outdoors for some fresh air while it was still light out. She located her now daisyless flip-flop, and then hastily turned her shirt around before stepping outside onto the porch. After skipping down the steps, Dakota lifted her face to the warmth of the sunshine and smiled, barely resisting the urge to spin in a circle like Julie Andrews in *The Sound of Music*. Then she laughed out loud while thinking that fatigue was probably making her a little slaphappy. But for the first time in a long while, she felt a sense of purpose and hope.

As she crossed the gravel road, Dakota couldn't resist looking over at Trace's cabin, hoping she might catch a glimpse of the cranky cowboy. Her heart thumped harder when she spotted him walking, bare-chested and wearing low-slung board shorts, across his back deck. His halting gait reminded her of his leg injury, and she realized he was going for a soak in a large hot tub visible from the road. As if feeling her eyes upon him, Trace suddenly looked her way. Like a shy schoolgirl, Dakota averted her gaze and quickly entered the wooded trail that led down to the shoreline.

"He's just a guy. Stop being so silly," she grumbled to herself as she walked down a well-worn path, but then smiled when the glistening blue lake suddenly came into view.

With an excited intake of breath, she hurried forward but then tripped over an exposed root. She let out an alarmed cry as she thrust her arms forward in anticipation of landing hard, and fell in a puddle of mud from a recent storm. She stood up, but winced when her rubber soles sank in the muck. Something weird was on her tongue and she spit it out, dearly hoping it was a leaf. Letting out an exasperated sigh, she stood there for a minute and willed her heartbeat to slow down. *So much for a leisurely stroll*, she thought.

"Are you okay?"

Startled at the sound of the deep voice, Dakota staggered backward, but her flip-flops stayed suctioned in the mud, and she landed on her butt. She looked up at Trace as he took a step closer and frowned down at her.

"Dakota, what exactly are you doing?"

"Thought I'd do a little frog gigging," she answered breezily, while attempting to wipe the mud off of her hands. "A girl's gotta eat."

"Really?" he asked incredulously.

"No!" she answered with a chuckle, and waited for him to join in, but he only frowned. "I fell, okay? I'm not normally this clumsy, but I'm a bit out of my element."

He nodded as if in agreement.

Dakota tried to shake the mud off her hands, but managed to fling some onto Trace's bare chest, which she noticed was very nicely defined. As were his abs. She cleared her throat and said, "How in the world did you get down here so fast?"

Trace jammed a thumb over his head. "There is a direct path from the back of my deck. I heard you yell." He crossed his arms over his chest, making his biceps bulge as big as softballs, and gave her an annoyed sigh. "Then I thought I'd better see what happened. Again."

Okay, that did it. She lifted her chin a notch. "I'm fine. You can go now."

He extended his hand but failed to smile. "Come on. My path is easier."

"Yeah, that's what they all say," she muttered. Briefly, Dakota thought about refusing his offer, but didn't want to appear petulant, so she allowed him to help her up.

"Follow me," he said, but quickly released her hand and turned around before she could refuse.

A little irritated at his attitude, Dakota felt like rushing past him, but in mud-caked flip-flops and wet jeans, it was all she could do to keep up. She also knew that her attention should be fixed on the lumpy path, but she couldn't quite tear her gaze away from a butt you could bounce quarters off of. That's when she tripped on another pesky root and thrust her hands out in anticipation of falling, just as Trace came to an abrupt halt on the hill.

She was saved from falling by grabbing his butt, which felt as firm as it looked.

Dakota quickly righted herself as he pivoted to face her. "Sorry!" She blinked up at him, but suddenly found the situation unbearably funny. "Really," she continued, while laughter bubbled up in her throat, but she somehow managed to control herself. "I didn't mean to do that."

"I almost believe you," he replied in a deep deadpan tone, making Dakota wonder if he possessed a sense of humor at all. Her smile faded, and she decided to make it her goal to squeeze a smile out of him somehow, some way as she followed him up the path to his deck.

"Sorry to have interrupted," Dakota said with a glance at the hot tub. The steaming water looked inviting, but when he didn't make any offer for her to join him, she said, "I'll, um, be going now."

"Okay," he answered with a guarded expression that for some inexplicable reason made Dakota want to reach out to him. But of course she didn't, and when he turned around, she hesitated, searching for something to say, but then walked away.

When she reached the porch, she kicked off her muddy flip-flops, and after locating her toiletries, headed straight for the shower. She suddenly felt too exhausted to even think about spiders and mice, and even though it was still early, she ate a bag of pretzels for dinner and then headed for bed, hoping she would get a good night's sleep.

After a restless night of tossing and turning, Dakota woke up to the sound of birds chirping. While rubbing her eyes and yawning, she considered staying in bed longer for some much-needed sleep, but wanted to get started on cleaning the place up. Although still shaken by her unusual encounters with Mr. Tall, Dark, and Broody, she felt measurably better about her current situation, which, unfortunately, still wasn't what one would call *good*.

After changing into denim shorts and a yellow T-shirt, she scrounged around in her purse for something to eat since she didn't want to go to the marina kitchen just yet. "Yes!" She smiled when she located a slightly mangled but edible oatmeal granola bar, and gobbled it up. The need for coffee was almost too dire to ignore, but Dakota made do with a can of Diet Coke left over from her drive.

"Okay, then," While dusting her hands together, she took a look around. The furniture was old but sturdy and had a certain rustic charm, and with some buffing the hardwood floor could gleam and shine. The plaid curtains her mother had sewn years ago were faded and needed a good washing, but complemented the cozy furnishings.

To the rear of the living room was a breakfast nook with a round oak dining table and four high-backed chairs. Dakota smiled at the plaid cushions that matched the curtain fabric, and remembered her mother humming as she sewed. Dakota had helped her tie them to the chair rungs with neat little bows, and then proudly showed them off to her daddy after he returned from fishing. The soft cotton had gone from bright red to muted rose, but only added to the charm of the cabin.

The colorful, soft touch of her mother's hand was everywhere, and Dakota suddenly missed her so much that it felt like a deep ache in her chest. It wasn't the first time that she wondered if the few years of fame had been worth the cost. In fact, she had entered the Miss Teen pageant on a whim, never really expecting to win, much less to become a singing sensation. Luckily, her mother had traveled with her early on, and instead of being a momager terror, she had protected Dakota from being exploited. Later, when Dakota had been advised to move permanently to L.A., her mother had returned home because of her father's heart issues.

Oh, how she had worried about her father and had missed her mother. She had desperately wanted to come home, but her parents had insisted that she stay and not give up what they thought was her dream. "Oh, boy," Dakota muttered as she leaned against a chair, shaking her head and chuckling without humor. Now she was faced with reinventing herself and returning to the road, or risk having to sell Willow Creek Marina. But the mere thought of bulldozers touching the pristine property had her pushing away from the chair. "No way!"

Dakota bit her bottom lip and massaged her fingertips to her temples, wishing she had gotten a better night's sleep. Swallowing hard, she pivoted to the right and entered into a galley-style kitchen. Knotty pine cabinets flanked a small sink with a window above overlooking a deck built by her daddy years ago.

A sloped backyard abutted tall trees that offered lush green shade in the summer, but that turned to burnt orange, deep red, and bright yellow in the fall, Dakota's favorite season and one she had sorely missed while in sunny California. Winters in Tennessee were generally mild, but not without an occasional ice or snowstorm that brought stark beauty to the lake. Although trips to the cabin in harsh weather had been few, memories of hot chocolate, games of Scrabble, and crackling wood in the fireplace brought another smile to her face.

And then an unexpected vision of Trace snuggled up with her in front of the hearth snuck into her brain. Frustrated, she turned away to explore the rest of the cabin, checking out the bathroom and closets while making mental notes of items to purchase. But when she entered the master bedroom and eyed the rumpled covers on the big brass bed, another vision of Trace had her putting fingertips to her lips.

"Ohmigod, just stop!" While grabbing the bedpost, she closed her eyes and then told herself once again that she had best stay far away from testy Mr Temptation. She was here on a mission, and the last thing she needed was to be sidetracked. She rested her warm forehead against the cool brass and groaned, "Mmmmm."

"So, there you are," Trace said behind her.

Startled, Dakota spun around so fast that she lost her balance, and in an effort to regain it, squeezed the bedpost hard. But her hands slid on the slippery brass and she fell to her butt with a thump on the hardwood floor. *Dear God! Not again!* She'd fallen more in the past two days than she cared to remember, and it was always in front of Trace. He certainly had an effect on her sense of balance. "Ouch!"

"Are you okay?"

Dakota glared up at him. "I'm fine," she answered tightly. "Must you keep asking me that?"

His dark brows came together. "Need some help?" he asked as he extended his big hand.

"No," she answered wearily. She wanted to hide her face with her hands, but he wrapped firm, warm fingers around her wrist anyway, and then gently tugged her to her feet. "Don't you believe in knocking?"

"I did knock."

"Really? I must have been . . ." She angled her head at him while trying to give him an I-wasn't-daydreaming-of-you-in-my-bedroom look. "I must have been thinking of song lyrics or something. So, when I didn't answer, you decided to enter anyway?"

He shrugged. "I brought some mousetraps and wanted to set them." He drew in a deep breath. "I have some work to accomplish at the marina, and I didn't want to have to come back later."

"Oh." The wind went out of her sails and she felt a bit childish. "Well, thanks."

He jammed his thumb over his shoulder. "I'm going to go set them now."

Dakota wrung her hands together at the thought of a little mouse trapped in such a painful way. "Okay," she said slowly, but when Trace turned to leave she added, "Ew, wait. Stop. No."

Trace turned around slowly. "Dakota," he began, and was about to shrug and let well enough alone, but the thought of her being in a cabin with rodents scurrying around didn't sit well with him. "The mice will get into your food. They carry germs."

She closed her eyes and pressed her lips together. "Can't I just get a cat?" she asked in a small voice.

"And just what do you think the cat will do?"

Her eyes opened wide as she looked over at him. "But that's nature, you know?"

"Look, you need to let me do this. You'll sleep better," he added when he noticed the dark smudges beneath her eyes. He gave her a level look while thinking how she had engaged him in more conversation in a few minutes than he normally had in an entire day. She was breaking through his carefully constructed armor, and he had better put an end to it right now.

"I'm setting them," he told her firmly. "I'll come by tomorrow, and hopefully after that, you should be rodent free."

Trace pivoted on his boot heel and left her sputtering her protest. When she didn't follow, he figured it was because she really did want the mice gone but didn't want to witness him setting the traps. Or then again, perhaps she simply didn't want to be around him, he thought, and waited for the feeling of satisfaction that just wouldn't come.

"Dakota?" he called after setting traps where she wasn't likely to see or step on them. When she failed to answer, he thought about simply leaving. But her lack of response somehow bothered him, and so he went looking for her. He walked to the bedroom and was about to inform her that the deed was done, but he stopped in his tracks when he saw her. She was curled up in the middle of the mattress, sound asleep, and for a long moment he stood in the doorway and simply stared.

Her golden hair had come completely undone and
fanned out against the green and white patchwork
quilt. She had one hand beneath her cheek and the
other one was balled in a fist near her mouth. Something hot and intense unfurled in his gut that went beyond sexual heat. She was doing things to him that he
couldn't quite comprehend or maybe just didn't want
to acknowledge. Unnerved, he glanced away, but the
sound of her soft sigh drew his gaze right back to her
sleeping form.

He knew he should turn on his heel and leave, but
the morning breeze blowing through the open window
was still rather cool, so he walked quietly over to the
bed and pulled up the edge of the quilt and draped it
over her. She stirred, murmured something, and for a
heart-thumping moment he imagined her opening her
eyes and reaching for him. . . .

Trace shook his head, trying to clear it. Even before
the accident, he wasn't a touchy-feely kind of guy, and
yet he longed to lean down and caress her hair, kiss her
forehead. And these tender feelings floored him. He
didn't even really know her yet. He shoved frustrated
fingers through his hair. There was no *yet*. He was not
going to get to know her.

She might have lived in L.A., but there was a girl-
next-door sweetness about her that was no match for
a scarred and jaded cowboy like himself, he thought
darkly. Trace turned and quickly left the room.

He closed the door quietly, thinking that she really
must not have slept much last night, and decided he'd
tell Sierra to come up and at least sweep out the dust
and cobwebs and bring some fresh linens and a few
basic supplies. As much as he didn't want to admit it,
Dakota was the owner and his boss. The least he and

the staff could do was make the cabin presentable for her, he decided, and then headed over to the kitchen to locate the camp cook.

"What the—!" Just as Trace pushed open the kitchen door, Gil, the fishing guide's dog, came blowing by him with a big bone hanging out of his mouth. Gil was closely followed by Sierra running after him with her fist in the air.

"Outta my way!" Sierra warned Trace, but before he could sidestep, she shoved him hard in the chest and he stumbled back into the open doorway. "Git back here, you mangy-ass dog!"

Gil, the full-blooded Australian shepherd, however, kept right on running down the dock with his stolen prize. Sierra followed in hot pursuit. Shaking his head, Trace watched, wondering who would fall into the lake first.

Grady Green, who was walking down the dock, tugged his ball cap up to watch the mad chase. "What the hell?" he asked when he reached Trace's side.

"Seems like your dog made out with something from the kitchen," Trace answered.

"Oh, baby, there's gonna be hell to pay," Grady said with a grin.

"You or Gil?"

"Both," Grady answered with a grimace. "Course I always seem to be gettin' in trouble no matter what I do, where Sierra's concerned." He scratched the side of his chin, which was shadowed with dark blond stubble. "Never done a damned thing to her, and yet she's always ridin' my ass for some reason or another." He paused and pointed. "Whoa, she almost had him caught!" Grady shook his head while chuckling. "Damn. Course she's a little bitty thing, so she's quick."

Trace turned with Grady and watched Gil take a sharp turn up the hill. Sierra gave it a good effort, but the dog quickly gobbled up some ground, leaving Sierra bent over and panting. Finally, she raised her fist and then slowly started to make her way back toward the dock. Trace noticed that she paused with her hands on her hips and looked at Dakota's BMW parked in the driveway, and then made her way down the gravel road.

"We best not be caught gawkin'," Grady advised. "Sierra might be little, but she sure is a spitfire when she gets riled up."

"You got that right." Trace nodded in agreement and followed Grady into the kitchen. Sierra was young, about twenty-three or so, but had a slew of brothers and could hold her own with the rowdy men at the camp. She might be small in stature, but nobody messed with her, and he had been telling the truth to Dakota about Sierra being treated pretty much as one of the guys. "Musta taken a soup bone," Trace commented when he saw the ingredients for vegetable soup on the long cutting board. "I think it was on the menu for tomorrow's lunch."

"*Was* is the operative word here," Sierra grumbled and then swiped at her damp brow as she walked through the back door. Strands of her dark hair pulled back in her customary no-nonsense ponytail were coming loose and curled around her face. She impatiently tucked a lock behind her ear and gave Grady a glare. "Your mangy dog snatched my soup bone."

"Sorry," Grady offered. "You want me to take you into town and get you another? You could ride with me and pick out whatever you need."

Sierra's green eyes widened just a bit and she suddenly flushed and looked away from Grady. "No, it would be too late to start the soup by the time we'd get back. I'll have to make something else instead." With her lips pressed together in agitation, she started gathering up the variety of vegetables.

"I'm really sorry," Grady offered again, and adjusted the bill of his black baseball cap, which sported a big fish and the phrase KISS MY BASS. "Is there anything I can do?"

Sierra paused and then pointed a carrot at him. "You can keep your dog under control, that's what you can do. This isn't the first time he's run off with my food."

"I'll do my best," Grady promised with his usual good-natured smile. "Gil's a good dog, Sierra, and you know it. Back me up here, Trace."

Trace raised his palms in the air while firmly shaking his head. "I'm staying outta this one." Although he had a bit of a hell-raising, wild streak, Trace liked Grady. He was a hard worker, and when he wasn't doing his fishing-guide duties he performed general maintenance around the marina, doing anything asked of him without complaint. In addition, he had disclosed to Trace that he was saving his prize money from fishing tournaments in hopes of owning his own bait and tackle shop.

"Yeah, well, maybe he is, and you're not a good owner," Sierra grumbled.

"Aw, come on, Sierra. How 'bout if I buy you a beer later on tonight down at Dewey's Pub to make it up to you? You headin' that way after work? Playin' some pool with the boys?"

"You mean you don't have one of your hot dates you're always braggin' about?" Sierra asked with a sassy little head bop.

"Naw," Grady admitted.

It might be Trace's imagination, but he thought Sierra looked pleased at Grady's no-date. Trace suddenly wondered whether Sierra secretly had a crush on Grady. She was such a tough little no-frills cookie and fit in so well with the guys that Trace sometimes forgot she was a girl. Maybe they all did, including Grady.

"But the day's not over," Grady added with a wink.

Sierra lowered her eyes, but not before Trace noticed the disappointment, and he suddenly knew he was right on the money. Funny, he thought, but he never would have picked up on it before his little encounter with Sleeping Beauty up at her cabin. Just the thought of her sent his dormant sex drive into full throttle.

"Earth to Trace," Sierra prodded with a shake of her head.

"Hmm?" He hoped she thought the sudden heat he felt in his face was from the kitchen stove.

Sierra flicked Grady a glance before turning her attention back to Trace. "I said to tell the guys that we're having chili instead of vegetable soup. Luckily, I have some ground beef in the freezer."

"Oh, sure, no problem."

"Your chili kicks ass," Grady commented. "You're not afraid to make it blazin' hot, just the way I like it."

Sierra's cheeks turned pink at his compliment, reconfirming Trace's suspicion. "Well, it's what you'll be gettin', like it or not."

"And corn bread?" Grady pleaded. "Please say yes. Your corn bread is better than my mama's, but don't tell her I said so."

"Yeah, and honey butter," Sierra promised, and started to smile, but then seemed to catch herself and frowned instead. Trace knew the feeling, and wondered what she had in her past that kept her guard up too? Something he hadn't thought about until now either. He shook his head, thinking that Dakota had really gotten under his skin in more ways than one.

"Trace, just where has your mind wandered off to again?" Sierra asked.

"Oh, did you ask me something?"

"Yeah, I was wondering what brought you to the kitchen. Was there something you wanted?"

"Oh yeah. When you get the chance, could you head up to Charley Dunn's cabin and sweep it out? Maybe bring some fresh linens and a few basics, like soap and toilet paper?"

"Are Charley and Rita Mae in town?" she asked hopefully.

"Mmm, no. Actually, it's Dakota Dunn, their daughter. She's been living in L.A. She owns the marina, remember?"

"Oh." Sierra's eyes widened. "Yeah. Hey, wasn't she famous or somethin'?"

Trace shrugged. "She had a few hit records a while back when she was a kid. Says she's here for the peace and quiet and to reevaluate. Whatever that means."

Sierra scrunched up her nose. "Sounds like some sort of new age mumbo jumbo."

"Is she hot?" Grady asked.

Trace realized that Grady was just being Grady, but for some reason his question pissed him off, and so he shot him a quelling look.

Grady took his ball cap off and laid it on the kitchen counter, and then ran his fingers through his slightly damp wavy blond hair. "Hey, I was just askin'."

"She's your boss, Grady," Trace reminded him firmly.

"Dude, I was just curious." He shook his head. "You two are too intense. Lighten up."

"Yeah, well, whatever." Feeling silly at his overreaction, Trace suddenly wanted to escape. "I'll see you two later."

Sierra nodded. "I'll head up to the cabin and give it a once-over and leave some supplies."

Trace nodded. "Thanks. See ya around, Grady."

"Yeah, see ya. Hey you wanna come into town tonight and shoot some pool? Toss a few back?"

Trace shook his head. Grady had been asking the same question every Friday and Saturday and always got the same answer. "No, thanks."

"I tried. One of these nights you're gonna come with me and have some fun."

"Someone needs to be here and keep an eye on things," Trace argued, even though that excuse was wearing thin. Although he didn't mind hanging out with Grady and Sierra occasionally at the marina for a few beers, he had no interest in going into town to socialize.

"Okay," Grady said with a shrug. "Maybe next time."

"Sure," Trace answered, even though they both knew he wouldn't. He didn't want to talk about his glory days or his accident, and he sure didn't want to go trolling for women. No, he was content right here, spending quiet nights at the marina.

4

Slip Slidin' Away

"What did you come here for, Grady?" Sierra asked after Trace left.

"A cookie," he admitted with a crooked grin. "I'm not beyond stealing one just like Gil, but I can't run as fast and you'd catch me and whup my ass. Can I have one . . . or three?"

"What?" Sierra frowned.

"Aren't those your homemade chocolate chip cookies I smell?"

"Oh, shit! The cookies!"

Sierra picked up a pot holder, ran over to the oven, and yanked it open. The cookies were browner than she liked, but not ruined. She grabbed the cookie sheet and quickly pulled it from the oven, but in her haste she touched the metal pan with her fingertips. "Ouch! Damn!" she grumbled. She set the cookie sheet on the kitchen island with a solid clank and then glared at the pot holder as if it were the culprit.

"Hey, are you okay?"

"I'm fine," she lied, feeling stupid. Her fingertips

tingled and she longed to blow on them, but refrained. "I must have forgotten to set the timer when Gil ran off with my soup bone."

"Here, you need ice on that," Grady insisted, and opened the big side-by-side freezer. After retrieving some ice, he came over to her side. "Let me see." Before she could protest, he took her hand and pressed the cold cubes to her tender fingers. "Better?"

Sierra swallowed hard and tried not to be affected by his nearness. "Yeah," she answered gruffly. "It's no big deal. Burned fingers go with the territory." She shrugged while he held her hand in his and rubbed the ice back and forth. "I'll live."

"Yeah, well, you'll feel better living without blisters." Grady looked up from his task and grinned. "You know, for a minute there I thought you were gonna catch Gil and wrestle that bone right outta his mouth."

"Yeah, there woulda been hell to pay," she responded, trying to sound angry, but her breathless tone blew that all to hell.

"I don't doubt it one bit," he agreed, and his grin widened to a full-blown smile. His teeth were white and straight, unlike the ones of some of the local guys Sierra knew who dipped or smoked. "And I think Gil realized it."

"He got me going up the hill. Guess I'm outta shape."

He chuckled, as if recalling the mad chase. "Are you kiddin'? You were like greased lightning." He frowned at her fingers, and then gently rubbed some more. He smelled of the outdoors and a hint of spicy aftershave and . . . *dear Lord*, did his eyes have to be such a vivid shade of green? Wavy blond hair that reminded Sierra of Paul Walker's in *The Fast and the Furious*, curled at the nape of his neck, just begging a girl to run her fingers through it. "You were hell on wheels, that's for sure."

"You're damned straight," she responded, trying again to sound big and bad but failing miserably. Water from the melting ice ran down her hand and dripped onto the floor, but she didn't care. It was a small price to pay for Grady's undivided attention.

"I hope you don't blister," Grady commented, and continued to soothe her pink fingertips. "Nothin' worse than a burn."

"Oh, I'll be fine," Sierra assured him, and had to hold back a shiver that had nothing to do with the ice. She knew he wasn't affected by their close proximity the way she was, nor did she kid herself that he was flirting, which kind of stung, because the attraction seemed so one-sided. But she would take what she could get.

Sierra had witnessed firsthand the type of girl Grady went after—tall, blond, and busty. And she was the polar opposite. While she stayed toned and slender due to physical work and endless energy, she wished for womanly curves that turned male heads. She tamed her unruly dark curls in a ponytail, dressed in jeans and T-shirts, and wore very little makeup. In truth, she longed to be more feminine, but her mother had run off when she was just a child, leaving her daddy and three older, rough-and-tumble brothers to raise her. She had always been treated as one of the guys and didn't know any other way to dress or act.

"There," Grady said after the ice melted to a mere sliver. "That should do the trick," he added hopefully, and then gently dried her hand with a dish towel.

"Sorry to have caused you so much trouble, Sierra. I know you work real hard and don't deserve this drama." Grady's usual cocky smile suddenly seemed tender, and when he reached over and unexpectedly ran a fingertip down her cheek, Sierra wanted to tilt her face into the palm of his hand and sigh. But she knew he was simply feeling guilty about Gil's behavior and nothing more, so she took a step back before she did something silly that she would later regret.

"You're just trying to get on my good side for some chocolate chip cookies," she scoffed, and turned away before he could read the truth in her eyes. She rose up on tiptoe to retrieve some Ziploc bags and then busied herself with sliding several crispy cookies into the plastic bag. "They're a little on the crunchy side," she warned as she handed him the cookies. "Might need some cold milk for dippin'."

"Thanks," Grady said, "but I can tell ya, they won't last till I get home. I'll eat every last one while drivin' in my truck." He grinned. "And I promise to give Gil a what-for on the way home too."

Sierra waved a dismissive hand at him. "Oh, don't bother. I get riled up quick but get over things quick too. But you'd better guard those cookies. That dog of yours will eat anything. He ran off with a stalk of celery the other day!"

Grady laughed. "I think he just wants your attention. Can you blame him?"

Sierra opened her mouth at his comment but was so flustered by it that she didn't know how to answer. But if Grady noticed her reaction, he chose to ignore it.

"See ya around," he said, and turned toward the door, but then paused before leaving. "Hey, the offer still stands for that beer. I'll be headin' in to Dewey's tonight after a power nap and a shower." He held up his bag. "And thanks for the cookies."

All Sierra could do was nod. After Grady left, she put her palms on the cool kitchen island and inhaled a deep breath. She suddenly pictured him in the shower with water sluicing down his body.

"Mercy," she murmured, and then wondered whether she should head into town later and take him up on his offer. The hard part, she mused, would be seeing the local girls hang all over him. Grady had been a star point guard at Tall Rock High School, leading the hometown team to a state championship. Even though he didn't go on to play college basketball, he was still considered somewhat of a hometown hero. Sierra had been two grades behind him in school but never missed a game, not that he would know it.

Sierra had been pretty much a loner in high school, never really finding her niche. It didn't help her social life that she had worked in her daddy's diner from the time she was able to fill salt shakers and sweep the floor. Because she hated waiting tables, she ended up in the kitchen instead and had learned her cooking skills alongside her father, until they were forced to close when they could no longer compete with the big restaurant chains that caused many of the mom-and-pop businesses to fold.

With a sigh, Sierra pushed away from the kitchen island and mumbled, "Better quit mooning over Grady Green and get my work done." Feeling a little drained, she reached in the fridge for a Mountain Dew and popped the top. After a long swig, she felt better. Then she slipped a Kid Rock CD in the boom box for added inspiration. In no time, she had the rest of the cookies

baked and spicy-hot chili simmering on the stove in a
big pot.

While rubbing the small of her back, Sierra glanced
at the digital clock on the microwave and wished it was
later in the day. She winced when she remembered she
was supposed to sweep out Dakota Dunn's cabin and
take her some supplies. "Well, hell's bells." Grumbling
under her breath, she gathered up some linens and
soap along with a few other basics and loaded them in
the golf cart that she used when cleaning the cabins.

Even though Dakota's car was still parked out front,
no one answered her knock. But wanting to complete
her task and head home, Sierra opened the front door
with her master key.

"Hello?" she called out, but when she discovered
that Dakota was sleeping, Sierra closed the bedroom
door, thinking it must be nice to be able to sleep in this
late. She decided to do a quick, quiet once-over and
leave the supplies. While humming softly, she broom
swept the floor and then lightly dusted the furniture.
Since they didn't offer daily maid service at the fishing
camp Sierra didn't have to clean on a regular basis, but
even so she had the drill down to a science. And so
her mind wandered, usually about what her menu was
going to be or supplies she needed in town. But today
visions of Grady filled her head.

As Sierra spruced up the bathroom, she wondered
how it would feel to be in Grady's arms and to kiss
him. But after wiping Windex from the mirror, she
paused to gaze at her reflection and shook her head
slowly. "Lordy, I need help," she whispered.

Wayward curls that had escaped her ponytail had
started to frizz, and her dark eyebrows, she knew, were
in need of plucking. She decided her mouth was one

of her better features, and she shrugged, thinking that her nose was okay. Not too big or small. She put her fingertips to her high cheekbones but had no idea how to play them up. And while she knew that her eyes—vivid green flecked with gold—were unusual, they were her best feature. But makeup and fashion left her totally clueless. Her few experiments with eye shadow had left her looking as if she should be standing on a street corner, and so she had quickly given up.

"Oh, well," she mumbled, and dropped her gaze from her reflection to the sink and finished up. After placing a small bar of soap in the dish, she leaned over to put a fresh roll of toilet paper in the holder when a high-pitched "Ohmigod!" startled her from her thoughts.

Sierra stood upright so fast that she lost her balance and grabbed for the shower curtain, which came loose. She landed with a painful thump in the bathtub. Groaning, she struggled to free herself from the clear plastic decorated with fish, but had somehow become entangled in it.

"Ohmigod!" Dakota yelped. "Are you hurt?"

"How the hell do I know?" Sierra looked up through the plastic and saw a blurry but clearly startled Dakota with her hand to her mouth. "Well, don't just stand there! Give me a doggone hand!"

"Oh! Okay." She started to bend over, but then paused. "Hey, just who are you anyway?"

"The damned maid service for your ass!" Sierra grumbled, sounding muffled behind the swimming fish. Then she reluctantly remembered that Dakota was her boss. "I mean for *you*. Hey, come on and help, would ya?"

Dakota reached over but tripped over the cleaning-supply caddy and stumbled. Sierra's eyes widened when Dakota reached for something—anything—to break her fall, and yelled as Dakota turned on the cold-water nozzle before tumbling into the tub.

"Holy crap, are you trying to kill me?" Sierra grunted after taking an elbow to the gut.

"Sorry! God that water is freezing!" she sputtered.

"Get off!"

"I'm trying! It's slippery!" Dakota yelled as the cold water pelted them. "The tub is filling up. Unplug the drain! I'm gonna drown!"

"You're not gonna drown!" Sierra shouted, and reached for the soap holder to hoist herself up. "Just stop squirming and calm down!"

"Easy for you to say. Whatever you do, turn the doggone water off!"

5

A Fish Out of Water

As Trace passed Dakota's cabin on the way to his own, he heard a little scream come from an open window. He paused on the gravel road and sighed, and then saw Grady pull up in his battered pickup truck and hop out.

"Hey, Trace, you got any cold beer in your fridge, buddy?"

"Isn't it kind of early?"

Grady laughed. "It's five o' clock somewhere."

Trace hesitated, thinking he had already experienced more conversation and interaction than he wanted for one day, but then nodded. "Maybe we can toss back a couple later on," he reluctantly agreed. If Grady was put off by his short answer and lack of enthusiasm, it didn't faze him.

"Cool—I'm on it," Grady said, and slapped Trace on the back. "Been a long-ass week, and I'm ready to cut loose. How 'bout you?"

"Thought you were going into town later on to cut loose?" Trace asked, but was saved from once again telling his young friend that his partying days were a thing of the past when another high-pitched scream followed by a lower-pitched curse came loud and clear from the small side window.

"That cussin' sounded like Sierra," Grady commented with a frown.

"Yeah, there's her golf cart," Trace commented while shading his eyes in the direction of Dakota's cabin.

"Wonder what the hell's goin' on?"

When they heard another scream, this time higher pitched and seeming to echo in the trees, Trace said, "We'd better go check it out."

Grady nodded. "Yeah."

Trace knocked on the front door, but he and Grady didn't wait for a response and quickly entered the cabin. They followed the sounds of the commotion coming from the hallway and paused at the closed bathroom door. Trace raised his hand to knock, but his fist paused in midair when Dakota said, "Move to the left. Dear God, I'm soaking wet!"

"I'm trying, but it's damned slippery and my hand is stuck," Sierra answered.

"Higher! Left!" Dakota said, and then she groaned. "You were so close!"

Trace turned to Grady, raised his eyebrows and mouthed, *What the hell?*

Grady stared back at Trace with wide eyes and shook his head. Grady and Trace turned their attention to the closed door and strained their eyes, as if hoping for X-ray vision.

"Right there?" Sierra asked. "Oh yes, I feel it too."

"Now wrap your fingers around it. Yeah, you're doing it! Whatever you do, don't stop! You've almost got it!"

Trace blinked and Grady gulped. *I hear water. Are they in the shower?* Grady mouthed.

Trace shrugged and tried not to think about the image that came to mind.

"Arch your back. Yes! Right there!" Dakota yelled enthusiastically, then she groaned. "Ugh, it's no use!"

Trace elbowed Grady and mouthed, *We should go.* He jammed his thumb over his shoulder.

"Not on your life," Grady whispered fervently, and cocked his ear toward the door.

After a thump and a muffled curse, Sierra said, "Maybe we can get the guys to help. Damn, I'm starting to shiver too."

Trace turned to Grady and whispered, "Help?"

"I'm willin'," Grady offered with a grin, and reached for the doorknob, but Trace stopped him with a sharp shake of his head.

"Are you crazy?" he whispered, and pulled Grady's hand back.

"No, man, but you must be! I've dreamed of something like this." He lifted his hands skyward. "Thank you, God!"

"It's hard to get my hand down this wet denim. Oh, damn, the battery's dead."

Dakota groaned. "We're going to have to yell for help."

"This sucks," Sierra grumbled.

"Okay, on the count of three, we're going to yell *help* at the top of our lungs."

Trace looked at Grady and whispered, "What are we gonna do?"

Grady grinned. "I don't know about you, but I'm able-bodied and willin'."

Trace rolled his eyes and thought to himself that Dakota Dunn was going to turn his orderly life upside down.

"Okay," Dakota began, "one, two, *three*!"

"Hel—" she began, and Trace and Grady burst through the door.

"That was quick!" Sierra said with narrowed eyes.

"What the hell?" Grady murmured from where he stood in the small confines of the bathroom directly behind Trace.

"Girls, what's going on?" Trace asked when he got an eyeful of sopping wet Sierra straddling Dakota. The shower curtain was twisted around them like a candy wrapper, with the rod just below Dakota's chin.

"Holy shit," Grady said, and got an elbow from Trace.

"We had a little mishap," Sierra grumbled, as if that explained the strange sight. "Would you two quit your gawkin' and give us a hand, for pity's sake?"

Trace took a step closer, wondering where to start. *Wet women wrapped in plastic . . . hmmm.* "Yeah, but how did you two get all tangled up like this?" He wanted to know, and glanced down at Dakota.

Her cheeks flushed a firecracker red and she said, "It was an accident."

"But—"

"Trace!" Sierra grumbled. "Ask questions later, will ya? We got us a situation here."

"You sure do," Grady commented with a sense of wonder but a tinge of disappointment in his tone. "Not exactly what we tho—" he began, but got an elbow to the gut and grunted. "Damn, that's gonna leave a mark," he complained while rubbing his midsection. "Okay, Trace, where do we begin?"

Trace rubbed his chin with his thumb and forefinger. "Sierra, can't you just stand up?"

"Right," she said testily. "I'm just doin' this for shits and giggles. My leg is trapped. Sorry there wasn't any hanky-panky goin' on, boys."

"We didn't think anything of the sort," Trace said, and tossed Grady a look of warning.

"Course not," Grady said in a mock-serious tone, and then arched backward to avoid another shot to the ribs.

"Right," Sierra grumbled.

"Grady, you grab Sierra, and I'll try to slide Dakota out of the tub."

Grady nodded. "Gotcha." He wedged himself between the toilet and the tub and then slid his hands beneath Sierra's armpits.

Trace pressed his back to the tile wall and bent his knees until he could lean over, and slid his hands behind her shoulder blades. "Damn, you're cold."

"Ya think?"

When she shivered, he felt the need to get her out of the cold water quickly, and looked up at Grady. "Okay, ready, Sierra?"

"Yep."

"Here goes, girls," Grady warned, and hefted Sierra upward. But when nothing much happened, he jerked a little harder.

The shower curtain made a suction sound and then suddenly unwrapped. Sierra popped free from the wet plastic so fast that Grady stumbled backward and hit the wall with a thud while still holding on to her.

Dakota thrashed in the cold water. She finally calmed when Trace yelled, "Hold still!" He grumbled and shot her a glare, but it was difficult to stay angry as she stood up, shivering, in her T-shirt. He inhaled a deep breath and tried not to notice how the wet cotton outlined her lacy bra, but he failed miserably and had to avert his gaze as he offered his hand to assist her out of the tub.

When she shivered again, he had the urge to wrap her in his embrace and warm her up. He had to wonder what kind of spell she had cast over him. *Damn!* "Here," he said gruffly, and tossed her a towel.

"Th-th-thank you," she said through chattering teeth, even though the towel hit her in the face.

"I've had champion bulls give me less trouble than you."

"I didn't mean—"

"Save it," he said rather curtly, and turned away. "Now that whatever the hell crisis this was seems to be over, I'm heading back to work."

"Hey," Grady said cheerfully, and dropped his arms from around Sierra. "How 'bout we all head over and warm up in your hot tub? "

Trace shot Grady a look that should have shut him up, but Grady just grinned.

"These girls are freezin', and I don't know 'bout you, but I gotta know the story behind all this. So whaddya say, Trace?"

No! the sane part of his brain shouted, but when Sierra and Dakota looked at him with wide, hopeful eyes and shivering bodies, "Okay, but for just a little while," came out of his mouth instead. He shrugged. "I've still got work to accomplish," he added, not wanting them to think this was something he really wanted to do. He didn't socialize, and they needed to know it. He was merely being nice. No, not nice. He didn't do nice. Accommodating.

"A hot tub!" Dakota's smile did more damage to his gut than being rammed by the shower curtain rod. "Oh, heaven!" she said with a long sigh followed by a shiver. "Thank you!" she gushed and clapped her wet hands together.

When Dakota looked as if she might hug Trace, he took a giant step away from her and almost tripped over the supply caddy. The bathroom was too damned small for four people, he decided, and backed out through the doorway. "I'm heading over to the cabin," he said quickly, and then hurried out the door.

Dakota scrunched her nose at Trace's back. "Well, he could be a little less testy about the whole thing," she muttered, but then noticed that his limp looked a bit more pronounced as he walked away, and felt a sharp pang of sympathy.

Sierra shrugged. "It's just his way. He's been through some major stuff," she said a little defensively.

Grady angled his head at Sierra. "Yeah, I get that, but Trace needs to loosen up. Get rid of that chip on his shoulder. Seems like the man hates the world."

Sierra pushed away from the wall and shook her wet head at Grady. "Don't judge when you haven't walked in someone's shoes."

"I'm not judging him, Sierra. Damn, girl, you need to lighten up too. You coming over for a soak in the hot tub?"

"I've still got work to do." Dakota noticed that Sierra's cheeks turned pink and she had to hold back a grin. "Plus, I don't have a swimsuit."

"No problem. Swimsuits are optional," Grady said with an arch of one eyebrow.

Sierra's cheeks flushed a deeper shade of dusky

rose. "Right, so will *you* be wearin' one?" Sierra shot back.

"There's only one way to find out," Grady answered with a wink.

"Sierra," Dakota said, "I have a whole slew of swimsuits. We just have to find what box they're in. We seem to be close enough in size."

"I should get back to work," she said with a glance at Dakota, but then shivered.

"I'm calling an executive meeting together at Trace's hot tub," Dakota announced with a grin.

"I'm likin' our new boss." Grady gave Sierra a nudge as he squeezed past her to the doorway, but then turned around. "Come on over and get warmed up."

"I don't think so."

"Suit yourself," he said. "Or then again, leave the suit off," he joked. But then he added, "Ya know, it's not often we can talk Trace into hanging out with us. Sierra, he needs the company whether he wants to admit it or not."

Dakota watched Sierra's expression soften and knew that Grady had found her weakness. "We'll be over in a few minutes," Dakota answered for them both. "Have the hot tub ready and waiting."

"Gotcha!" Grady said with a good-natured grin and then turned to leave.

After Grady was out of the room, Sierra inhaled a deep breath and said, "Just who do you think you are answering for?" She put her hands on her hips and stared at Dakota.

"Oh, come on. You're into Grady. Admit it."

"I admit no such thing!"

"Then you're lying to yourself. This is your opportunity."

"My opportunity for what?"

"Flirting with him, for goodness' sake!" She took Sierra by the hand. "In a hot tub! Come on. Let's find you a sexy swimsuit."

Sierra's eyes rounded and she tugged back. "No way, Dakota! I don't do sexy. They all think of me as one of the guys around here, Grady included." She shook her head. "Don't you get it? I don't have a sexy bone in my damned body."

Dakota dropped her hand and glumly admitted, "Me neither." While averting her gaze, she squeezed excess water from her hair and into the tub.

"What?" Sierra sputtered and shoved Dakota's shoulder. "You gotta be kiddin' me. Look at you! And weren't you famous or somethin'?"

"Yeah, right. That's why you have to *ask me* that question." Dakota rolled her eyes and motioned for Sierra to follow her. "After winning the Miss Teen beauty pageant, I was the princess of pop for a little while, with a wholesome, girl-next-door reputation. I had some hit records and made a lot of money in a short period of time, and then"—she paused and snapped her fingers—"poof, it was all gone in a flash."

Dakota kept talking as she looked through some boxes for swimsuits. She shook her head when she found a stack of old teen magazines. "Here," she said, and slid the box toward Sierra. "That was me. And no comments on the hair, please."

Sierra picked up a magazine. "Wow, you were on the cover! How cool is that? So were you like Miley Cyrus?"

Dakota shook her head. "I never got that big. You don't remember me? You're younger, but you would have been the demographic we were aiming for."

A shadow of sadness seemed to pass over Sierra's face, but then she shrugged. "I wasn't much into girlie things," she answered, but Dakota sensed there might be more to it than that. "So, do you miss bein' famous?"

Dakota hadn't ever really considered that. "I miss the music more than anything, I guess."

"Yeah, but wasn't it amazing singing up on stage?"

Dakota nibbled on the inside of her cheek for a second. "You know what? I never really did feel comfortable in the spotlight. I'd rather be strumming my guitar on the front porch. In fact, I can't wait to do just that." She found a cute bathing suit and tossed it at Sierra. "Try this one."

"So, then it all went to hell in a handbasket?" Sierra persisted as she caught the royal blue tankini that Dakota knew would look great on her.

"You could say that." Dakota looked down at a yellow bikini, wondering if she had the nerve to wear it, and then looked back at Sierra. "Listen, you promise to keep this between you and me? I mean, we are the only girls here, and we have to stick together."

"Yeah, you got my word," Sierra answered so seriously that Dakota instantly believed her. Her green, expressive eyes widened in expectation, and Dakota wanted to tell her she had very pretty bone structure and with a little work she could knock Grady's socks off.

"I'm here to make myself over."

Sierra raised her eyebrows. "Here? I thought people left this small town to do that."

"I've been told to sex up my image in a kick-butt redneck way, like Miranda Lambert or Gretchen Wilson."

Sierra flipped a damp lock of hair over her shoulder. "So what does that have to do with me?"

"Well—and I mean this in a good way—you're a little rough around the edges. I need to be more like you."

Sierra gave her a slow smile. "And I need to soften up a bit. Be more like you." She pointed at Dakota.

"Yeah. We need to tutor each other. I'll show you how to style up a bit. And you can show me how to be a really cool redneck chick."

Sierra pursed her lips. "What about the whole bein' sexy stuff?"

Dakota shrugged. "Guess we'll both have to practice up on that." She angled her head toward the door and wiggled her eyebrows. "Now is a good opportunity."

"So you are into Trace. Thought so."

"I barely know him." She arched one eyebrow, leaned forward and whispered, "But he's sexy as all get-out."

Sierra's expression faltered. "He doesn't think so."

"Because of the scar?"

"And the limp."

Dakota frowned. "That's silly. I barely noticed."

"Really? What if it were you?" She shook her head. "He was like a rock star on the PBR circuit. He was on top of the world for a while too. Had buckle bunnies chasing him down right and left."

"Buckle bunnies?"

"Rodeo groupies. No one has been bangin' down his door since the accident. Dakota, bull riding was his life. Now Trace is a loner. Won't even venture into town. It's like his spirit has been broken."

Dakota felt unexpected emotion well up in her throat. "Well, then, let's venture over to his hot tub and flirt our butts off."

"Think we can do it, little Goody Two-shoes?"

"Sure," Dakota scoffed. "I sang before crowds of thousands. This will be a piece of cake."

"You gonna wear that tiny bikini?"

"I wear it all the time."

"Liar," Sierra said, and laughed.

"And you know this how?"

"Hello, the tag is still hangin' from it." She laughed harder and slapped her knee.

"Oh." Dakota snickered. "Busted."

"You're not gonna wear it, are you?"

Dakota held the little scraps of yellow fabric up and scrunched up her nose. "No." She bent over and found a more modest pink two-piece and nodded. "This will have to do."

Sierra shook her head. "You'd never know you blew in here from L.A."

Dakota pursed her lips. "I was a fish out of water there. Come to think of it, I'm always a fish out of water."

"Me too," Sierra said softly, and then quickly contained herself. "Now let's get on over there before they drink up all the danged beer."

Dakota wrinkled her nose. "Beer? Isn't it a little early for drinking?"

"Oh, Dakota, beer drinkin' is Redneck 101. None of that sissy wine drinkin' stuff. And it's never too early for a beer. Remember that."

"Okay. I'll choke one down."

"One?" Sierra waved a hand in her direction. "Girly-girl, you got some learnin' to do."

Dakota laughed, and for the first time in a long while, she felt a measure of excitement that she had made the right decision in coming home.

6

Get My Drink On

"Damn, this cold beer feels good goin' down," Grady announced, and took another swig from his longneck.

Trace, who had experienced enough conversation for one day, merely nodded. He was a little ticked at himself for letting Grady talk him into inviting Dakota and Sierra over. He didn't want to socialize, and he sure as hell didn't want to see Dakota Dunn in a bathing suit. Well, he did, and that was the problem. He hadn't been able to get her out of his head from the moment he laid eyes on her, and the last thing he needed was her hanging out in his hot tub.

"How in the hell do you think those two got themselves all tangled up in the shower like that?" Grady asked with a low chuckle.

Trace took a swallow of his beer. "Beats me," he finally answered. "My guess is that it was Dakota's doin'. That woman has been a walking train wreck since she arrived—and she just got here. Claims I'll never know she's here. Yeah, right."

"Good luck with that one," Grady agreed. "She's flat-out gorgeous."

For some reason, Grady's comment set Trace off. "Don't even go there. She's off-limits."

Grady raised his bottle in the air. "Whoa there, Trace. I'm not making a play for her. I can tell she's on your radar."

Trace scooted up so fast that he sloshed water over the edge of the tub. "She's on my radar, all right. That little pop princess is a royal pain in the ass," he growled. "She's gonna be nothin' but trouble."

"If you say so," Grady said in a breezy I'm-not-buying-your-crap tone. "Guess they're not comin' over anyway," he added glumly.

"Good!" Trace took another swallow from his bottle, pretending he wasn't disappointed. "Now we can just relax," he said, and eased back down into the frothy, churning water. "I suddenly feel like getting my drink on," he announced, and tossed his empty into the nearby trash can. After it landed with a thump, he snagged another longneck from the cooler behind his head. "I know it's early, but what the hell. I don't do this much anymore, and today I feel like it." Thank God Charley Dunn had rescued him before alcohol had become a crutch. "You ready?"

Grady nodded and tossed his own empty in the trash and then held his hand up for another. "Yeah, buddy!" He caught the bottle midair and twisted off the cap. "Damn, that tastes good after working hard."

"Yeah, like fishing for a living is work," Trace said.

"Somebody's gotta do it. Might as well be me," Grady answered, and clinked his bottle to Trace's.

"I hear ya," Trace responded, and for a moment almost felt like his old self, when Saturday nights meant cutting loose with friends and having fun. For a while, some of his bull-riding buddies had tried to get him out, but when Trace flatly refused again and again, they had eventually given up. He had always known he was tempting fate every time he strapped himself to the back of a bull, and he had suffered his share of injuries and then some. What he hadn't been prepared for was to be cut down in his prime. Instead of facing his family, his friends, and his fans, he had chosen to lick his wounds in private. But right now he had to admit it felt damned good to hang out with a friend. "This beer sure is going down easy."

"You got that right." Grady sighed as he looked up into the trees. "Only thing better than this would be if we had us a couple of girls in this steamy, hot water."

Trace answered with a disgruntled snort. "Women are shallow creatures with a personal agenda."

"Whoa now, wait a minute. Sounds like you're describing me." Grady pointed his bottle at his chest and laughed.

"If the shoe fits," Trace shot back, but knew Grady Green much better than that. The young fishing guide might put on like he was a carefree kid, but in reality was a responsible, hardworking, all-around nice guy who deserved a good woman—if there were such a thing. Trace had his doubts.

"All the same, I wouldn't mind," Grady began, but then trailed off. He finished, "Well, hot damn."

Trace followed Grady's gaze, and his brain echoed the sentiment. Walking across the deck were Sierra and Dakota. Although they were wrapped in towels, bare shoulders and legs indicated bathing suits were underneath.

"Howdy, boys. Got any beer left in that cooler?" Sierra asked in her usual don't-mess-with-me tone, but Trace noticed she seemed a bit nervous.

"Sure do," Grady answered with a grin. "Glad you girls could join us."

"Well, hand a couple over," Sierra said in her gruff way, but suddenly seemed petite and feminine snuggled in the fluffy pink towel that must have belonged to the pop princess who was standing there quietly and wrapped in a matching towel. And then it suddenly occurred to Trace that, *hello*, Sierra was a girl. She fit in so well with the all-male staff that he usually forgot that fact.

"Bud Light?" he asked.

"Sounds good," Sierra responded.

"Dakota?"

"Oh, um, yeah. Bud Light would be fine."

"Comin' right up." Trace leaned back and shoved his hand in the cooler. He fished around in the sloshy ice for a couple of light beers and extended them to Sierra and Dakota. When they both stood there for a moment eyeing the beer, he realized that they would have to drop the towels in order to grab the bottles. He wondered why two perfectly fit women would worry about being seen in bathing suits. It occurred to him that he would never understand the opposite sex, but couldn't help but find their timidity somehow appealing. Women he had known would have been flaunting their bodies in his face.

"Hey, hand Trace your drinks while you climb up here in the tub," Grady offered. When they still hesitated, he said, "Girls, I think I can vouch for Trace when I say we're not gonna bite." He wiggled his fingers. "Come on, let me give y'all a hand up."

"We're comin'," Sierra said a bit defensively, and

Trace noticed that she gave Dakota a discreet nudge with her elbow. Then they both let the towels slide from their shoulders to the deck.

Although both swimsuits were modest, Trace heard Grady suck in a breath and had to fight from doing the same thing. Dakota's pink two-piece revealed just enough torso and cleavage to be sexy, but left enough to the imagination to remain enticing. Sierra's royal blue tank top exposed a few inches below her belly button, and the high-cut bottom made her legs appear long. Although Dakota's body was curvier, Sierra was definitely *not* one of the guys. And judging by Grady's dropped jaw, he noticed too.

"Well, don't just stand there. Come on in." When Grady offered his hand to Sierra, Trace felt compelled to do the gentlemanly thing and assist Dakota up the two steps into the hot tub. He tried not to dwell on how amazing she looked, but couldn't tear his gaze from her body until she slid beneath the churning water.

"Here you go," Trace said, and returned a cold bottle to each woman.

"Thanks," Sierra replied, but her gaze flicked over to Grady. Her cheeks were pink and Trace somehow doubted it was because of the hot water. It occurred to him that she was much prettier than he had ever realized, and knew that Grady noticed too.

"Mmm, yeah. Thank you," Dakota responded, and released a throaty sigh when the water warmed her chilled skin. She took a long pull from the longneck and found it surprisingly refreshing. She wasn't much of a beer drinker, but the ice-cold brew felt good going down. She drank about a third of the contents before coming up for air, and burped just as the jets turned off. And it wasn't a delicate burp, but a deep rumble that sounded even louder at the sudden silence.

"Oh! Excuse me!" Dakota said, but the unthinkable occurred when the end of her high-pitched *me* slid into another unexpected burp. Dakota turned wide-eyed to Sierra, who tried to keep a straight face, but then laughed so hard that she sputtered beer right out of her mouth.

Still laughing, Sierra leaned over and clinked her beer bottle to Dakota's. "Ohmigod, I wish we could rewind and see you do that again. You're gonna be a quick study."

"You think?" Dakota asked while wondering if she should be appalled or proud. Probably neither.

"Yeah! I could not have done better!"

"Um," Grady said while looking from Dakota to Sierra, "have you girls already been drinkin'?"

"Now, why would you think that?" Dakota asked, and just had to laugh. She took another long swig from her beer bottle, and for the first time in a very long while actually started to relax. Crazy, when here she was sitting in a hot tub, drinking beer early in the afternoon (and burping!) with virtual strangers. And yet somehow it didn't feel that way.

Dakota took another, more careful sip of her beer and looked at Trace beneath her eyelashes. It might have been her imagination, but she thought he appeared more relaxed as well. When he suddenly smiled at a joke Grady was telling, his features softened, making him look young and approachable. But just as quickly, Trace seemed to catch himself and his smile faded. She hated that he worried about his scar and longed to tell him that she had been surrounded by physical perfection and it was overrated.

As if knowing she was thinking about him, he glanced down at his bottle and then over at her. Their eyes met, and something unspoken passed between them, something soft and warm, something with a hint of sexual awareness that felt to Dakota like *hope*. When Trace's eyes widened just a fraction, Dakota knew he had felt it too. But when she smiled in invitation, Trace turned his head, showing his scarred side as if telling her to not go there.

Dakota felt a hot surge of disappointment and wanted to tell him that she might be frightened of spiders and rodents, but she wasn't afraid of him. And yet his obvious rejection stung, and so she turned her attention back to Sierra and Grady, who were bantering back and forth. Dakota smiled, realizing that Sierra might think she was simply giving back what Grady was dishing out, but in reality she was flirting.

"Now, Sierra, just what were you and Dakota doin' in the shower?" Grady asked.

"Just havin' a little girl time," Sierra answered, and then wiggled her eyebrows.

"You know you're killin' me," Grady responded with a groan, and sent a small splash her way.

"Hey, watch the beer!" Sierra warned, and put her hand over her bottle as Grady laughed.

The rest of the afternoon passed in a blur of beer and so many Grady Green jokes that by the end of the day Dakota's sides hurt from so much laughter.

"Well, I don't know what time it is, but it must be late," Trace finally announced.

"We're not goin' till the beer is gone," Grady protested, and slapped the water.

Trace leaned back and swished his hand around

in the cooler. "Well, we seem to have depleted my supply."

"Damn," Grady mumbled, and leaned back with his arms on the edge of the tub. The top half of his nicely defined chest was above the water, and Dakota noticed that Sierra was taking full advantage of the view. "Time for a beer run."

"I'll go with you," Sierra offered. "We can take the golf cart."

"No way," Trace said sternly. "You can still get a DUI."

"In that golf cart? I can walk faster than that old thing," Sierra scoffed. "Seriously?"

"Yeah, you can," Trace answered. "Grady, you're gonna have to stay here at the marina for the night. I don't want you driving your truck. Understood?"

"Yes, Dad." Grady gave Trace a sharp salute.

"Cabin ten is vacant. You two can bunk there."

"B-both of us?" Sierra stuttered. Her green eyes widened and she looked at Dakota. "I'm just gonna stay with Dakota. If that's okay with you." She kicked Dakota beneath the water.

Dakota wrinkled her nose and kicked Sierra back. "I don't recommend it. The spare bedroom hasn't been cleaned yet. I'd stay in cabin ten."

"I can get some fresh linens," Sierra protested.

Dakota shook her head. "And then you'd have to strip the bed and all that stuff. Don't you have to be here in the morning to fix breakfast for the fishermen anyway?"

"Sierra has Sundays off," Trace spoke up. "It's doughnuts and coffee for breakfast. I'll heat up the leftover chili for lunch, and then pizza later when the new crew of guests arrive."

Grady suddenly stood up, sloshing water everywhere. "I'll settle this right now," he announced, and then extended his hand to Sierra. "Come on, now. I told you I don't bite. I'm off tomorrow too, and we can sleep in. I will be the perfect gentleman," he added.

"Yeah, right, like you even know how," Sierra scoffed, but then swallowed hard and stared at Grady's hand.

"Hey, I resent that," Grady said, and tried, but failed, to pull off an offended expression. He leaned over and grabbed Sierra's hand. "Come on, Sierra, we're buddies. I'm not gonna try anything."

Dakota watched Sierra's face fall, but then she allowed Grady to hoist her up. "Yeah, like I'd let you. Try anything, buster, and I'll kick your ass."

"I bet you could," Grady said and laughed.

"You know it," Sierra shot back as she stepped over the side of the hot tub. She grabbed her towel and wrapped it around her wet suit. "I have to put dinner out for the campers. Luckily, it's chili, so no big deal."

"I'll help." Grady picked up his own towel, dried his chest and then slapped it over his shoulder. "See y'all later," he said, and waved in the direction of the tub, but then continued to banter with Sierra all the way across the deck and down the driveway.

Dakota was so intent on listening to their conversation that it took a moment for it to sink in that she was sitting alone with Trace—in a hot tub, no less. When Trace tipped the bottle up to his mouth, Dakota watched the long column of his throat as he swallowed. Her gaze dropped to his broad shoulders and then to his muscled chest that seemed deeply golden next to the blue water. His nearly shoulder-length dark hair was damp and slicked back from his bronzed face.

Male perfection, save for the scar that somehow made him seem starkly masculine and added an edge of danger that awakened something deep and wanton in Dakota's blood.

She inhaled a sharp breath, drawing Trace's attention just as the jets ceased. Her gaze locked with his. Sexual tension crackled between them, making Dakota want to slip through the water, slide onto his lap and straddle him. She imagined her hands on his chest and her mouth on his neck, licking droplets of water.

And then his deep voice interrupted her wayward thoughts with "I have some work to catch up on. You should go, Princess."

"Yes, I should. Sorry, I was just in a zone." She waved her fingers in the air, explaining what that meant for her. "I do that sometimes. I think I'm just really tired. It's been a long day." Knowing that she was talking way too much and that her face must be glowing as red as the end of a matchstick, Dakota decided to make a quick exit. She quickly stood up and sloshed water to the deck, knocking over several empty beer bottles. They clanked and thumped, making Dakota worry about shards of glass.

"Oh, no!" Dakota slipped back into the water and kneeled on the seat as she peered over the edge. "The bottles don't seem to be broken," she assured him over her shoulder, and then realized that her butt was perched and positioned just a few feet from his face.

Dear God.

Embarrassed, Dakota tried to turn around, but slipped on the slick surface of the molded seat and fell back in the water with a hands-flailing splash. She broke the surface, coughing and sputtering, and then flopped forward, falling facedown in his lap. Her knees throbbed but her injured pride smarted even worse, and she pushed up hard against his thighs in a frantic effort to back away, unwittingly thrusting her breasts mere inches from Trace's face.

Dakota caught the widening of Trace's eyes as she managed to push to her feet and back away to the opposite seat. Water swished and churned as if a sudden storm had risen from the steamy hot tub, but Dakota sat very still, afraid to cause yet another face-flaming moment.

"What was that all about?" Trace asked in a deadpan tone, making Dakota wonder whether he was amused or annoyed or truly wondered what the hell she just did.

"Water aerobics," she answered, and then flipped a lock of wet hair over her shoulder. Trying to remain flippant but dangerously close to tears, she inhaled a cleansing breath and said as calmly as she could, which wasn't calm at all, "I do believe I'll go home now." She managed a smile that trembled only slightly, stood up slowly, and oh so carefully stepped from the tub. With all the dignity she could muster, she wrapped the towel around her shoulders, gave Trace a brief nod, and then walked away with her head high and her back ramrod straight.

Dakota walked across the deck and down the driveway in the dark, refusing to think about beady little eyes staring at her from the surrounding woods. Then she shook her head while thinking she had been living in the city way too long.

"The spiders are gone and the mice are sleeping," she whispered as she flicked the closest switch. She turned the lock and leaned against the door, swallowed hard, and closed her eyes. Clenching her hands

into tight balls at her sides, she gritted her teeth and
fought tears of frustration, fear, and fatigue. But even
though the urge to slither to the floor and melt into a
puddle was strong, she refrained.

"Get hold of your sorry self," Dakota muttered
darkly, and then using the last bit of energy and determination left in her body, she pushed from the door
and walked to the bathroom. After turning on the light,
she looked at the shower curtain crumpled in the bathtub and put a hand to her mouth. The crazy events of
the past two days tumbled through her head, and she
once again wondered if she should laugh or burst into
noisy tears.

She decided to laugh.

Laughing made her feel measurably better, but as
she peeled her swimsuit straps down, she paused,
leaned against the sink, and peered at her reflection.
Frowning, she put her fingertips to the cool mirror and
said, "Just who are you, Dakota Dunn?" She had been
telling the truth to Sierra when she said she had been a
fish out of water living in Los Angeles. In that moment
she realized that for a long time she had been living her
life externally.

It was about time she started writing the songs she
wanted to sing, wearing the clothes she wanted to
wear, and discovering herself as a grown woman. She
narrowed her eyes and gave herself a silent challenge
to figure out what she really wanted out of life and
then to go for it, no holds barred.

Trace Coleman. His name popped into her head and
she smiled. "Now, there's a challenge," she said with
an arched eyebrow. "Are you up to it, girlie?"

Dakota was still thinking about Trace after she
changed into dry clothes. "He's as tough and hard-

nosed as they come," she warned herself, but those light blue eyes of his told a different story, drawing her to him in ways she couldn't even begin to explain. But she had promised to keep out of his way and to basically remain invisible around the marina, and that's what she intended to do. She would keep her word.

In the meantime, she decided to locate her guitar. It was about time to jump-start her career and her life.

7

Straight to the Heart

"I thought I smelled coffee," Grady said, causing Sierra to whip around at the sound of his voice.

"Good mornin'."

"Same to ya." Shirtless, Grady leaned one shoulder against the kitchen doorframe and grinned, causing Sierra to clutch her Styrofoam cup so tightly that the lid popped off.

Grady chuckled. "That was a cool trick."

"Been practicing it all mornin'," she said, trying to sound unaffected by his half-dressed appearance. Although she had seen him bare chested in the hot tub, in the light of day it somehow felt intimate. Trying not to blush, she discreetly allowed her gaze to travel over dark blond hair lightly covering his chest in a wedge that narrowed to an enticing line heading south. Worn Wranglers rode low on his hips and molded to muscular thighs, and for some reason Sierra found his feet to be sexy as hell. "One of those for me?" He nodded to another cup sitting on the counter.

"Oh yes, here." Sierra handed it to him and watched

him tip it back and take a sip. It wasn't fair that he appeared so amazing while sleep rumpled and unshaven, and she felt as if she needed a shower. She self-consciously reached up and tried to smooth her tangled hair. Loose from her customary ponytail, she knew it was a mass of untamed curls spilling over her shoulders.

"Mmmm, thanks." He held up his coffee cup in a salute. "So, we have doughnuts too? What did I do to deserve to wake up to this?" He gave her a lingering look, making Sierra wonder whether he was flirting or just joking around. Knowing how mussed she looked, Sierra decided the latter.

"I guess it's your lucky day," Sierra replied, trying not to be ticked at how delicious he had the nerve to appear this early in the morning. It just wasn't fair.

"Sure wasn't my lucky night," Grady replied as he walked over and snagged a cruller.

Sierra's heart thudded in her chest. "What do you mean?" came out of her mouth before she could stop it.

"Doggone raccoons kept me awake half the night." He took a bite of his cruller and licked the flaky sugar off his thumb. "How'd you sleep?"

"Like a baby." Of course, that was a big, fat lie. She had tossed and turned for hours, thinking of him sleeping on the other side of the hallway. She was beginning to get annoyed that she had lost a good night's rest over someone who obviously was totally unaffected by her in the way she was drawn to him.

"You go get breakfast dressed like that?" He nodded his head in her direction.

"Like what?"

"In my shirt?"

Sierra's eyes widened and she looked down at the

University of Kentucky T-shirt that he had discarded last night. "I didn't have any dry clothing, and you tossed this on the bathroom floor." She shrugged. "I didn't think you'd mind."

"No, I don't, but hand it over now," he requested, and reached in her direction.

Sierra's mouth moved, but at first nothing came out. "Are you serious? I don't have anything on underneath this!" Sierra sputtered, and then immediately wished she had kept her big mouth shut. "My swimsuit is wet."

"Sierra, I'm kiddin'," Grady replied calmly, but then had the nerve to grin. "Wow, you sure aren't a morning person, are you, twinkle toes?" Still grinning, he shook his head. "Why is it that I'm always in trouble around you?"

"Well," Sierra started to answer, but became distracted when he licked icing off his bottom lip. "You," she tried again, but when he leaned one hip against the counter and scratched his chest, her train of thought took a totally different path.

"See, you can't think of one little ole reason you need to give me a hard time." He polished off his cruller and dusted his hands. "Can you?" He took a swallow of coffee and said, "By the way, thanks for going after breakfast."

"I didn't," Sierra admitted, glad to have a change in the subject. "Trace must have brought the coffee and doughnuts."

"You think so?" Grady arched his eyebrows and seemed surprised.

Sierra nodded. "Yeah, he'd grumble if you thanked him, though. He acts like such a badass, but underneath it all he's a great guy. He just doesn't want anyone to know it," she added, but when a slow smile spread across Grady's face, she narrowed her eyes and said, "Okay, I'll bite. Just why are you grinnin'?"

"Nothin'." Grady rubbed his hand over his chin and then angled his head at her. "Just sounds like someone else I know." He gave her a pointed look.

"Oh, go on with ya," she scoffed, but then made the mistake of giving Grady what was meant to be a playful shove. When her palm made contact with his bare chest, a hot shot of pure longing traveled from her fingertips to her toes. And when she tried to pull her palm away, Grady surprised her by capturing her hand in his and bringing her fingers so close to his mouth that she could feel the warmth of his breath on her skin. "What are you doin'?"

"Checking your burn," he explained. "A little pink, but no blisters. Good. The ice did the trick." He examined Sierra's fingertips and then nodded with satisfaction. But when he looked at her face, he suddenly swallowed hard and seemed to forget to release his grip. "You know, I don't think I've ever seen you with your hair down," he murmured, seemingly more to himself than to her.

"At least not literally," Sierra tried to joke, but her voice came out breathless. She pointed to her mass of curls. "And now you know why. My hair takes on a life of its own while I sleep. Especially when I toss and turn."

His eyes met hers. "Thought you said you slept like a baby."

Sierra felt the warmth of a blush steal into her cheeks and looked away while desperately hoping for a snappy comeback. She might have come up with one, but Grady put his thumb and forefinger on her chin and gently forced her to look at him. "I guess I lied."

Grady seemed to search her face for a moment. "Me too," he said softly.

Sierra's heart pounded so hard she thought Grady must surely hear it. "So you got a good night's sleep after all?"

He shook his head slowly. "No, but it wasn't the raccoons that kept me up, Sierra."

"What, then?" Dear God, his eyes were focused on her mouth as he oh, so slowly lowered his head. With a sigh, he threaded his fingers through her hair, lifting the heavy mass of curls from her neck and cradling her head in the palm of his hand before capturing her mouth in a soft, sweet kiss.

"That's what kept me awake," he whispered in her ear, making her all but melt. "Wondering what you would taste like."

"Oh." Sierra was well aware of the fact that Grady Green had the reputation for being a big flirt. She knew she should guard her heart, but his warm skin beneath her palms felt too good. Still, she would have stepped away, but when Grady kissed the tender part of her neck beneath her ear, she was powerless to move. Then when he pushed her hair to the side and nibbled on her earlobe, a hot tingle shot down her spine, making her cling to his shoulders. To her horror, a little whimpering noise bubbled up in her throat and came tumbling out of her mouth.

With a little growl of his own, Grady pulled her against the length of his body. Sierra slid her hands up his back, loving the ripple of muscle beneath smooth, supple skin. Grady groaned, dipped his head and captured her mouth in a searing kiss that took her breath away. His palms slid to her ass, kneading and pushing her closer with only thin cotton between him and her skin.

As if reading her mind, Grady slipped his hands beneath the hem of the shirt and cupped her bare bottom. Sierra gasped, arched her back, pressing her breasts to his chest. She reached up and wrapped her hands around his neck, coming to her tiptoes to compensate for her lack of height while giving him better access to her bare body. "Mmmm." Her fingers found the hair at the nape of his neck, thick and silky soft.

"God, Sierra," he said, and then lifted her to the counter. She gasped when her hot skin hit the cool surface. "Wrap your legs around me," he pleaded in her ear. "God, you're driving me crazy. Such a little sex kitten in the mornin'. And damn that hair. I want to see it spread across white sheets. Bury my face in it," he said, and then scooped his hands beneath her ass cheeks and lifted her off the counter. "By the way, you look damned good in my shirt."

"I feel good in your shirt." Sierra, who wasn't much of a giggler, suddenly laughed with abandon when he whisked her toward the bedroom.

"Gil," Grady ordered, "git your sorry ass out of my bed."

Gil moaned, did a big, wheezing doggy yawn, and shot Grady a bleary-eyed you've-gotta-be-kidding look, but then obediently hopped to the floor and trotted out of the room.

"I'm beginning to like that dog better," Sierra commented, and squealed when Grady tossed her to the bed where he had slept the night before. The rumpled covers looked sexy and inviting. His male scent—musky, spicy—filled her head as she gazed up at him, breathless and heart pounding and unable to look away.

Sunlight streamed through the curtains and glinted off of Grady's blond hair. His chest was tanned to a deep bronze, and although tall and lanky, he appeared whipcord strong, born out of years of outdoor labor. He had an easy smile and warm eyes that looked down at her with such longing that Sierra suddenly felt unaccustomed moisture behind her eyelids. She had waited for a man to look at her this way for so damned long. Knowing it would be a mood killer, she blinked back the tears and gave him a trembling smile.

And then she reached out for him. "Come here."

Grady looked down at Sierra and wondered how in the world he hadn't realized how beautiful she was until this very moment. While she wasn't the Barbie doll type he typically went after, he realized that her beauty radiated from within. She was a hard worker and gave him a rough time because he was good at dishing it out. Come to think of it, Sierra was the only woman who really *got* his humor and tossed it right back at him. She was a tough little cookie, but looking down at her right now, with her green eyes wide and luminous and her full lips curved in a trembling smile, Grady realized with what felt like a shot straight to the heart that she might appear rough-and-tumble on the outside, but like Trace, she had a soft side that she carefully kept hidden.

And he had the power to hurt her.

All at once, Grady realized how much he had come to care about Sierra over the past couple of years, and she deserved more than a roll in the sack.

He couldn't do this.

"Sierra," Grady jammed his hands in his pockets and then frowned down at her.

Her eyes widened. She swallowed and let her arms fall to the bed. "Ohmigod," she mumbled, and pushed up to her elbows, ready to scramble off of the bed.

"No, listen."

"I'm all ears." She looked at him with wary, questioning eyes.

"Um," Grady searched his brain for something to say, but this was foreign territory. "I . . ."

"Oh, just go." She pointed a shaky finger toward the bedroom door.

"Wait—"

"Get the hell outta here!" she said through clenched teeth, and tried to glare but blinked rapidly as if holding back tears.

"Sierra," Grady attempted again, feeling like a complete jackass. He took a step back when she came up to her knees on the mattress. She had fire in her eyes and color high in her cheeks. The thought went through his head that she was magnificent when angry, especially with her hair a riot of curls tumbling over her shoulders. He was beginning to regret his decision. "Let me—"

"Get out! And take your mangy-ass dog with you!"

"Sierra, I didn't mean to—" he began, but had to duck when a pillow came flying his way. It hit the wall.

"Get out!" She was breathing hard, and when she leaned over to grab another pillow, her shirt hiked up, giving Grady a tantalizing peek at her cute little ass. With a squeal, she hefted the plump pillow over her head and swung it with all her might, this time hitting him in the head.

"Ouch!" he protested, playing on her sympathy even though it didn't really hurt. His ploy apparently didn't work, since she fiercely flung another pillow his way. Anticipating her move, he caught the pillow and decided to lighten the mood and toss it back at her.

Not a good idea.

The pillow plowed her in the shoulder, knocking her sideways and onto the bed harder than Grady intended. She bounced and came up cussing and swinging.

"Sorry, Sierra!" he said, not realizing he was a big guy and although she was a spitfire, in reality she was a little bitty thing.

"Why, you! You!" she sputtered but didn't finish, as if she couldn't come up with anything vile enough to call him. Grady took a step closer, intending to talk some sense into her, but had to duck when she took another fisted swing. When she came up with nothing but air, she spun around in a complete circle and came precariously close to the edge of the bed. "Whoa!" She teetered but caught her balance, and then looked around for more ammunition.

"Sierra! No!" His eyes widened when she hefted another pillow above her head and sent it sailing in his direction. Grady knew that the force of her throw would propel her forward, and so he lunged toward the bed, hoping to catch her before she tumbled to the floor. The mattress was perched pretty high off of the ground, presenting real danger.

Between Grady lunging forward and Sierra tumbling toward him, the impact of their bodies colliding packed quite a wallop. Grady grunted as he caught her in midair, and landed on the bed with a bounce. She straddled his waist, but her arms flopped outward onto the mattress and her breasts squished against his upper chest. The shirt scooted up her back, and Grady's hands somehow landed on her bare butt. The smooth skin and firm, rounded muscle compelled Grady to squeeze, bringing a screech of protest from Sierra. She pushed up with her palms, causing her hair to trail across Grady's cheek and down his chest.

"Get your hands off my ass," she grumbled, but her husky, breathless voice sent an entirely different message to Grady.

"What if I don't want to?" Grady asked in a teasing tone, knowing he should let go and allow her to run out the door, but he just couldn't help himself.

"I'm warning you."

"Ask me nicely."

"Kiss my ass."

Grady grinned. "Gladly." In an instant he flipped her over onto the bed. It was his intention to give her a smacking kiss on each cheek, give her a swat and then let her go, mad as a hornet at him, so that she would never allow herself to get in this situation with him again. Getting girls came easy to Grady, but relationships did not, and she deserved better than the likes of him. Ah, but when he laid eyes on her sweet little rump, his kisses lingered. She moaned, clenched her hands in the sheet when he pushed her shirt up higher on her back and kissed a moist trail up her spine.

"Though you look good in my shirt, Sierra," he said as he tugged it up to her shoulders, "you would look even better without it." He leaned down to her ear and whispered, "Take it off for me."

Sierra inhaled sharply when he slid his palms up her back. She hesitated, though, suddenly feeling insecure, but then turned over to face him. "What's goin' on here, Grady?" she asked softly. "Are you messin' with me?"

Grady felt guilt wash over him. He should not have sex with Sierra for a lot of reasons. She was his friend. They worked together. And he cared about her.

Sierra inhaled deeply and closed her eyes for a moment before looking up at him. "Thought so," she said, mistaking his reasons for hesitation. "Let me up, and you get your butt on back to your Barbie doll bimbos," she added while pushing at his chest.

Grady caught her hand and wouldn't let her budge. He gazed down at her and wanted to thread his fingers through her thick curls and kiss her senseless. But the longest he'd ever dated a woman was about three months, and that was stretching it. "Sierra," he said, prepared to tell her that she shouldn't get tangled up with a guy like him, when a little voice in his head whispered that maybe it would be different with her. Maybe it wasn't him, but the women he dated. Why not give it a shot? "Hey," he began, "maybe—"

"Maybe nothin'," she told him with a firm shake of her head. "Let me up, Grady." She pushed harder at his chest.

"I wasn't toying with you, Sierra." For some reason, he couldn't stand her thinking the worst of him, even though it had never really bothered him what women thought of him before this.

Her expression softened. "Look, we got caught up in the moment. As far as I'm concerned, it never happened. Deal?"

"Okay, deal," Grady said, but then felt a shot of disappointment in his gut when he realized she was giving him an easy out when she had a real reason to be ticked. She truly was different than women he dated and that, he suddenly realized, could be a very good thing. "But—"

Sierra stopped him with a finger to his lips. "But nothin'. I'm not your type, and we both know it. This would have been a mistake," she said, but something flickered in her eyes, and he had to wonder if Sierra had feelings for him.

"Okay." He realized too, that this was a way for her to save her pride, and so he nodded in agreement and then moved to allow her to get up.

"I'll wash your shirt and bring it to work tomorrow."

"Okay, thanks."

She gestured toward the bed. "And don't worry about the sheets. I'll change the linens too. Just toss the coffee cups and trash when you're finished with breakfast."

"Gotcha," Grady said, but felt a sense of loss after she left that he couldn't shake. He flopped back down onto the bed and stared at the ceiling. A few minutes later, Gil trotted into the room and hopped up to join him. "Hey there, buddy," he said absently. Gil, not one to be ignored, nudged Grady's arm with his nose. "Aw, okay," he said, and scratched his loyal dog behind the ears.

With a sigh, Grady mulled over the events of the morning, trying to make sense of his feelings and reactions to a woman he had always considered one of the guys—a buddy, someone to joke with or shoot a game of pool with. But the feel of her silky skin beneath his hands let him know that tough little cookie or not, Sierra Miller was all woman and then some.

It suddenly occurred to him that he always looked forward to seeing Sierra, and, in fact, bantering with her had been one of the many things he enjoyed about working at the marina. He dropped in on her every day just to say hi.

"I hope we can go back to the way things were," Grady said to Gil, who looked at him with eyes that seemed to understand, even though Grady knew his dog was probably daydreaming about soup bones and

chasing cars. "She said she would pretend this little incident never happened. Think we can do that, Gil?"

Gil yawned and rolled over, begging for a belly
rub. "Oh, all right." Grady came up on one elbow and
obliged. "I mean, I'd hate to lose her friendship, ya
know? And she's right. She isn't my type at all," he continued, but then remembered how amazing she felt in
his arms. "Damn." Grady shook his head, trying to get
Sierra's sexy and sleep-rumpled image out of his head.
"Who knew she was hiding that hot little body beneath
sweatshirts and jeans?" Grady glanced at Gil, who was
in doggie heaven. "I know what you're thinkin'. What
about friends with benefits? Think she'd go for that?"
He stopped long enough for Gil to give him a deadpan
stare. "Yeah, you're right. Not gonna happen. She'd
probably knock me right on my can."

Grady flopped back onto a pillow, tucked an arm beneath his head. "Guess I'll have to head on into Dewey's
later on and find me a sweet little thing to get Sierra off
my mind. Sound like a plan?" he asked, even though
the prospect didn't hold much appeal, and deep down
he knew why. He glanced down at Gil, who had fallen
asleep on his back with his paws dangling at his sides.
"Damn, dog, you've got the life," he commented with
a chuckle.

8

Busted

Boom, boom, boom, boom.

"What the heck?" Dakota mumbled and sat up in bed. Disoriented, she shoved her hair out of her face and blinked into the sudden sunlight invading her pupils. "Where in the world am I?" She glanced at the other side of the bed and then sighed with relief, remembering she was in her daddy's cabin and no longer in California. "Thank goodness."

She put a relieved hand to her chest, since she had thought for a wild moment that Trace might be lying beside her. She might have drunk dialed him a few times. Or maybe she'd just dreamed of being in his arms. Whatever. He had been on her brain when she went to sleep and continued to be so even in the light of day. She shook her head and tried to recall the events of the night before, but they were fuzzy. Oh yeah, she had located a bottle of Chardonnay and had consumed most of it.

Boom, boom, boom.

"Dakota! I know you're in there. Open the doggone door!"

"Sierra?" Dakota scrambled from the bed and hurried down the hallway. "Hold your horses, I'm coming!" she shouted when Sierra knocked again.

"Are you deaf?" Sierra demanded after Dakota let her in.

With a wince, Dakota wiggled her finger in her ear. "I might be now! What is your deal?" she asked, and then noticed the big blue T-shirt and pointed. "Ohmigod! You slept with Grady, didn't you?"

"No." Sierra pursed her lips in a pout. "Just with his shirt."

"Oh." Dakota eyed her skeptically. "Are you sure?"

"Are you blond?"

Dakota put her fists on her hips, but it was difficult to look tough in her little pink nightie. "Well, last night is a bit fuzzy for me, what with all the drinking, and now you're wearing nothing but the man's shirt."

"You drank three lousy beers!"

"I do believe it was four." She held up her fingers to prove her point. "And I drank some wine later on!"

"Wine?" Sierra rolled her eyes. "Whatever, lightweight. We will have to work on your redneck skills." Sierra glanced around the room and then wrinkled her nose. "Ew. Aren't you going to get rid of that?"

"Get rid of what?" Dakota asked. She followed Sierra's gaze, put her hand to her chest, and screamed.

Trace tossed Grady the T-shirt he had asked to borrow and then stopped in his tracks. "Hey, did you just hear a scream?"

"Sure did," Grady answered, and looked toward the open front door. "Came from Dakota's cabin." He pulled the shirt over his head and tugged it down his torso. "Imagine that."

"Not again." Trace shook his head and then walked out onto his front porch. An awareness washed over him just thinking about Dakota, and it annoyed him. He couldn't sleep for thinking about her last night, and she was already on his mind this morning. Shading his eyes, he peered across the road and then asked over his shoulder, "Looks like Sierra is over there again. Think we need to check it out?"

Grady jammed his hands in his pockets and rocked back on his heels. "Mmm, I'm not too sure Sierra will be all that happy to see me."

Trace narrowed his eyes. "Did you sleep with her, Grady? If you hurt her, I'll tear you a new one."

"Hey, hold on there, hoss." Grady pulled his hands from his pockets and raised his palms in the air. "I didn't sleep with her, even though I could have."

"You expect me to believe that?"

"I'm a lot of things, but I'm not a liar," Grady replied with a touch of anger. "You know me better than that."

"You're right," Trace conceded. He wanted to know what happened, but decided it was none of his business. "She's a good girl, though, Grady. She doesn't deserve—"

"I know, I know. She doesn't deserve the likes of me," Grady said, jamming a thumb at his chest. "Think I don't realize that?" He folded his arms across his chest and gave Trace a level look. "You know, I think it's pretty safe to say that it takes one to know one. I've heard the stories about your PBR days. Buckle bunnies in every city?"

Trace sat down on the porch railing and rubbed his

thigh, which suddenly started aching. "Yeah, but those women knew what they wanted and so I didn't give a damn. Dakota is different."

"Dakota?" Grady arched an eyebrow.

"I meant to say *Sierra*."

"Did you?"

"Yes," Trace insisted, even though he knew he was busted. He was saved from further explanation when another scream came from Dakota's cabin. "I'm gonna have to check out what the hell's goin' on over there," he grumbled, and pushed up from the railing. "You comin' with me?"

"Guess I better."

The gravel crunched beneath their boots as they hurried across the road. Dakota and Sierra's voices carried through the screen door as Trace and Grady approached the cabin in a déjà vu moment. Trace was about to knock, but Grady put a hand on his arm. "Wait," he whispered. "This might be good."

Trace thought better of it, but hesitated and then listened.

"Come on, Dakota, sweep it onto the dustpan."

"It moved!" Dakota insisted, and then squealed.

"Dakota, it's a little bitty mouse. And it's deader than a doornail. Now sweep the damn thing into the dustpan."

"What I need is a cat, and then I wouldn't have this problem. Maybe we should call Trace. He said he'd do this for me."

"We don't need to be botherin' Trace," Sierra replied, prompting Trace to nudge Grady and jerk his head toward the road.

We should go, Trace mouthed, and Grady nodded in agreement, but then reared back his head and sneezed.

"Damn!" Grady winced and got a glare from Trace. "Busted again."

"Did you hear that?" Dakota asked from inside, and a moment later was at the front door. "What are you guys doing here?"

"We heard screams," Trace explained. Dakota stood there in a pink silky-looking thing. He opened his mouth to further explain, but one spaghetti strap slipped off her shoulder and all coherent thought fled his brain. In her excitement, she didn't seem to notice, however, and eagerly opened the screen door.

"We caught a mouse!" she explained with wide eyes, and padded across the hardwood floor in bare feet. Dear God, the pink thing she was wearing was thin enough for him to see matching pink short-shorts underneath—a combination of sex and innocence that had him breaking out into a sweat despite the cool morning breeze blowing through the open windows. "There!" She pointed and then swallowed hard.

"We coulda handled the situation ourselves," Sierra declared. Trace noticed that she avoided looking at Grady, but Grady, on the other hand, had no problem gawking at her. Not that he could blame him. With her dark hair tumbling over her shoulders and wearing nothing but Grady's T-shirt, she looked uncharacter-istically sweet and feminine, and he would have been gawking too, if he didn't think of Sierra as a baby sister. What Trace did feel was protective of her, and would kick Grady's ass if he made even one teardrop fall from her too-trusting face.

"I thought I saw it move," Dakota declared in a

stage whisper to Trace, "or we would have taken care of it a while ago."

"It's dead, Dakota!" Sierra announced, and rolled her eyes. "Guts are comin' outta his mouth!"

Dakota put a hand to her stomach. "Oh! You didn't have to tell me that!"

Trace noticed that Sierra seemed a bit embarrassed at her outburst and she glanced at Grady, who had taken it upon himself to sweep the trap into the dustpan.

"I'm just sayin'," Sierra continued with a small shrug. "The mouse is toast. He wasn't gonna hurt ya."

"Grady, check the trap in the kitchen, will ya?" Trace asked, and then turned to Dakota but carefully kept his gaze on her face. "I'll set new traps later today, and then you should be rodent-free."

"Thanks." Her smile seemed sweet and genuine, touching a chord in Trace that he never knew existed. "Sorry to be such a bother. No more screaming. I promise," she said, raising her hands in the air. When Sierra snorted, Dakota shot her a look and said, "I'm trying to acclimate myself. Give me a few days, okay? You might not be so huffy if you were in L.A.," Dakota challenged, even though she had never quite felt at home in L.A. either, and Sierra knew it.

"Oh, whatever, Pop Princess." She wiggled her fingers in the air.

"Kiss my grits, Kitchen Queen," Dakota shot back with her hands on her hips.

Trace and Grady watched the sparring as if it were a tennis match.

"Kiss my grits?" Sierra sputtered with a shake of her head. "Dakota, you have to do better than that, for Pete's sake! *Day-um*, my work is gonna be cut out for me."

"And you think mine won't be?" Dakota replied, but then put a hand to her mouth as if she were revealing some big secret.

Trace frowned. "What are y'all talkin' about?"

"Nothing!" Dakota insisted, and gave Sierra a look of warning, making Trace wonder what the two of them were up to. But he refrained from asking. He needed to stay as far away from Dakota as his job would allow.

"Okay," Trace said, "well, I think we're done here." He glanced at Grady. "You ready?"

Grady nodded. "Yeah, see you ladies around."

Trace nodded to Dakota, but noticed that Grady stole a glance at Sierra before they walked out the door.

"Just what do you think those two are up to?" Grady asked before whistling for Gil, who was running around in the woods.

"Damned if I know," Trace commented, "but it's gonna involve trouble. You mark my words."

Grady threaded his fingers through his hair and nodded slowly. "I do believe you're right. Well, I'm headin' out. Gonna crash for a while, since I didn't get much sleep last night," he admitted with a yawn, and opened the passenger's door of his truck for Gil to hop in.

"Sounds like a good idea," Trace agreed, knowing just how his young friend felt. "See ya tomorrow."

Grady walked over to the driver's side, but paused before getting in. "Hey, I'll most likely be goin' in to Dewey's to shoot some pool later on. You wanna come?"

Trace hesitated. For the first time in a long while, the idea held some appeal, but then he shook his head. "Got some paperwork to do tonight."

"Okay," Grady said, but gave Trace a lopsided grin.

"But you hesitated this time. I think I'm finally wearin' your sorry ass down. If you change your mind, give me a holler."

"All right," Trace agreed, wondering just what the hell was coming over him. . . . But then again, he knew it wasn't *what* but *who*. After Grady drove away, Trace glanced back over toward Dakota's cabin and sighed. She was making him wish for things he didn't want to long for, and he didn't like it one bit. With a little growl of frustration, he entered his cabin and was met with the same silence that always greeted him, but instead of the sense of peace that he usually found in the quiet, Trace felt empty. Lonely.

While fisting his hands at his sides, he inhaled sharply and shook his head. Keeping the marina and fishing camp in the black was difficult enough without dealing with Dakota on the side. If she kept poking around, she would realize the slim profit margin and perhaps consider selling. And then where would he go? What would he do?

The muscles in his bad leg tensed up, causing an intense ache that pulsed and throbbed. "Damn!" Trace limped over to the sofa and sat down. While staring blankly out the window, he absently attempted to massage the pain away.

The logical part of his brain whispered to him that this self-imposed loner lifestyle he had been leading was ridiculous and there was no reason not to slide back into the land of the living. He didn't even fully understand where the anger in him was coming from, but then again he had been knocked from his pedestal at the top of the PBR circuit as if a sniper had taken aim and hit the bull's-eye. He had wanted to retire the sport in a blaze of glory, waving to the adoring crowd like Justin McBride did at the PBR World Finals in Vegas.

Imagining that shining moment had gotten Trace through grueling and painful rehab. The doctors had warned him that he would never ride again, but Trace was a competitor, a champion, and never once doubted he would get back on the bull riding circuit or have the opportunity to best the bull who had done this to him. For Trace, this had been the ultimate failure that he still could not accept, even though he knew he should face the facts and move on. It was so much easier to hold on to his anger and hide from the world. He had been doing a good job of it until Dakota Dunn landed here at the marina, shaking up his life in more ways than one.

Trace uttered a dark oath when the image of Dakota in pink silk slipped back into his brain. He didn't want to think, to feel, to want. To need. "Stay the hell away from her," he warned himself. "Running the marina is a big enough challenge," he added for good measure, while reminding himself that her well-being was not his responsibility.

Trace inhaled a deep breath and blew it out. If only she weren't Charley and Rita Mae's daughter, he could probably buy into his reasoning. But she *was*, and dammit, he couldn't allow any harm to come to her, even if it was something as silly as a doggone mouse. While rubbing his thigh, he told himself to be polite but distant, and for God's sake never to invite her for another soak in his hot tub.

"You can damn well do this, Coleman," he mumbled under his breath. How hard could it be?

9

Cowgirl Up

"That's good enough, already," Sierra whined from her perch on the toilet seat.

"You said you wanted me to make you pretty," Dakota responded, and plucked another hair from Sierra's eyebrow.

"At this rate, I'm not gonna have any eyebrows left!"

"Hold still!" Dakota grabbed her chin, tilted it up, and examined her work. "You're supposed to be the tough one, remember? Ever had a bikini wax?"

Sierra narrowed her eyes. "Don't even think about it."

Dakota laughed. "Okay, fine. Hey, much improved! Turn around and look into the mirror. Sexy, huh?"

Sierra's perfectly arched eyebrows rose when she gazed at her reflection. "Wow," she said, and blinked in amazement.

"I know." Dakota felt a sense of accomplishment and smiled. "Are we still going to Dewey's Pub tonight?"

Sierra frowned at Dakota in the mirror. "It can be

a little on the rough side. You think you're ready for this?"

"I've got wing-tipped cowboy boots, sugar-glazed Wranglers, a racerback white tank, and a very cool concho belt." She tapped her thumb to her chest. "I'm rip-roarin' and ready to go."

Sierra rolled her eyes.

"Overkill?"

Sierra nodded.

"Okay, I'll tone it down a notch."

"Seriously, Dakota, you can't be so perky at Dewey's. You'll get our butts kicked. Just play it cool, okay?"

Dakota nodded eagerly, but then made an effort to appear subdued. "Right. Play it cool. I can do that."

"There are some sketchy characters who hang out there, so be careful who you flirt with."

"Gotcha."

"Just follow my lead, okay?"

"Okay," Dakota agreed, and then clapped her hands lightly. "This is going to give me some material to start songwriting," she announced in an excited, high-pitched voice.

Sierra shot her a look.

"Right." She put her hands out, palms facing the floor. "Play it cool."

"Okay, that gesture you just did? If I do that to you tonight, you know to back it down." Sierra demonstrated.

Dakota nodded seriously and then brightened. "Can we have a special handshake too?"

Sierra gave Dakota a deadpan stare and pointed to her own face. "Hurry up and make me pretty. I need me some hot wings and cold beer."

Dakota turned to her wide array of cosmetics purchased for Sierra. She rubbed her palms together and said, "I feel like Carmindy."

"Who?"

Dakota picked up an eyeliner pencil and said, "The makeup artist on *What Not to Wear*. You should watch. Okay, tilt your head up. And don't look in the mirror. I want you to be dazzled by your reveal."

"Whatever that means, but okay."

Dakota played up Sierra's green eyes with smoky eye shadow, chocolate eyeliner, and a generous coat of mascara. She used a sheer mineral foundation, since Sierra's skin was amazing, and added just a touch of dusky pink blush to the apples of her cheeks. "Wow," Dakota commented, but held Sierra's chin firmly when she attempted to turn around for a peek in the mirror. "Not yet. I have to do your lips and then tame that hair."

"You know I'll never be able to do this on my own," Sierra complained.

"Yes, you will," Dakota promised. "You just need some practice," she reassured her as she dabbed on rose-tinted lip gloss. "Now, I'm going to sweep your hair back in a looser ponytail, a little sloppy, but in a sexy way. This look will tame the curls, but we'll let some hair escape to give it more of a feminine appeal. Sound good?"

Sierra nodded, then nibbled on the inside of her cheek as if she were nervous. She looked so hopeful, but with a vulnerable edge, that Dakota wanted to lean in and hug her, but she didn't. Sierra needed to slide her way into this friendship, and the last thing Dakota wanted to do was frighten her away with too much touchy-feely affection.

"All right, turn around." Dakota's heart thumped in anticipation as she stepped back and watched Sierra's reaction.

"Oh." She breathed, swallowed hard and then blinked as if holding back tears.

"Don't you dare make your mascara run," Dakota said, but her own voice was husky.

"I'm not gonna cry," Sierra protested, but her badass tone was busted when she gingerly put her fingertips to her cheeks and gazed at her reflection with a sense of wonder. She blinked up at Dakota and whispered, "Do you think I'm pretty?"

"No, Sierra." Dakota shook her head. "You're not just pretty, you are gorgeous."

"Oh, shut up! I was bein' serious!"

"So was I," Dakota shot back, but then sniffed hard. "Course this all happened because I'm a makeup artist genius. It's got nothing to do with your bone structure, thick mane of glossy hair, or pouty mouth." Dakota put her hands on Sierra's shoulders and said, "Or the inner beauty that radiates from within."

"You are so full of it," Sierra said, but her bottom lip trembled.

"Grady is going to melt into a puddle at your feet."

"Good, and I'm gonna give him the cold shoulder and flirt with every cowboy in the place."

"Two little redneck girls out on the town." Dakota squeezed Sierra's shoulders.

"Listen," Sierra advised, and then spun around on the toilet seat. "None of this sugar-and-spice stuff, you hear me?" She reached up and tapped her on the chest. "I wanna see some gunpowder and lead!" Sierra angled her head. "Give it a don't-mess-with-me attitude.

You know, a pointed stare. An arch of one eyebrow. None of that perky, pop-princess crap."

"Gotcha." Dakota nodded, but then changed the direction of her head. "I'll never pull it off. I might as well call my manager now and tell him to forget this nonsense."

Sierra stood up and put her hands on her hips. "The hell you say! Dakota, you might look like a little powder puff, but there's a hidden strength that you don't let anybody see. It took some balls to get up there onstage and do the stuff you did. Am I right?"

"I guess."

Sierra shoved Dakota hard. "The answer is: damned straight! Now, cowgirl up!"

"What's that mean?"

"It's the chick version of *cowboy up*. In bull riding terms, it means 'get ready, have the courage to climb on, and give it your all.'"

"All righty, then," Dakota said, and tapped her knuckles to Sierra's. "Cowgirl up!"

Sierra nodded. "Listen, I'll drive my truck, but if we get to drinkin' too much, we'll have to get us a ride home."

Several minutes later, they were out the door. As they were walking down the driveway to Sierra's truck, Trace happened to be walking toward his cabin. He stopped in his tracks when he saw them, and Dakota wasn't sure if he was more surprised at her attire or Sierra's makeover, but his eyes widened before he could stop himself. When he waved but didn't comment or ask where they were going, she felt a stab of disappointment and turned away. But just when she was reaching for the passenger's door handle, she heard the crunch of gravel behind her.

"Where you ladies off to?" Trace asked while trying to keep his voice casual. In truth, he was stunned by Sierra's sudden transformation from grunge to gorgeous and Dakota's sexy cowgirl attire.

"Dewey's Pub for a bite to eat," Dakota answered, and turned around, giving him an up-close view of her in a little white tank top and hip-hugging Wranglers.

"Dewey's?" Trace finally asked when he found his voice, but couldn't help but frown.

"Yes, why?" Dakota asked with a defiant lift of one eyebrow.

Trace leaned around her so he could look inside the truck where Sierra sat in the driver's seat, gripping the steering wheel as if anxious to leave. "You're taking Dakota to Dewey's?"

"You got a problem with that?" Sierra asked with her usual bluntness, even though her appearance was nothing but feminine. It was then that it occurred to Trace that both women were going to be out of their element. While Dewey's drew a mixed crowd and wasn't exactly dangerous, the later the night wore on, the more likely there would be a bar fight or young cowboys hitting on the girls. He didn't relish either Sierra or Dakota in that atmosphere, and so he had to ask even though he really didn't want to, "So, you plannin' on bein' out late?"

Dakota shrugged. "We might."

"Trace, if we get to drinkin', we won't drive."

"Oh." He liked this scenario less and less. "Well, just how will you get home, then?"

"I'm sure we can get a cab or something," Dakota assured him as she climbed up in the truck, giving him a mouthwatering view of her butt.

"They're hard to come by in Tall Rock," Trace warned them.

Sierra sighed. "Trace, I will know half the people in Dewey's. We'll work it out."

"Yeah, and they will all be drinkin'. Not a very good plan," he grumbled. "Call me and I'll come and get you," Trace offered, even though he didn't want to. But if anything happened . . .

Dakota looked out the open window at him in surprise. "You don't have to do that, Trace."

"I realize that," he answered a bit sharply. "But I offered, so take me up on it, okay?"

"We can take care of ourselves, you know," Dakota shot back.

Sierra leaned forward so Trace could see her. "Trace, I'm a regular there, playin' pool with the boys. We'll be fine."

Yeah, but not looking like that, he thought, but nodded and stepped back from the truck. "Call me, okay? Don't take any chances. And don't let anyone mess with you."

"Trace, nobody messes with me," Sierra reminded him with a low chuckle and a thumb poked at her chest. "Just a little girl's night out is all we're havin'. See ya around." She wiggled her fingers and drove away with gravel crunching and a cloud of dust left behind.

Trace stood there for a minute with his hands jammed in his pockets and watched the truck fade into the distance. For some reason, his gut warned him they were going to get into some sort of trouble, and his gut rarely lied. It didn't help matters that Sierra was looking anything like one of the boys, and Dakota was totally out of her element in a honky-tonk bar. With an oath, he sent a rock flying with the toe of his boot.

"It's not your problem, Coleman," he growled, but it hit him hard that he cared about both of them. Lifting his gaze to the deep blue sky, he inhaled a deep breath and then made his decision.

He was heading into town.

10

I Love This Bar

"I'm so excited," Dakota declared as they pulled into the parking lot of Dewey's Pub. While the outskirts of Tall Rock had their fair share of development and strip malls, Main Street downtown looked much the same as it did when Dakota had left for California, and she found the quaint old buildings charming. "I've never been in Dewey's, but I've heard stories!"

"Squash the perkiness," Sierra reminded her, but then laughed. Her smile faded, however, when she caught a glimpse of her reflection in the rearview mirror. She gulped and then looked over at Dakota. "I can't go in there lookin' like this."

"You mean looking amazing?" Dakota angled her head at Sierra in confusion.

She shook her head and put a trembling hand to her chest. "This isn't me."

Dakota thought about saying something kind or profound but then shook her head and slapped the cracked leather seat so hard that it hurt. But she refrained from yelping in pain, because she was supposed to be a badass. "Bullshit!"

"Say what?" Sierra raised her perfectly plucked eyebrows in surprise.

"You heard me." Dakota twisted on the bench seat to face Sierra. "We need to break out of our routine and go after . . ." Her voice trailed off, and she shrugged.

"What?"

"I'm not quite sure, but I think we'll know when we find it." Dakota put her fists forward for a knuckle tap. "Come on. Cowgirl up."

Sierra looked down at Dakota's fists and then nodded firmly and tapped knuckles. "Cowgirl up! Okay, now let's go before I lose my nerve."

They slid from their seats in the truck and approached the door. Music, laughter, and the clinking of glasses filtered out to entice them, but it was the aroma of bar food that drew them in. "Something smells good."

"Bar food. Everything is deep-fried. Even the pickles."

"Pickles?"

"And deep-fried mac and cheese."

"Holy cow." Dakota put a hand to her stomach and hoped it was up for the challenge.

"Come on—I'm starvin'. Let's quit standing here like a couple of dorks." Sierra put her hand on the door, and Dakota grabbed her arm.

"Just so you know, people are going to stare," Dakota said.

Sierra's eyes widened. "I forgot that you are freakin' famous."

"Sort of. By now people narrow their eyes and wonder how they know my face, and then usually snap their fingers and ask if I was on *American Idol*." Dakota sighed. "But they do stare, just to give you fair warning."

"You'll be fine," Sierra said and squeezed Dakota's hand. "Let's go!"

Dakota entered Dewey's and stopped to look around. She had been in lounges and to cocktail parties, but a neighborhood honky-tonk remained virgin territory until now. "This is so cool!" Dakota squeaked in Sierra's ear.

"I told you to stop with the perkiness, Princess!" Sierra grabbed her hand and yanked her forward.

"Okay," Dakota said in a forced lower tone, and followed Sierra, but looked around with unabashed interest. At the moment, Rascal Flatts blasted from a jukebox, but the stage at the far end of the room appeared set up for live music. It had been years since she had performed, and looking at the microphone gave her a nervous flutter in her stomach, so she quickly glanced away. In the right corner, a couple of weathered cowboys were shooting darts, and to her left an old-school pinball machine dinged and blinked. "I want to play that," she told Sierra, and pointed.

"Later. I need food and a tall beer. And for God's sake, stop pointing!" Sierra said as she led Dakota past tall stools occupied by people of various shapes and sizes, making Dakota think of Toby Keith's "I Love This Bar." She tried to soak it all in, and couldn't wait to people-watch, in hopes of gaining inspiration for songwriting. She suddenly realized how much she missed the creative side of music and felt the itch to sit down with her guitar.

"Over here." Sierra suggested a table set up for dining in the bigger room beyond the main bar. The pool hall could be seen through a big archway, and Dakota angled her head to see inside, but Sierra leaned forward with her hands on the maroon vinyl tablecloth. "Stop gawking. You'll bring attention to us," Sierra said, and looked left and right.

"Sierra, people know you here," Dakota said, and patted her hand. "Relax and have fun. So you're wearing some makeup." She shrugged. "So what?"

While drumming her fingertips on the table, Sierra nodded. "I know. I'll be okay after a couple of beers." She glanced around again as if waiting for someone to recognize her, and said, "Hey, let's do a shot."

Dakota raised her eyebrows. "What?" She shook her head hard and wagged a finger at Sierra. "Oh no. I don't think so."

"Suit yourself. But I'm going to."

"Sierra," Dakota began in a tone of warning, but stopped herself. For a long time she had been living on the outside looking in, and tonight she decided she was long past due in cutting loose and having a wild time. What was the harm of one little old shot anyway? Maybe like a Buttery Nipple or something. But after listening to Sierra place her order, Dakota proudly proclaimed, "I'll have the same thing. A shot of Maker's Mark, followed closely by a Bud Light in a bottle, and an order of hot wings, but with the exception that I want extra celery and blue cheese, and skip the fries. Oh, and put an order of deep-fried pickles on my tab for us to share." She said this primly, as if she were in a four-star restaurant, and then unfolded her paper napkin onto her lap.

For a minute, Sierra blinked across the table at Dakota, as if pondering whether this was a good idea or could lead to disaster, but then she grinned. "I think we just set the mood for the night."

"And what might that be?" Dakota inclined her head politely just as their shots and beer arrived.

"Only one word comes to mind."

"Yes?"

"Ca-raaa-zy!" Sierra proclaimed. When she raised her shot glass, Dakota followed suit.

They clinked together, and Dakota watched Sierra so she did the deed in the correct fashion, and prayed to God that she didn't sputter it all over the table. As Dakota brought the glass to her lips, she told herself that if she could eat sushi, she could surely toss back a shot of good Kentucky bourbon. She inhaled sharply, sending the pungent aroma straight to her head just as she opened her lips and flung the entire contents into her mouth and swallowed. For a second it wasn't too bad—just strong—and she actually liked the flavor. She started to smile. But then it suddenly felt as if there were a trail of fire in her throat that just might explode in her stomach.

Dakota gasped and blindly reached for water, but there was none so she grabbed her longneck and took deep, soothing gulps of the ice-cold liquid until brain freeze forced her to stop guzzling. She set the bottle down with a thud and looked across the table while blinking away the water in her eyes. "Snap!" Dakota managed, while holding one hand to her forehead and the other to her stomach. "That was intense! Whew!"

Sierra grinned and looked none the worse for wear. "You'd better slow down there, Princess."

"Don't worry. I will," she said, and reached for her beer after her brain thawed out. She took a leisurely sip and then smiled when the wings arrived. "These smell heavenly."

"They are spicy hot, so be warned."

Dakota waved a dismissive hand. "I love spicy food," she said, but after taking a bite of a tiny drumstick, her lips felt tingly and she reached for her beer again.

"Too spicy for ya?" Sierra teased, and Dakota watched with a sense of wonder while Sierra ate a wing and leisurely licked her fingers.

"Not at all," Dakota replied, and determinedly took another rather dainty bite. Her eyes watered and her lips burned, but she bravely consumed the entire drumstick before soothing her palate with celery and a generous dollop of cool and creamy blue cheese. The bourbon and beer made her feel warm and relaxed enough to get up the nerve to try a deep-fried pickle. She reached over and picked up a golden brown spear from the basket and looked at it with interest.

"Dip it in the ranch dressing," Sierra advised.

"Okay." She dunked it in the little bowl and then took a tiny bite. "Hmm, interesting," she commented, and took a bigger bite. "Good, actually. I like it!"

Sierra laughed, and snagged a pickle and took a healthy bite before wagging it at Dakota. "I wonder who thought of these anyway. Genius!"

Dakota laughed back and dunked hers in the dressing, but when she glanced up, she suddenly realized that they were slowly becoming the center of attention. She nudged Sierra beneath the table to alert her to what was happening and gave her discreet hand signals to look around. Sierra's eyes widened, and she self-consciously reached up to touch her hair as if she had forgotten about her altered appearance.

Dakota noticed that a group of young guys who could see them from the main bar were elbowing each other and obviously talking about them. She leaned forward as if her goal were to snag one of Sierra's

French fries and whispered, "Do you know those guys staring at us?"

Sierra nodded. Following Dakota's lead, she leaned forward and grabbed a celery stick, but said in a low voice, "I play pool with them sometimes." She looked at the celery stick as if she really didn't want it, but then took a crunchy bite.

"Well, don't look, but one of them is heading our way."

Of course she looked, and whipped her head back around.

Dakota leaned forward and took another fry. "I told you not to look!"

Sierra reached for another celery stick. "I don't mind very well."

Dakota leaned over and dipped her fry in Sierra's ketchup. "Ya think? Just play it cool."

"How?"

"Small talk."

"I don't *do* small talk!" she protested between clenched teeth.

"Wing it!" Dakota considered holding up a hot wing as a prop, but that might have been overkill so she refrained.

"Dear God!"

"It's not that hard," Dakota assured her, and sat back up straight, but not before stealing another forbidden fry. She had been schooled to watch her weight since her pop-princess days, and the salty, crunchy fries made her want to moan. "Here he comes," she mouthed before taking a swig of her beer.

A moment later, the bravest of the pool-shooting bunch twisted a chair around and plopped down, straddling it. "How y'all doin'?"

"We're doin' all right," Sierra responded in a calm voice, but Dakota noticed that she nervously toyed with her napkin.

"Wait. Sierra Miller?" He tilted the bill of his Carhartt ball cap up and turned it slightly cockeyed.

"Danny Dixon, you've known me since sixth grade," Sierra chided with a shake of her head, but Dakota noticed pink color bloom on her cheeks.

"Hi, Danny," Dakota interjected, to get his attention off Sierra so she could compose herself. She stuck her hand out. "I'm Dakota Dunn."

"Nice to meet ya," he said, and then narrowed his eyes the way most people did while trying to place her. "You from around here?"

Dakota smiled. "I grew up in Tall Rock, but I've been away for a few years."

"Oh," he said while scratching his chin, but continued to look at her in question. "Thought I recognized you." He tilted up his longneck with two fingers and took a swig.

"Would you like some wings or deep-fried pickles?" Dakota offered. "I'm afraid our eyes were bigger than our stomachs." She noticed that Danny's buddies were watching with interest, even though they pretended to be taking in a baseball game on a nearby television suspended from the wall.

"Don't mind if I do," he accepted with a grin that Dakota thought was charming. There was no pretense—just good-ole-boy earnestness that Dakota had forgotten existed. After he polished off the wing, he licked his thumb. Dakota was struck by the fact that the spicy hot sauce didn't even faze him in the least either, making her feel rather wimpy. "Hope you ladies will save me and my buddies a dance or two later when the music starts."

He looked at Sierra, who appeared stuck for words, so Dakota jumped in. "Sure we will. Might cost you a beer," she added, and was proud of herself for sounding saucy.

"It'd be well worth it," Danny flirted back. Then he winked at Sierra and added, "You sure are lookin' bangin' tonight. Catch you ladies later." He scooted his chair back and paused to give Sierra a wink before heading back to the main bar, where he got a few elbows to the ribs and shoves to his shoulders.

"He was cute," Dakota commented as she picked up another pickle. "And he sure did like you."

Sierra waved her off. "Oh, he was put up to it by his buddies. Just messin' with me."

"You are so wrong, Sierra," she said, and then widened her eyes when two more shots came their way. "Did you order this?"

"From the boys at the bar," the waitress answered, then nodded toward Danny and his partners in crime, where they were perched on high stools. They lifted their beer bottles in salute and waited in anticipation.

Dakota looked at the amber-colored bourbon while dearly wishing for a Buttery Nipple, and then glanced over at Sierra, who grinned and lifted her glass. Knowing she was throwing caution to the wind—or more like spitting into the wind—Dakota drew in a deep breath, brought the glass to her lips, and tossed it back.

11

Hit Me with Your Best Shot

"Holy shit," Trace muttered when he and Grady entered Dewey's and spotted Dakota and Sierra through the archway, sitting at a table. "They're doin' shots."

"Yeah, this could get ugly," Grady agreed with a shake of his head.

Trace flicked a concerned glance at Grady and was glad he had asked him to come along. "Let's get them the hell outta here."

"Just hold on," Grady said, and put a restraining hand on Trace's arm. "I can pretty much assure you that Sierra won't leave unless she damned well wants to. Trying to strong-arm her outta here will only make her want to stay. I say we go over there in the corner where they can't see us, and keep an eye on things." He shrugged. "Besides, she's a regular here and can take care of herself."

Trace angled his head at Grady. "Has she ever been in here lookin' like she looks tonight?"

"What do you mean?" Grady asked, and squinted to get a better view of Sierra.

"Dakota must have done some sort of makeover on her, because she sure looks hot."

Grady turned and narrowed his eyes at Trace.

"Hey, it's an observation. She's like a sister to me. Damn, Grady, you've got it bad."

"Like you don't?" Grady asked in a low voice, so as not to draw attention to them. "I've tried forever to get you here, and all it took was knowin' Dakota was in the house and in need of your protection." While batting his eyes, he put his hand to his chest. "My hero," he crooned in a high-pitched voice, and was rewarded with an elbow jab to the gut. "Ouch!"

"I feel an obligation to her mama and daddy to keep an eye on her. That's what got me here."

"Right. And I'll buy that swampland you're sellin' too."

Trace was about to snap back when he noticed the young guys at the bar watching Sierra and Dakota. "Those dudes musta bought them the drinks."

Grady looked in the direction Trace indicated and growled, "Let's kick us some ass."

It was Trace's turn to put a hand on Grady's shoulder. "Chill, man. I really don't want any trouble if we can help it. Let's stick to the plan of kicking back and keeping an eye on things." He didn't add that he didn't really want to be recognized or talk to anyone.

"If you say so," Grady reluctantly agreed, but then raked his fingers through his hair and sighed. "Don't know what the hell's gettin' into me. You go sit down over there in the corner, and I'll get us some beer."

"Okay." With his long hair and dark stubble shading his face, and given the dim lighting of the bar, Trace hoped he would fly under the radar, especially in the corner. He really didn't want to talk about his glory days or the inevitable question of whether he would return to bull riding. He also really didn't want to see expressions of pity at his scar or feel eyes on his back when he limped. The fact that he also didn't want to witness guys hitting on Dakota slammed into his brain when a couple of cowboys swaggered over to their table and started chatting them up.

Trace clenched his teeth together and almost stood up when the taller of the two put his hat on Dakota's head. She laughed and accepted the beer he handed her. Trace shook his head when Grady sat down. "She's already over her limit," he grumbled. "I can tell." He looked across the table and said, "Maybe you're right and we should just drag them outta here."

"Well, I don't think those boys would take kindly to that, Trace. Drink your beer and calm down. It's Sunday, so it should clear out early and we can get the girls home."

Trace nodded. "You're right." The beer tasted good and cold, but he knew he could drink only a couple and drive home, and he sure as hell wasn't going to let Dakota or Sierra hitch a ride with anyone but him or Grady. So far no one had recognized him sitting in the shadows, and after he polished off the beer he relaxed just a tad.

"Oh, shit," Grady said when a couple of the young guys started to argue. "I smell trouble."

"Just sit tight," Trace warned, but he was on full alert since the shoving was going on very close to Dakota's table. He had a sneaking suspicion Dakota was going to take it upon herself to say something, and he was right.

"Guys!" Dakota shouted. She stood up and wobbled slightly. "Stop it! Can't we all just get along?"

"Sit down!" Sierra said, and pointed to Dakota's chair.

"No. This is silly!" Dakota protested with her hands on her hips, and then gave her attention to the boys. The Toby Keith–style hat she still wore slipped to the side of her head when she said, "Stop it this minute! Fighting is . . ." She paused as if struggling for a word, and finally raised a finger in the air and loudly proclaimed, "Stupid!"

By this time, everyone in the bar had stopped doing their various bar activities, including the band that was setting up, and turned their attention to Dakota and the anticipation of a fight. Trace looked around for the bouncer, who must have used the only moment he was needed to take a trip to the men's room.

"What should we do?" Grady asked.

"I don't—" Trace began, but when the argument heated up and Dakota decided she should put herself between the two cowboys with her hands extended, he knew he had to step in.

"Get outta the way, little lady," one of the cowboys warned in a John Wayne–sounding voice. While his attention was diverted, the other guy took a swing at him way too close to Dakota for Trace's comfort.

"Dakota, sit your ass down!" Sierra shouted.

"Damn it!" Trace pushed his way into the room and snagged Dakota around the waist just as one of the cowboys took another swing. He saw the punch coming and twisted her out of the way, but ended up getting clipped on the side of his face. He staggered sideways and came down hard on his bum leg, nearly losing his balance, but braced his hand against the wall and remained upright. His arm remained around Dakota, and when she started to wiggle away he held her tightly and said in her ear, "Stop it. You're going to get me into a fight."

"But—"

"But nothin', Dakota. Now, are you comin' peacefully or do I have to toss you over my shoulder?"

"Peacefully," she assured him.

"Good," he said, and eased his grip around her waist, but remained at her side as she walked back over to her table. Grady was with Sierra, who was busy paying the tab. The big, bald bouncer hurried into the room and hefted both boys toward the door and then turned to Trace.

"Trace Coleman?" he boomed, and extended a big, beefy hand. "Bo Mason. Man, it's good to see you in Dewey's. I hope you come in more often. I'll make sure people don't bug the hell outta ya."

"I appreciate that," Trace said, and shook the bouncer's hand. In truth, he was surprised that he didn't really want to leave.

"Thanks for steppin' in," Bo said, and gave Dakota a stern look. "You should stay outta bar fights, Princess."

Dakota shook her head. "Why does everyone call me P-Princess?" She tried to look up at the bouncer, but the rim of the hat tilted forward and shaded her eyes. "Huh? Why? My princess days are done. Over. Now I'm just . . ." She sighed heavily and continued, "I don't know what I am." She twisted to look up at Trace. "What am I?"

"Well," Trace held back a grin. "You're drunk—I can tell you that much."

She gave him a pout. "A teensy bit tipsy is all I am."

"Right."

Bo the bouncer chuckled. "You'd better get your girlfriend home, Trace."

"Good idea," Trace responded, and didn't correct Bo on the girlfriend comment, figuring that the big guy would keep a careful eye on Dakota when he wasn't around if he thought they were together. He turned to Grady and said, "I'm getting her home. Are you giving Sierra a ride?"

Grady nodded. "Actually, I've convinced Sierra to hang out here for a while. But yeah, I'll get her home."

Trace looked at Sierra. "You okay with that?"

She nodded but appeared a bit flustered. "Yeah, I'll get my truck tomorrow," she assured him, and walked over to Dakota. "Cowgirl up," she said, and then lifted her hand to give Dakota a high five.

"Cowgirl up!" Dakota replied, but pretty much missed hitting Sierra's hand and stumbled forward with the momentum. Trace slipped his arm around her waist and held her up.

The cowboy hat tumbled to the floor, but when Dakota leaned forward to pick it up, Sierra said, "You go ahead. I'll get the hat to its rightful owner."

"Thank you, Sierra. You're a good friend." She blinked as if ready to cry and said, "I messed this up, didn't I? God, I am such a *bad* cool redneck chick. I suck, don't I?"

"You don't suck."

"Yes, I do," she complained.

"Okay, you sucked a little," Sierra admitted, and gave Trace a sympathetic you've-got-your-hands-full wince. "Just don't hurl in Trace's truck."

Dakota leaned back heavily against Trace, but tilted her head up to look at him. "I won't. I have a very strong constitution. Wait, is that the right word?"

"Yes, and I hope you are right. Now let's get you some fresh air, okay?"

"Yep. Just help me walk just a tiny bit." She turned and gave a pathetic little finger wave to Sierra and Grady.

"Just lean on me," Trace said, and held her firmly around the waist. He wished he could simply carry her to his truck, but he didn't want to draw any more unwanted attention to them, and he wasn't sure how his damned leg would hold out. "We don't have far to go," he reassured her as he approached the front door.

"Take care of your lady," Bo the bouncer said as he opened the front door for them.

"I will," he answered, and assisted Dakota across the parking lot. When he got to the passenger's side of his truck, he opened the door, but then said, "Are you feeling okay, or should we sit here for a few minutes while you get some air?"

"I'll be fine," she said. "I told you I have a very strong disposition."

"Constitution."

"Yeah, that too." She sighed and looked at the big step up. "It sucks to be short. Help me up, okay?"

"Sure," Trace said, and spanned his hands around her waist. He made quick work of hefting her onto the seat, but not before his body reacted to having her slide up against him. After closing the door, Trace inhaled a deep gulp of air, trying to get her soft, sultry scent out of his head. He knew he had to maintain control. It wasn't fair to take advantage of her inebriated state; he had come here to protect her from exactly what was going on in his head that very moment.

God, I want her.

Trace told himself it was simply because it had been

so long since he had been with a woman, but deep down he knew it wasn't true. He didn't want just any woman. He wanted Dakota Dunn, and he was going to have to fight like hell not to give in to his desire. So when he slid behind the steering wheel, he didn't even look at her, and kept his attention on the road.

"I know I'm disgusting," she said in a small voice after about a mile of driving.

Trace reluctantly turned to look at her, but she was gazing forlornly out the passenger's window. "You're not disgusting," he quietly insisted, even though he didn't want to show kindness or care. He wanted to keep his damned distance.

She sighed and turned his way. The impact of her luminous eyes and her sweet smile hit him with hurricane force. "You're just being nice." She sighed again. "I just wanted to fit in for once. But I never do."

"You don't have to fit in, Dakota. Just be yourself."

"That's the problem," she said softly, and God help him, but a fat tear slid down her cheek. She sniffed and turned her head back to gaze out the window. "Don't mind me. I've had too much to drink. What was I thinking, doing shots?"

Trace gripped the steering wheel harder. "You were just having fun. No harm done," he added as he turned up the hill toward the marina.

"I'm sorry for ruining your night. Just drop me off and head back to have some fun of your own," she said, but when he remained quiet, she turned her attention back to him. Knowing that looking at her would be a mistake, he kept his eyes on the road. "I'm really very sorry. I assured you I wouldn't be a pain in the ass, and that's all I've been. I promise to stay out of your hair from now on," she stated firmly, but with a quaver in her voice that he couldn't ignore, especially when he knew she had mistaken his silence for anger.

"I'll walk you over to your cabin," he said curtly after killing the engine.

"I'm fine," she responded with a lift of her chin, but when she reached for the door handle, Trace leaned over and put a restraining hand on hers.

"Stay put until I can help you down. It's a big step, and I don't want you to fall."

"Okay," she said, but he could read in her eyes that she was going to yank on the handle as soon as he let go.

"Oh no you don't," he said, and slipped his arm around her waist. He opened his door with his other hand and scooted her across the bench seat with him.

"Hey!" she protested, and kicked her feet when he easily hefted her over his shoulder.

"Stop!" he said, and gave her a swat on the butt.

"Why, you!" she sputtered, but he just laughed.

It wasn't until he had her on her own porch that he realized he hadn't even given a thought to his leg. He wasn't too happy that she had left her front door open, but he took advantage of the fact and carried her inside and flicked on a light.

"Put me down!" Dakota insisted with some real heat in her voice. "Right this instant!"

Trace answered with another chuckle. He was glad to get her good and pissed off, so she would kick him out on his ear before he did something stupid like kiss her. "I will when I'm good and ready."

"You—you—the hell you say!" She squealed and wiggled so hard that he lost his grip and she tumbled onto the sofa. She bounced and flopped onto her back for an instant before coming up to her knees and then her feet on the cushions. Before he had time to say that he was sorry, he realized too late that she planned on launching an attack.

"Dakota!" he pleaded, but she had fire in her eyes and hopped up as if she were on a trampoline, bounced pretty doggone high, and then, holy shit, launched herself at him. He caught her in midair and stumbled backward. He had to twist so that he softened their landing, hopefully onto the sofa. "Whoa!" He fell backward over the armrest that caught him at the back of his knees and then landed on the cushions, with Dakota on top of him. The impact wasn't too bad until he smacked his head on the opposite armrest with a painful thump.

"Ohmigod!" Dakota gasped, and pushed up from his chest. All of her anger evaporated and she somewhat sobered up. "Are you okay?"

"I think I need to dig out my Kevlar bull riding vest and wear it around you." Trace reached back and rubbed his head. "Well, it's not as bad as kissing the bull, but it hurt like hell."

"Kissing the bull?" She frowned down at him. "Why would you do that?"

"It's when your face hits the back of the bull's head," he explained, intending to let her know that he was really okay, but when she angled her head and gently traced the thin red scar that ran from the outside corner of his eye and bisected his cheekbone, his heart thumped hard in his chest.

"Is that how you got this?" Dakota asked softly, and when Trace nodded and tried to turn his head, she wouldn't allow it. "Ohmigod, and you have a bruise on the other side where that guy clipped you in Dewey's!" She shook her head and squeezed her eyes shut.

"This is all my fault. I should never have come here and disrupted your world."

"Maybe I needed my world disrupted."

Trace's quiet admission had Dakota opening her eyes wide. When she gazed down at him, Trace lowered his gaze, as if he wished he had kept his thoughts to himself. But when he tried to turn his face again, she held his chin firmly. She looked at him for a heart-stopping moment, and then leaned over and gently brushed her lips to his. Her intention was to immediately pull back, but the mere touch of his mouth sent tingling heat radiating through her body, closely followed by longing— an ache she couldn't ignore. Instead of pulling back, she opened her mouth in invitation and trailed the tip of her tongue over his full bottom lip.

Trace groaned as if giving in. Or maybe he was letting go of something she didn't fully understand. Although Dakota knew he was fighting his feelings for her, she didn't care. All that mattered was the touch of his lips, the taste of his mouth, and the incredible need to heal. She licked and nibbled, coaxing a kiss from him that started off soft and sweet, but when he slid his hands up her back, all bets were off.

Dakota deepened the kiss while moving ever so slightly against him. Her breasts tingled and liquid heat oozed like warm honey through her veins. She drank him in while melting against his body, and kissed him as if there were no tomorrow. Trace cupped her ass, pushing her even closer, letting her know the extent of his desire. She pulled her mouth from his and gasped when he tugged her shirt from her jeans and splayed his big, warm hands on her bare skin. She wanted—needed—to have those hands on her breasts.

While straddling him, she sat up and peeled her tank over her head, and then tossed it over her shoulder. But when she arched her back and reached around to unhook her bra, Trace leaned forward to a sitting position and said, "No—wait."

12

Hurricane Dakota

"Allow me," Trace requested, and even though he knew he should put a stop to this madness, he was powerless to do so. Still, he looked into her eyes, searching for hesitation or regret, but all he saw in the amber depths was heat, longing, and need.

And it was the need that pushed him over the edge.

When was the last time someone needed him? God, how he wanted to be valued, to be desired, and to be missed when he was gone. When his bull riding days ended so abruptly, it was as if his personal stock plummeted and he became worthless. And although Trace loved the sport and missed the glory, he wanted to be respected for more than his ability to ride a bucking bull for the required eight seconds.

As if somehow reading his mind, Dakota placed her palms on his cheeks, leaned in, and kissed him softly. "Relax and let this happen. You don't have to think past right now."

"You've been drinking."

"Yes, but more than that, I've been feeling. Something I don't think either one of us has done in a long time. Trace, I won't regret this, and I won't be sorry tomorrow no matter where this goes."

Trace looked at her for a long, heated moment, and when he bestowed upon her one of his rare smiles, it went straight to her heart. Dakota made a vow to herself that she would find a way to make him smile whenever she was in his presence. And when she wasn't around, she hoped he would think of her and smile.

"Are you going to take my bra off or not?" she asked with what she hoped was a saucy arch of one eyebrow. "Okay, did that look silly? Be honest."

Trace laughed and answered, "In due time. First, I want to simply look at you."

"Oh." The heat in his gaze made her feel sexy and bold, and so she scooted back a little bit. "Well, then," she offered with the slight lift of one shoulder, "look your fill."

And so Trace did, beginning with her face. He lingered on her mouth and then continued downward, leaving a trail of heat on her skin that felt almost tangible, like a physical caress. Dakota said a silent thank-you to Victoria's Secret when Trace took in the soft swell of her breasts, which spilled above the cream-colored satin fabric of her push-up bra. A tiny, demure bow seemed to beckon him, and when he reached out and traced it with his fingertip, Dakota sucked in a breath.

"Touch my skin," she pleaded softly.

"Gladly." While looking into her eyes, Trace barely grazed the sensitive skin behind her ear with the back of his hand. He continued a path down her neck and proceeded to the valley between her breasts. Then he cupped her fullness and rubbed the pads of his thumbs over the soft swell directly above her nipples. Dakota's eyes fluttered shut and she arched her back, needing more.

"Take my bra off," she whispered, but he continued to tease with his thumbs, and then made her all but melt when he began a moist, hot trail of kisses where his fingers had been. Just when she was ready to reach around and unhook the bra herself, Trace finally did it for her. "Oh!" Her breasts tumbled free and her breath caught in her throat.

"God," Trace breathed, and tossed the bra to the floor. "You are magnificent."

"Good word."

"It fits." He caressed her skin while swirling circles over her nipples with his thumbs.

Dakota was already so sensitive and aroused that when he leaned up and took her into his hot mouth, she all but came undone. With a breathy sigh, she threaded her fingers through his long, surprisingly silky hair and leaned forward, filling his mouth with her softness. He licked her lightly, flicking his tongue back and forth until she came up to her knees and pulled at his shirt. "I need your skin next to mine."

Trace didn't protest when she tugged open the snaps on his western-cut shirt with a decisive yank, exposing his chest. "Oh, my." She traced a fingertip over a long scar along his ribcage, and then looked at him for explanation.

"A head thrower got me with his horns," he told her.

"Head thrower?"

"A bull that tries to hit you with his head or horns while you're on your back."

"Bastard," she muttered so vehemently that Trace laughed, but his laughter faded when she leaned down and gently kissed the scar.

When she lifted her head to look at him, Trace tried for humor, something he used to be good at. "I have lots more of those."

"And I will kiss each and every one. Stupid bastard bulls."

Trace chuckled softly. "I guess you could say stupid me for trying to ride two thousand pounds of solid muscle with razor-sharp hooves and pointed horns."

Dakota eased the shirt over his shoulders while shaking her head. "I understand when something is in your blood and can't be denied. Music is in mine."

"Yeah, but it's a lot less dangerous," he joked again, but the thought of her in danger set his teeth on edge.

"Good thing! I think I've already established that I'm a little bit wimpy. So the hooves are razor sharp?" She winced.

Trace pointed to a curved scar on his arm. "I've got several on my calves where they always seemed to find me," he said.

"Then I have my work cut out for me," Dakota said, and reached for his belt buckle. She wasn't kidding. Once she had him naked, she planned on kissing each and every scar where he had been sliced, diced, or trounced upon.

Trace found Dakota's breathy trail of kisses erotic, and yet she touched a chord much deeper than sexual gratification. She cared. And because she cared, Trace knew he was venturing into dangerous territory, but he couldn't bring himself to push her away. He wanted this too damned much, and maybe she was right—maybe it was time to start feeling again.

"Not here," he told her. "I want you in bed."

"Okay." Dakota nodded and stood up, but instead of walking, he scooped her up in his arms. "Trace! Your leg!"

"I'm fine," he told her, and was surprised by only a slight twinge as he carried her into her bedroom. He would probably pay for this tomorrow, but it would be worth it. One small bedside lamp cast a soft glow in the room, and the cool night breeze blew in through open windows, bringing in the scent of earth and water. He let her slide down his body, loving the feel of her bare breasts against his chest.

"Sit down on the edge of the bed," he requested, and kneeled down to remove what were obviously new boots. His heart thumped when he reached up to unzip her jeans. She raised her hips for him to pull the tight denim downward, and he sucked in a breath when a cream-colored stretch-lace thong emerged at eye level.

Unable not to, he reached over and ran his fingertip beneath the edge of the lace. Dakota gasped and fell back to her elbows. She closed her eyes and caught her bottom lip between her teeth, and for the life of him, Trace couldn't remember ever seeing a more erotic sight. She was beautiful but had a vulnerable edge that tugged at a protective male side that up until now he didn't even know he possessed. She had somehow managed to find a chink in his armor, and although he didn't know her full story, he had the impression she carried some baggage too.

Perhaps this was meant to be, Trace thought as he leaned over and kissed her just below her navel. Her belly quivered in response, so he kissed her gently again. But then the jaded side of him reared its ugly head. It had just been too damned long since he had made love. No, *had sex*, he sternly corrected himself. This was sex. And once he had her out of his system, he could go back to his usual routine. Plain and simple. Cut-and-dried.

Yeah, right. When Dakota let out a sultry, sexy sigh and threaded her fingers through his hair, Trace looked up and was lost in the amber depths of her soulful eyes. God, and then when she smiled, her lips trembled slightly, reminding him that his heart wasn't the only one at stake here.

That's why this was insane.

His intention was to end this, but Trace inhaled a deep breath and her scent filled his head, chasing away all coherent thought. Instead, he stood up and unzipped his jeans, finishing the task that Dakota had begun. She watched him undress through half-lidded eyes full of female appreciation for his male body. He knew he was in shape, with a thicker build than in his bull riding days, but it had been a long while since a woman had looked at him with desire, and it felt good. Once again she was breaking through his carefully constructed barriers, and at the moment he was powerless to fight it.

With his jeans kicked to the side, Trace stood before Dakota in his boxer briefs. Her eyes widened slightly at his obvious erection clearly outlined against the cotton, but when he started to peel off the briefs, Dakota came up to her knees and put her hands on his wrists. "No, I want to do it. Fair is fair." Her smile was shy, but she held his gaze.

Trace could only nod and manage a husky "Okay." Dakota's hands felt cool against his hot skin, and her warm breath on his abdomen teased and tickled. She hooked her thumbs in his waistband and pulled downward ever so slowly, baring him inch by inch. When she bent her head and slid the briefs down his thighs, strands of her blond hair, golden in the dim light, grazed his skin. The silky texture felt feathery soft and sent a hot shiver down his spine.

He mindlessly stepped out of his boxers while Dakota straightened back up. For a heart-throbbing moment, he thought she was going to take him in her mouth. She looked up, telling him with her eyes that she was willing, but he shook his head, knowing that her mouth on him would immediately send him over the edge. So instead he joined her on the bed, loving it when she wrapped her arms around him in a sweet but sexy way that wrangled another smile from him that he usually kept hidden.

"Dakota, do I need protection?" he whispered in her ear.

"No, I'm on birth control," she shyly assured him, and he instinctively trusted her. "Now kiss me." When she tilted her face up, he covered her mouth with his and kissed her deeply while sliding his hands over her soft skin. She shivered.

"Cold?"

"God, no," she answered.

When he took a nipple into his mouth, Trace was rewarded with a low moan. Damn, he was steely hard with need but he refused to rush, wanting her crazy for him. He teased her with his tongue until she arched her back and lifted her hips up from the bed. "Trace!" Her throaty plea let him know she was more than ready, and with a quick intake of breath, he came to his knees and then eased the lacy thong down her legs.

Trace took a long moment to drink in her beauty. Pe-

tite but with lush curves, she was every man's dream—
and yet, amazingly, seemed unsure of her appeal. He
was scarred and she was perfection, and maybe when
the bourbon wore off she would be sorry.

"Trace, you're frowning. I'm not"—she swallowed
and stammered—"not what you want in a—"

Trace put a fingertip to her lips. "You're perfect,
Dakota."

"What, then?" she began, and her eyes widened
in understanding. "Ohmigod." She put a hand on his
chest and shoved. Of course he didn't budge, because
she was no match for his size, but that didn't stop her.

"What are you doing?"

"This!" Dakota shoved again, hard enough to take
him off guard, and somehow, maybe because it was
one of those adrenaline-fueled miracles, she managed
to do as she intended and flipped him over onto his
back in a move that would have made Hulk Hogan
proud.

"What the hell?" Trace asked, and tried to rise from
the mound of pillows at his back, but she pushed his
shoulders and straddled him, breathing hard, and
pinned him with a glare. Trace had obviously pushed
some sort of button, and he wasn't quite sure where
this was going. "You're pissed?"

"Royally."

"At me, Princess?"

Her glare faded and she shook her head. "No.
I'm pissed at whoever made you stop believing in
yourself."

She was hitting way too close to home, but he didn't
let her know it. "I believe I can make you come three
times, so let's get to it," he said, armor intact, deliber-
ately rude. But when he slid a hand up her back and

tried to pull her head down for a kiss, she braced a hand on his chest and resisted.

"I have no doubt," Dakota replied. "I also believe you have the heart and soul of a champion. You were on top of the world, a cocky, hell-raising cowboy."

He wanted this conversation to end. Now.

"Trace, I know what it's like to be on top of the world, but I also know how much work and determination it takes to get there. But listen! There's so much more to you than—"

"Speaking of on top, do you like it there or do you—"

"Shut up!" Dakota said, and tried to scramble away, but Trace grabbed her wrists. She knew he was retreating into defensive mode, but this was too much for her to handle. "Let me go," she demanded. Her eyes shimmered with tears, and she tried to tug her hands away from his firm hold.

"I wish the hell I could," Trace replied. Instead he threaded his fingers through hers and pulled her hands over her head so that she landed flush against his chest.

And then he kissed her.

13

The Eye of the Storm

Dakota was well aware of his tactics. She shouldn't have played into his hands and allowed him to get to her, but she was completely out of her element on so many levels that she couldn't think straight, and it wasn't from the bourbon. Trace Coleman was more intoxicating than her two shots of Maker's Mark, and his kiss sent her head spinning. He let go of her hands so that he could cradle her head, but she remained powerless to escape.

She wanted this way too much.

Her anger, though, simmered beneath the surface, and she could feel his own frustration in his touch, his kiss, but Dakota understood. It was simple, really. His scars were emotional as well as physical, and she knew where he was coming from. . . . When you are no longer on top, you find out who your true friends are, and they are few and far between. Trace was angry because he didn't want to risk his heart by caring, but it was too late. Although he pretended to be a badass, she should let him know he was a big fat phony. But in order to do that she would have to quit kissing him, and she really didn't want to stop.

The man could kiss.

Still, Dakota knew he was pissed that he couldn't resist her, and she remained pissed that he had been such an ass, but their mutual anger only served to fuel their desire. The kiss was hot, deep, aggressive, and sexy as hell. And his half-sitting position against the pillows allowed Dakota's breasts to slide seductively against his chest. With a groan he wrapped his big hands around her waist and lifted her up so that she rested intimately against his shaft. He felt hot and hard—big and ready.

"I want to be inside you," he murmured, low and husky in her ear. "Do you want this, Dakota?" He guided her hips so she could rub against him.

"Yes." Dakota nodded. Her heart thumped and she ached with need, so she gripped his shoulders and watched his face while she lowered her body to his. "I want this," she gasped at the delicious sensation of him sliding into her slick heat, inch by glorious inch. She also knew he was going slowly for her benefit, her comfort, and she was moved by his concern and her anger evaporated. He was big; she was small, and, dear God, he felt amazing.

Dakota leaned in and kissed him softly while easing her body up and then slowly back down. Trace helped her, guided her with his large hands and strong body until desire took over. Her eyes fluttered shut and she moved faster, loving the feel of warm skin over hard muscle. She moved faster, needing more of him, all of him. Dakota squeezed his shoulders while he filled her, loved her until her pleasure climbed higher, escalated, and then exploded. When she cried out, he joined her, thrusting upward, climaxing with her before pulling her head down for a long, heated kiss.

Dakota fell against his chest and he held her there. They didn't speak, but he gently moved her to his side and pulled the covers up over them. "Are you going to stay with me?" she asked as she snuggled against him. He didn't answer, but she felt his muscles tense. "It's okay; you don't have to," she quickly added, but swallowed hard.

"I'll stay for a little while, but then I should go," Trace finally answered.

Not wanting him to hear the emotion in her voice, Dakota merely nodded. Sleeping with Trace Coleman probably wasn't the smartest thing she could have done, but she refused to beat herself up about it. Tomorrow she would dust off her guitar and knuckle down to do some serious songwriting, and stay out of Trace's way. And yet she snuggled in close, savoring the sensation of her skin next to his and knowing this might be the one and only time in his arms.

She felt the steady beat of his heart beneath her cheek and couldn't resist kissing him softly on his chest. He didn't respond, and at first Dakota thought he might be asleep, but the slight tensing of his arm curled around her let her know he was awake but didn't want her to know it.

A hot wave of sadness washed over Dakota. She had felt so alone, so lost, for such a long time, with no one to turn to. Her parents thought all was fine, and she intended to keep it that way because of her father's fragile health. She was a big girl and she was determined to find her way, and the last thing she needed was the entanglement of a relationship, especially with a broody, bruised, and battered cowboy who would likely fight her every step of the way.

You need each other; can heal each other, seemed to whisper to her on the edge of the night breeze. Emotion clogged her throat, and she wanted to reach up and pull his head down for a tender kiss.

But she didn't. Couldn't. Instead she lay very still, hoping he would think she had dozed off. After a few minutes, she did.

Trace could tell by Dakota's even breathing that she had fallen asleep. He kissed the top of her head, which was an oddly tender gesture for him to do and yet somehow felt right. He fully intended to ease from the bed, but she stirred, mumbled something like "Don't go." Or perhaps it was only his imagination. Still, he decided to stay until he could escape undetected. At least that's what he convinced himself. It wasn't because he didn't want to untangle himself from her body or hold her in his arms all night long and make love to her again as the sun peeked over the horizon. No, never that.

Dakota stirred, sighed, and her warm breath caressing his chest was almost enough for him to wake her and make love to her all over again. It didn't help that her shapely leg was tucked between his and her hand had slipped precariously close to his groin. Her scent, soft and alluring, filled his head and, although having her in his arms like this was incredibly arousing, Trace also found himself relaxing. He decided to allow himself this moment and leave then shortly thereafter, not giving a thought to falling asleep, since he often suffered from insomnia, especially if his leg ached. He'd just rest his eyes for a few minutes longer.

*   *   *

From somewhere far away, Trace heard his cell phone alarm beeping, and he moaned softly, not wanting to leave his warm cocoon of blissful slumber. Funny, though, since he always awoke before his alarm and used it as a backup just in case. His eyes fluttered as he slapped toward the nightstand where he kept his phone but came up with nothing but air. With another groan, this time of frustration, he opened his eyes and blinked in confusion.

This wasn't his bedroom. Um, and this wasn't his bed. Damn. And there was a very sexy little leg entwined with his. He had fallen asleep with Dakota. Trace ran a hand down his face and turned his head and took in her sweet, sleeping form. Sometime during the night she had rolled from his chest to her own pillow, but one small hand remained on his abdomen. Her blond hair was mussed and her lips slightly parted, and damned if she wasn't a gorgeous sight to wake up to, he thought with a reluctant smile. And he had slept like a baby. For the first time he could remember, Trace felt totally rested and relaxed. In the back of his mind he knew why, but he didn't allow himself to go there.

Trace took in the delicate curve of her shoulder, and he had the sudden urge to reach over and caress her cheek, making him wonder where all of these damned touchy-feely urges were coming from. Balling his hand into a fist, he refrained, but then she shifted, causing the sheet to slip down her back.

"Damn," he mumbled when the fact that she was stark naked slammed into his befuddled brain. Touchy-feely turned into touchy-he-wanted-to-jump-her-bones, and to make sure that wasn't going to happen, he had to get out of her bed quickly and, hopefully, without waking her up. Last night had been a mistake on too many levels to count, and he needed to escape.

Trace held his breath and slowly tried to scoot away from her body, but it wasn't easy since her leg remained entwined with his. Still, he moved, inch by inch to the side of the bed, and he was at the edge and about to put one foot onto the floor when she suddenly shifted and rolled toward him.

"Whoa!" In his surprise, Trace reacted too quickly and tumbled over the side of the bed, landing with a thump and an oath.

"What? Ohmigod, Trace?" Dakota mumbled, and leaned over the edge, rubbing sleep from her eyes and pushing hair from her face. "What happened? Did I kick you? I do weird things in my sleep." She covered her mouth with one hand, obviously forgetting her state of undress. She had a habit of doing that, Trace thought, and might have smiled if he hadn't been so embarrassed. "Hey, don't worry. I'm always doing stuff like that," she admitted with a sleepy smile, but then her eyes widened when she looked down and realized she was giving him quite a show. Of course, he was reciprocating.

Dakota scooted back under the covers. "Are you okay?" she asked in a husky, just-woke-up voice that was too damned sexy for words.

"My pride is about all that's injured," he admitted, and reached for his boxers that, thank God, were within reach, not that they could hide his obvious response to her nakedness.

"Thank you for staying," she said softly, and peeked over the edge of the bed once more. A cute pink blush warmed her cheeks, and he had a hard time not hopping right back into bed with her. "Would you like some coffee? I pilfered some from the kitchen," she offered with a bright smile that quickly faded when she read his expression.

"Dakota . . ."

She lowered her gaze and nervously plucked at the sheet wrapped around her body. "Oh, I think I get it," she said with a frown. "You fell asleep but didn't really have any intention of staying." At his silence, she glanced at him briefly to see if she was correct. She licked her lips, swallowed, and then nodded in what she probably thought was a businesslike manner. "No biggie. This was just one of those"—she cleared her throat and finished—"you know, things." She shrugged, but made the mistake of swinging her arm in a nonchalant arc, allowing the sheet to slip, baring one bodacious breast. She tugged the sheet back up, but then leaned over with her face flaming and said, "I did live in L.A., you know. In the"—she paused, as if searching her brain—"fast lane."

"Fast lane." He gave her a deadpan look as he sat up, and then chuckled.

"Okay, maybe not the fast lane, but definitely the middle lane." She made a wiggling motion with her fingers, giving Trace another nice peek of skin before she caught the sheet. Then she closed her eyes. "Fine, more like the slow lane," she admitted. She opened her eyes and looked down at him. "Look, the point I was trying to make is that I'm a big girl, Trace. I'm not going to cause any drama concerning last night. I'll go back to the staying-out-of-your-way-and-you'll-never-know-I'm-here plan." She reached up and crossed her heart. "I promise this time."

Not knowing what to say, Trace merely nodded, but when he looked up at her, he felt like an ass. It didn't help that she appeared lost and vulnerable, with her sleep-rumpled hair, heavy-lidded eyes, and white sheet clutched white-knuckle tightly at her chin. But added to the mix was the fact that Trace could see the outline of her breasts beneath the soft cotton. It hit him hard that he knew how those breasts felt in his hands . . . tasted in his mouth, and he had to suppress a moan. Her amber eyes were wide and expressive, but way too trusting. There was no way he wasn't going to keep tabs on her. He just wouldn't let her know it. But that was going to be as far as it went. "Well, if you need anything, let me know."

"Thanks. Will do. You probably need to get to work."

"Okay, boss lady."

"I didn't mean it like that!" She came up to her knees in the center of the bed, and damned if the sheet didn't slide to her waist. "Oh, dammit all to hell and back!" she cursed as she scrambled to cover herself, and wrapped up like a mummy. "In case you're wondering, I didn't mean to do that."

"I wasn't wondering."

"God, I am such a train wreck!" she muttered, more to herself than to him, and then turned away as if embarrassed at her admission.

Trace hated that she felt that way, and wanted to know more about the circumstances that brought her to the marina, but asking and caring were too dangerous and so he refrained. Trace knew he had to get the hell out of there before he made some stupid mistake and fell into bed with her again. For someone as disciplined as he prided himself on being, Trace had no willpower where Dakota was concerned. He tugged on his jeans, but the location of his shirt remained a mystery.

"In the corner," Dakota said glumly, and pointed with one finger.

"Thanks," Trace responded, and in spite of his resolve, she managed to get to him. So while he was snapping his shirt he said, "Dakota, you're not a train wreck."

"Be still my heart," she said, and snorted.

"Okay, that was lame," he admitted. "Look, about last night—"

"You did *not* just say that."

"What?"

"Just don't follow with 'I'm just not that into you.'"

"Dakota—"

She put a hand up in the air and sighed. "I told you I won't cause any drama, and I truly won't. It happened. You're off the hook, so just go, okay?"

"Yeah," he said, and knew he should feel relieved, but when he got outside in the warm sunshine, all he felt was an odd sense of loss. Deciding he needed some coffee to clear his head, he bypassed his office and walked in the direction of the kitchen, hoping that Sierra made this morning's batch good and strong.

14

Might as Well Be Me

Sierra's heart thudded when the screen door to the kitchen slammed shut. She turned around from thickening sausage gravy, thinking it might be Grady stopping in. But it was Trace, and damned if he didn't look as if he'd just lost his best friend. "Well, you're lookin' even more pissed off at the world than usual," Sierra observed, and turned to the oven when the timer buzzed. She peeked at the biscuits that were not quite golden brown yet and set the timer for another two minutes.

"I just need some coffee and I'll be right as rain."

"You know where to get it."

"It's strong, I hope."

"You know it. On a Monday morning I need an extra kick, especially since I stayed out too late last night," she admitted while slipping on an oven mitt.

"You and Grady stay long?"

"We played some pool," she answered, and turned away to take the biscuits out of the oven.

"And he drove you home?"

"Yes." Sierra busied herself stirring the gravy. She tucked a lock of hair behind her ear, and although she was back to her usual ponytail, it was the sloppy, sexy version, and she had taken some pains with her makeup the way Dakota had shown her. Instead of a loose fitting T-shirt and jeans, she wore a yellow tank top and cutoff denim shorts. There wasn't anything terribly revealing about her attire and it was perfectly acceptable on a warm June day, but she just knew if Grady walked through that door she would blush from her head to her toes.

"And?"

"For goodness' sake!" Sierra turned around, put her palms on the stainless steel island and leaned forward. "He didn't try anything." *Unfortunately,* she mused but kept that thought to herself. She pressed her lips together before giving Trace a knowing look of her own.

"What?"

She straightened up and fisted her hands on her hips. "Oh, like you didn't just come from Dakota's cabin!"

Trace shrugged and took a sip of his coffee.

"Spill, or I'll beat it outta ya!" Sierra pleaded, but inclined her head. She paused, waiting, and then rephrased in what Dakota called her indoor voice. "I mean, would you care to elaborate?"

"Not really."

"I wasn't really kiddin' about the beating it outta ya part," Sierra warned, but put her hand over Trace's and patted it. "Seriously, though, I'm here for ya. Anyone who gets mixed up with that girl will need someone to talk to," she added with a soft grin, and sighed. "You're not gonna spill, are ya?"

"Sierra," Trace didn't appear as if he wanted to elaborate, and Sierra felt a little guilty prying, but she was beginning to think that the two of them, however mismatched they appeared, somehow had potential. But then Trace shook his head. "Me and the pop princess? I don't think so." But there was something in his eyes that gave Sierra hope.

"She might be a princess"—she arched one eyebrow—"but you're no prince charming."

"I won't argue with you there."

Sierra reached over and lowered the temperature on the sausage gravy and gave it a stir. "And she does that annoying screaming thing that makes a person want to slap her silly, but still"—Sierra tapped the side of her cheek—"she has that cute Christina Applegate thing going on, don't ya think?" She didn't know why she was pushing this, but she felt compelled to for some reason.

"Christina Applegate?"

"Don't you watch any television?" Sierra asked while pulling apart the biscuits and tossing them in a big pan.

"No." He shrugged. "Well, except for sports. And the Food Network."

Sierra's eyebrows shot up.

"Hey, I like food. What can I say? Now, what were you getting at?"

She got another metal pan from the shelf and dumped the gravy into it. While breaking up the bigger lumps of sausage with a spoon, Sierra waved her other hand in the air. "Dakota reminds me of Christina Applegate, who happens to be sweet but sexy and a little on the flighty side, much like our resident owner."

"I hadn't noticed." Trace shrugged, and then paid way too much attention to his coffee.

"Right. Well, they sure did at Dewey's," Sierra mentioned briskly, and watched Trace's face for a reaction. He tried to remain calm, cool, and collected, but the muscle jumping in his clenched jaw totally outed him. Sierra had to turn away to hide her grin. Maybe, just maybe, the pop princess could bring Trace out of the world he had retreated into. While the marina was a beautiful place, a man who was once the best bull rider in the world needed more in his life to keep things interesting. Trace needed a challenge, and Dakota Dunn just might be the ticket.

"Well, Dakota promised me she would keep a low profile and let us go about our marina business while she does whatever it is she came here to accomplish."

Sierra lugged the pan of biscuits over to the warmer on wheels and put it in the open slot, and then did the same with the gravy. "And do you think she is capable of doing that?"

Trace heated up his coffee and added creamer. While stirring thoughtfully, he said, "I don't know why not. She seemed sincere enough to me."

Sierra nodded. "We'll see, I guess. I just don't know if she can pull it off. Trouble just seems to find her."

Trace nodded slowly. "Yeah, I'm afraid so."

Sierra added an egg casserole to the third slot and said, "I'd better wheel this out to the hungry fishermen. You want some first?" she asked, knowing that Trace never ate in the dining room with everyone else.

"Thanks. I'll take some of the casserole back to my office."

Sierra nodded and scooped a hearty portion onto a plate. "Catch ya later," she said, and waved as Trace headed out the door. She pulled the cart backward so she could bump the double doors open with her backside, but paused at the door and took a deep breath. Grady would be sitting with his morning group, giving tips about where to fish. She had done this drill hundreds of times, but facing Grady after what had gone down the past couple of days suddenly made her nervous. Still, this was her job, so she took a deep breath and paused to get her composure. She didn't want to enter the dining room with her face flaming.

Grady glanced at the double doors to the kitchen for the umpteenth time and looked up at the clock. Sierra was a little late with breakfast, and it wasn't like her not to be prompt. He wondered whether something was wrong, and shook his head. Ever since last night he simply could not stop thinking about her. She had looked so freaking amazing, and damned if he hadn't been jealous of the way other guys were fawning all over her. What was up with that? He simply did not get jealous.

You have to care to be jealous slammed into his brain, and he shook his head again. *I should have kissed her*, Grady continued to muse, and then shook his head even harder.

"What the hell's wrong with you, Grady?"

"Huh?" Grady turned his attention from the doors back to the table of guys anxious to talk fishing. Usually Grady couldn't shut up, but today he was totally distracted and couldn't keep a train of thought going. But he'd be damned if he'd admit it.

"Tied one on last night. Just a little hungover, so cut me some slack, okay?" Of course, it wasn't true, since he had only a couple of beers so he could drive Sierra home. *I have my pride*, he thought fiercely, but found himself looking back at the damned doors.

"Dude, you keep shaking your head and then staring at the kitchen."

"I'm hungry, okay?" he answered, just as a hush fell over the rowdy crowd and all eyes turned to the kitchen doors.

Grady joined them, and almost dropped his coffee mug when Sierra's very cute jeans-clad butt pushed through the double doors. She wiggled as she pulled the warmer into the room, and although he had never done so before, Grady scooted his chair back and headed over to assist her. "Need some help?"

"Oh!" Sierra looked up in surprise, lost her footing, and stumbled backward. Grady reached out and put his hands around her waist in order to steady her. She flushed a pretty shade of pink, but then frowned. "What the hell are you doin'?"

Grady shrugged lamely, feeling silly. "Thought you could use some help."

"I've done this a million times," she said, and then seemed to realize that all eyes were on them. "Thanks, though. I've got it."

Grady nodded and was about to sit back down, but instead he walked over to the other side of the warmer and helped her wheel it to the side of the dining room. She gave him another startled glance but didn't offer another protest, he supposed so as not to draw attention. But Grady noticed that all eyes remained on her progress, and he barely refrained from staring them all down.

Although on wheels, the warmer was surprisingly heavy for such a little shit like her to handle, and he felt guilty that he had never before offered to assist her. He thought about other times when he had seen her hauling in boxes or dragging out the trash and had never come to her aid, thinking, he supposed, that it was her job. It dawned on him that the main reason was that he had always considered her one of the guys—but those days were long gone.

When she bent over to get stacked plates from beneath the breakfast bar against the wall, there was a collective intake of breath. This time Grady couldn't help himself and whipped around to give the three tables of men a glare of warning.

"Need any other help?" Grady asked, drawing another look of surprise from Sierra.

"I'm fine," she answered, and then angled her head as if not quite sure what to make of his attention.

"Okay," Grady said, but stood there and stared at her mouth, which was shiny with some glossy stuff. Although her glorious head of hair was disappointingly pulled into a ponytail, several cute curls had already escaped and it was looser, more feminine.

"Grady?"

"Hmm?"

"You need somethin'?"

Yeah, a kiss, popped into his head and he almost blurted it out. "Um," he began, and wondered what she would do if he dragged her from the room, pressed her up against the kitchen wall, and kissed her senseless.

"You okay? Comin' down with somethin'?" She reached up and with concern in her eyes, felt his forehead. "You do feel a tad warm."

"Must be the coffee I just drank," he lied. "And I hurried to get over here, since I had to get a boat ready for Dakota."

Sierra's eyebrows shot up. "A boat for Dakota? I smell disaster."

"It was just a rowboat, for goodness' sake. You only have to be twelve to rent one, Sierra."

"Yeah, but what did she want a boat for?"

Grady shrugged. "She said she wanted to get out on the water. I told her not to venture too far." He waved a hand in the air. "She'll be fine."

"I guess." Sierra nodded, but didn't look convinced. "I sure hope you're right."

"Okay, then." Grady turned to leave, but paused and said, "Hey, I hate to ask this, but would you do me a favor?"

"Sure," she agreed without hesitation, one of the things he liked about her. He pulled her aside so that the men could line up and fill their plates, and—if he was honest—to give the impression that he and Sierra were together.

"It's supposed to really warm up today, and if the fish are biting I'll be out on the lake for a while. Would you mind making sure that Gil has water outside the kitchen door?"

"Sure," she answered with a smile that made Grady feel giddy, like he was a love-struck teenager. "If Gil gets on my good side, he might just get lucky and be rewarded with some scraps."

"Thanks," Grady said, and grinned. "Oh, by the way, just how does one get on your good side?"

"It's pretty simple," she answered with eyes that suddenly seemed serious. "Just be nice to me."

Her admission hit Grady in the gut as she hurried away as if she were embarrassed. He stood there, rooted to the floor, and watched her while his heart thudded. Grady knew Sierra's mother had run out on her daddy, and that they once owned the diner in town that folded a couple of years ago when she started working at the marina. He knew the Miller boys were good people but rough-and-tumble, and he just bet that Sierra didn't have it easy growing up in a house-ful of men.

"Holy shit," he said under his breath when he sud-denly had a lightbulb moment. Sierra was sick of being treated like one of the guys and had enlisted Dakota's help in getting all girly. He grinned and shook his head. And Sierra was giving Dakota lessons on tough-ening up. *Brilliant*, he thought, but then frowned when he remembered them together at Dewey's. *But damned dangerous*, he thought with a shake of his head. Both women were out of their element. No wonder Trace had been worried; it hit Grady that they were going to have to keep a close eye on both women as they ven-tured into foreign territory.

"Well, damn. *One of the guys*, my sweet ass." When Sierra came back into the dining room with a fresh batch of biscuits, all eyes were on her and Grady knew without a doubt that he and Trace were going to have their work cut out for them. But he smiled, thinking, *Hey, it's a tough job, but someone has to do it*. He watched Sierra's delectable derriere as she headed back to the kitchen, and grinned. "Yep, might as well be me."

15

Going Overboard

While humming a song she had been working on, Dakota paddled around the edge of the lake, hoping to get in touch with nature and encourage her creative juices to flow. It did her heart good to see that the water appeared as crystal clear as when she had spent time here as a child, and she felt a sense of accomplishment that she had a hand in keeping it from overdevelopment and the pollution that would have come along with it. Dakota realized that Pine Hollow Lake had always been the happy place where she and her parents had created so many memories.

My parents. At that thought, she closed her eyes and sighed. She had snowed them into believing she was living off endorsements and royalties when, in fact, she couldn't even score local commercials, and except for the random placement of some of her songs in movie sound tracks, royalties were a thing of the past as well. A few B-list reality show offers had come her way, but she had refused to go that route. And while she despised lying to her mother and father, she hated for them to worry even more.

Besides, she told herself as she hummed and rowed, she had a plan. "Country music star," she said with a firm nod. If Jessica Simpson could do it, so could she, right? Dakota shook her head and decided not to think about her problems and issues, and to simply enjoy a nice little cruise around the lake.

The sound of water lapping against the shore and birds chirping overhead caused a sense of peace to wash over her in a way she hadn't experienced for a very long time. The sunshine felt warm on her skin and the air smelled earthy and clean. She inhaled deeply, turned her face up to the clear blue sky, and smiled.

And then a bird pooped on her.

Wincing, she lifted her sunglasses and angled her head to view a grayish-white splat on her shoulder, which was bared by her buttercup yellow halter top. After lifting the oars into the boat, she looked around, hoping to find a rag or towel of some sort, but came up empty. With a groan she glanced at the bird poop and wondered what to do.

"Well, duh," Dakota muttered, and looked down at the water, thinking she could splash off the offending goo in a jiffy. But as luck would have it, right after she leaned over the side of her little vessel and scooped up a handful of water, a tricked-out fishing boat went zooming down the center of the lake. The unexpected wake caused Dakota's boat to bob, and with a scream, she tumbled headfirst overboard.

The water felt shockingly cold on Dakota's sun-warmed skin. With a muffled curse, she surfaced, sputtering and coughing, her hair covering her eyes. Taking a deep breath, she dipped beneath the surface to untangle her hair and smooth it back from her face while wondering how she was going to hoist herself back up into the boat. She realized she could swim to shore without too much effort, but hated having to go to Trace for help yet again. Before she could think more about her plan, a strong arm snaked around her waist and yanked her to the surface of the water.

"What?" she sputtered and looked back over her shoulder. "Trace? Where in the world did you come from?"

"I was making my rounds in my boat when I saw you fall in. Don't worry, I've got you now," he said, skillfully treading water while holding Dakota.

"Got me? You thought I was drowning?"

"Well, yeah!" His chest moved up and down, and she could tell he was really worried.

"Trace, my daddy taught me to swim when I was a toddler. I've been coming to this lake since I was a baby," she assured him, but felt a warm and fuzzy feeling that he was so concerned.

"Then why in the hell did you fall in if you are such an expert?" he asked, clearly annoyed. "I about broke my neck haulin' ass over here!"

The warm and fuzzy feeling evaporated, and she twisted around in his arms, refusing to feel guilty. "A bird pooped on me! I was simply washing it off when some jackass came flying across the water and forced me overboard."

"That jackass was Grady taking paying customers out to fish!" he ground out, and shook his head. "So much for your promise of keeping a low profile, Dakota."

"I didn't ask for, nor did I need you to, rescue me."

"Well, you screamed. Again. To me, a female scream

means a cry for help. For you, a scream is normal conversation."

"Look, I'm sorry," she said, and wanted to push away but knew she couldn't hoist herself up into the boat, so she was at his mercy. "All I wanted was some peace and quiet. I love it out here on the water." She shrugged. "I didn't mean to cause you any trouble. Now, if you would just shove me up into the boat, I'll be on my way," Dakota said, and wished his bare shoulders didn't feel so good beneath her hands. He was shirtless and, she guessed, in swim trunks. With his dark hair slicked back from his face he looked starkly masculine, and the urge to pull his head down for a hot kiss made her push at him and twist from his hold. "Okay, give me a shove." She turned and angled her butt at him.

The thought of putting his hands on her ass made Trace so hot, he wondered why steam wasn't rising from the water. And it sure didn't help that Dakota's cotton halter top molded to her like a second skin, making it obvious that she was braless.

"Well?" she asked over her shoulder, and then said, "Oh no! My flip-flop's floating away!" Without warning, she started swimming out into the lake.

"Dakota, wait!" Trace saw the ridiculous flower-topped flip-flop bobbing in the water. The problem was that there were several fishing boats out, and this area was a no-swimming zone. A speedboat coming by wouldn't be watching out for swimmers, and his heart pounded with the same fear he experienced when he saw her fall into the water.

Truthfully, he usually made his rounds to check up on things later in the day. It had been *her* he was checking up on this morning. "Dakota, get back here!" Trace shouted, but she kept swimming toward the rubber shoe. With a curse, he shot out after her, but she was a strong swimmer and had a head start on him. "Dakota! It's dangerous!" he tried to warn as he swam as fast as he knew how. Sure enough, out of the corner of his eye he saw a boat zipping toward her.

Trace doubled his efforts while praying the driver spotted the sun glinting off of her blond head. She reached for the flip-flop, but must have heard the whine of the engine and froze for a second before turning and swimming like the hounds of hell were after her. The boat passed a good six or eight feet from Dakota just as Trace reached her side, but in his mind it was still much too close for comfort.

"Ohmigod!" she shouted, and with wide eyes threw her arms around his neck and clung while waves from the wake washed over them.

Trace wanted to be angry, but she shivered in his arms. "Hey, you're okay," he soothed, and tightened his hold on her. "Let's get you back to the boat."

She nodded into the crook of his neck. "Where did he come from?"

"He shot out of a cove over there. Dakota, Willow Creek is strictly for fishing on this side, so the boaters don't look for anyone swimming. It isn't a no-wake zone this far from the marina, so they tend to fly like a bat outta hell down the main channel of the lake. I should have a talk with Grady about slowing things down."

Dakota shook her head. "No, don't ruin their fun on account of my stupidity." She blew out an exasperated sigh. "I am such a train wreck!"

"Stop saying that," he murmured in her ear, and if they hadn't been bobbing near the middle of the lake, he might have kissed her. "Come on, swim next to me."

"Okay," she glumly agreed, and moments later they were back at the boats. "All right, toss me up there, and I swear I'll stay out of trouble. Maybe I'll just head back to the cabin and crawl back in bed."

Now, that was an image he didn't need in his head. "No, you come with me. There's a ladder on my boat over there," he said, and pointed to his Sea Ray Sun Sport. "We can tow the rowboat back to shore."

"All right." She reluctantly nodded, and swam over to his boat.

Trace unfolded and lowered the metal ladder before moving to the side so she could climb up onto the swim platform.

"Nice boat," she commented.

"Thanks," Trace managed to answer, but he just about swallowed his tongue when he saw that her thin white shorts were all but transparent from being wet, allowing him to see the outline of her panties. He swallowed a groan and willed his body not to have an immediate reaction that would be embarrassing in his board shorts that laced up the front. He should have averted his gaze, but simply did not have the will power not to keep his eyes glued to her ass.

Trace opened his mouth to tell Dakota he was going to swim and pull her rowboat over to his when her hands slipped off the top rung.

"Whoa!" she shouted, and her very cute butt landed on his surprised face. Poetic justice for his ogling, he supposed, as he sunk beneath the water with Dakota in tow, since for some reason he felt compelled to grab her around the waist. They surfaced together, tangled in each other's arms and legs.

Trace rubbed his face. "You could have simply said 'Kiss my ass,'" he said, and she giggled. "And I suppose you're going to tell me you didn't mean to do that," he commented dryly.

"No, I didn't," she answered. "Truly," she whispered, and looked at him for a long moment. "But you know what?"

"What?" he asked, and could not take his eyes off of her mouth.

"I do mean to do this," she told him, and then pulled his head down for a kiss.

Trace was taken by surprise, but then again, her taking him by surprise was becoming a habit. He couldn't, however, even begin to turn away from the feel of her soft, warm lips pressed against his mouth. She was shy at first, but then groaned and opened her mouth in sweet invitation. Trace dug deep for willpower, but when the tip of her tongue touched his, any last shred of resistance melted.

Trace grabbed the ladder with one hand and slipped his other arm around her waist. He pulled his mouth from hers just long enough to whisper hotly in her ear, "Wrap your legs around me." When she complied, he cupped one hand around her ass and then crushed his mouth to hers while kissing her with a passion he hadn't experienced in a long time.

The water lapped sensuously against them, cool and silky against warm skin. Trace moved his mouth from her lips to her neck and started a hot trail downward to her cleavage. He licked the warm, soft skin and dearly wanted to untie the knot around her neck, but was afraid that someone would see them, and so he pulled back and rested his forehead on hers while trying to regain his composure. "Dakota, I'm going to tug the rowboat back to shore and then you can go on my rounds with me, if you want to. I'll show you some coves and secluded places where you can go for real peace and quiet."

She nodded and gave him a shy smile. "That sounds lovely."

"Good," he said, all the while wondering why he was inviting her along with him when he had vowed to keep his distance. "You'll find towels down in the cabin," he offered.

Dakota looked at him in surprise. "Cabin?"

Trace nodded. "It's small, just a weekender, but serviceable. There's a head, if you need it too."

"Nice," she said, and made her way up the ladder, this time without mishap.

"Toss me a rope," Trace requested when she was inside the cockpit.

"Here you go," she said, and disappeared from view.

Trace swam over and secured the rowboat to his Sea Ray, climbed up the ladder and folded it back into place. A moment later, Dakota, wrapped in a towel, emerged from the cabin.

"It's nice down there. Bigger than I thought," she said. "Having a bathroom is sweet."

"You mean a head."

"Right. There's even a kitchen."

"Galley," he corrected her with a grin. "Get with the program, Princess."

"Whatever you say, Captain," she said, and gave him a sharp salute.

"Now, that's more like it," Trace responded, and almost grinned again. "You may own the marina, but I'm the boss of this boat."

Dakota laughed. "Agreed," she said, and sat down in the passenger's seat across from Trace. She snuggled in the soft beach towel while they made their way back to the dock. Although the distance was fairly short, it was slow going with the rowboat in tow, but Dakota didn't mind. She entertained herself pretending to enjoy the passing scenery when she was really observing Trace from behind her sunglasses. His long hair blew in the wind, and in his blue board shorts and mirrored Oakleys, he appeared young and carefree—and he should be, she thought with a touch of sadness.

He stood up in front of the driver's seat and carefully drove at the required idle speed past boat slips and over to the side of the dock near the kitchen. Gil, who was lapping up water from a big bowl, barked in greeting as he ran over to meet them. A moment later, Sierra came out the back door with her hands on her hips.

"Gil, what the hell you barkin' about?" she shouted, but then waved in their direction. "What are y'all doin'?" she asked, and walked over to Trace's boat. She looked at the rowboat that Trace was tying up and then at Dakota, who remained wrapped in the beach towel. "Don't tell me you fell in the lake."

"Okay, I won't tell you," Dakota replied, but felt heat creep into her cheeks.

Sierra turned her attention to Trace. "Will you tell me what happened?" she asked in her usual no-nonsense tone, but Dakota noticed, with some satisfaction, that Sierra looked cute in her shorts and tank top. While her hair was in her customary ponytail, she had styled it artfully sloppily, and she also wore some subtle pink lip gloss and mascara. "Well?" She raised her arms in the air and looked at him expectantly. "This is gonna be good. I can tell."

While absently petting Gil, Trace said, "She leaned over and fell in."

"What? That's it?"

Dakota stood up and came to the side of the boat. "Now, wait a minute. A bird pooped on me, for heaven's sake! While I was leaning over cleaning it off, Grady went flying by in his fishing boat and *then* I fell in," she clarified, and gave Trace a look warning to not tell the flip-flop story. "Do not laugh," she warned Sierra. "Or I'll kick your butt."

Sierra rolled her eyes. "You gotta say it like you mean it, Dakota. And say *ass*, not *butt*."

"Okay, how's this?" She cleared her throat and stood up straighter. "Don't you dare laugh, or I'll kick your ever-lovin' ass!" She jutted her chin in the air for good measure.

"Should I ask what's going on here?" Trace inquired with a slow shake of his head.

"No," Sierra answered firmly.

"Then that means you two are up to no good," he replied. Gil put his paw on Trace's leg, begging for more, when Trace paused from scratching his ears. But Trace straightened up from his kneeling position and absently rubbed his thigh. Dakota had noticed, though, that he seemed to be walking a bit better, but she wasn't about to ask or comment on it.

"Lucky you happened to be out on the lake and spotted Dakota floppin' around in the water."

"I wasn't flopping around," Dakota protested, but it was now pretty obvious that Trace was out watching after her and not on his regular rounds. She knew he wouldn't like it if she called him on the fact, but felt another shot of warm fuzzies that he cared enough to take the time to keep her safe. He continued to be her reluctant hero, but was her hero yet again, like it or not.

Ever since her career went down the toilet, she had gotten used to no one caring. Sure, her mom and dad called, and she visited them in Florida when she could. They cared, but after that, the list was rather short. Caring, she decided as she looked over at Trace, was pretty damned sexy.

"Hey, Sierra," Trace said, "I'm going to show Dakota around the lake. Is there something in the kitchen you can toss us together for lunch?"

"Sure, I just made a batch of potato salad, and I'm having cold cuts, and cookies for dessert if Grady hasn't eaten them all. Sound good?" Sierra asked.

"Perfect," Trace answered. "A jug of sweet tea would be great too. That okay with you, Dakota?"

"Sure," she answered, "but are you sure about leaving your office? I don't want you to have a mountain of work staring you in the face on my account."

"I'm caught up," he promised her. "And I'll have my phone on, if anyone needs me. By the way, here's your tote bag from the boat," he said, and handed it to her. "I think I heard your phone ring."

"Thanks. I almost forgot about it!"

"I'll be back with your lunch in a few minutes," Sierra said, and when Trace tuned his back, she gave Dakota a thumbs-up, widened her eyes, and wiggled her eyebrows. When Trace turned back around, she schooled her face back into a serious expression.

Dakota covered her mouth to hide her smile and thought how much fun it was to have a girlfriend again. Her circle of friends from her singing days disappeared when her career took a tumble, and she missed female companionship. In a very short time, this little marina was beginning to feel like home more than L.A. ever did.

"Dakota, I'm going to pop in my office and check my e-mail while Sierra's packing our lunch. You need anything else?"

"No, I'm fine. I'll just dry off here in the sunshine," she said with a smile.

Trace didn't smile back, but she did get a brief nod. She had the feeling he wanted to spend some time with her, but then again was kicking himself in the butt—*ass*—for asking her to go on the cruise around the lake. She wasn't about to let him get out of it, though, and vowed that before the day was over, she would wrangle another smile from her cranky but oh-so-very-sexy cowboy.

And maybe a kiss or two as well.

16

Dakota Dunn's Day Off

"Don't do this to yourself, Trace," Sierra said as she handed him the big bag of food.

"Do what to myself?" he asked in a short tone.

Sierra pointed to his face. "Fret, worry. Turn that frown upside down."

"You did not just say that."

"Apparently, I've been hangin' around the princess too much. Listen, just enjoy an afternoon on the lake. The weather is amazing." Sierra put a hand on his arm. "The two of you need this." *Need each other* hung silently in the air.

"Right, I need this like I need another hole in my head," Trace grumbled, but took the bulging bag and thanked her. But as he walked down the dock to his boat, he racked his brain for a reason to back out. Not only did he have a hard time keeping his hands off Dakota, but also he was beginning to care way too much for his comfort. Taking her out on the water and into secluded coves like he promised spelled trouble. So when he approached her, Trace was prepared to tell her he had too much work to do after all.

But then she looked up from petting Gil and smiled.

And Trace was a goner.

"You ready?"

"Sure!" When she nodded, he offered her a hand up and was amazed that he was affected by even that brief contact. "Okay, let's go!" Her bright enthusiasm and eager smile lit a pilot light deep inside Trace that had gone out long ago, and he felt a sudden energy and lightness in his step.

Gil barked his protest at being left behind, since Trace often took the dog along, but he thought he would have his hands full with Dakota.

"Aw, Gil wants to come with us," Dakota said, and Trace was somehow pleased at her softhearted nature toward the dog. "Does he like the water?"

Trace nodded as he stepped onto the boat. "Yeah, I take him with me once in a while, but we'll be tying up or anchoring, and he tends to run off to explore. Maybe next time," he answered.

"Okay," she answered with a smile, and Trace could have kicked himself for mentioning a next time when he shouldn't even be doing a *this* time. "Here," she offered, and reached for the bag. "I'll stash lunch in the fridge while you get us up and running."

"It's heavy," he warned as he handed her the big bag.

"Got it."

When she disappeared into the galley below, he thought how in some ways this felt natural and couplelike. At times when he was with her, he totally forgot and let down his guard. He didn't think about his scarred face or his bum leg, and actually relaxed. The water had a way of settling him down too. Once Dakota was back up in the cockpit, he maneuvered them out of the marina and into the middle of the lake.

"You ready?"

"You betcha!"

"Okay, then." Trace opened up the engines, and when the boat leveled out, they skimmed across the water. He stood up to steer while carefully watching for other traffic and occasional logs floating on the water. The wind whipped through his hair and the sunshine felt warm on his shoulders and back. After a few moments, Dakota stood up as well and smiled over at him. When he automatically smiled back, she laughed with such pure delight that he couldn't help but chuckle and shake his head.

"Woo-hoo! Dakota Dunn's day off!" She laughed when the wind caught her hair. She twisted it around her fist and turned her face up to the sun, and Trace realized that Sierra had been right—they both needed this. He wasn't sure about the details that brought Dakota to Willow Creek Marina, but he sensed there was stress and heartache that she was trying to escape. While he had cautioned himself not to become personally involved, if she chose to confide in him, he would listen. Trace knew full well how destructive it was to keep things bottled up inside, and he did not want that for her.

After a while he slowed down and turned into one of his favorite coves, where the bank was jagged and steep. Pine trees seemed to defy nature and hugged the cliff, growing out of very little soil, scrawny but determined. Wildflowers added a splash of color in contrast to the vivid green trees and gray shale overlaid by limestone. The water became shallow in spots, so he navigated with caution before killing the engine.

"This is beautiful back in here," Dakota commented. "I seem to remember coming to this cove with my daddy." She inhaled deeply and said, "Will you listen to that?"

"What?"

"Nothing. Silence except for the rustle of the gentle breeze tickling the leaves."

"Tickling the leaves?"

Dakota laughed. "Yeah, I think I'll jot that down. I really need to start writing some songs."

"Do you write your own music?"

"Not all, but some. Actually, I've missed it. I had forgotten how much I loved the creative side of this business, and I'm itching to get started. I've already got some songs brewing in my brain and I can't wait to get them on paper."

"Do you want to head back?"

"To the marina?"

"To California," he said, and was surprised when his heart pounded in anticipation of her answer.

Dakota shook her head. "Heavens, no. This is inspirational and is clearing the smog out of my head."

Trace angled his head at her. "So you don't miss the bright lights, big city?"

"Some things." She sat down in her seat. "But I never felt at home there."

"And you do here?"

She tucked a lock of hair behind her ear and was silent for a moment. "That's what I'm trying to find, I suppose. A sense of home. Belonging."

Trace sat down and swiveled his chair toward hers. "What about performing?"

Dakota felt a shiver of anxiety at the thought and nibbled on the inside of her cheek. "It's been a long time since I've been up onstage. You know, though, I think I mostly miss making people happy. Standing up clapping, cheering, singing along." She nodded and looked over at him thoughtfully. "Yeah, now that I think about it, and to tell you the truth, I don't miss the glory of performing, but I loved making people smile. What about you?"

Trace thought her question about bull riding would bother him, since he avoided talking about it at all costs. But, surprisingly, it didn't. "Oh, I miss the glory," he flatly admitted.

"Really?" she asked softly.

Trace nodded. "I'd be lying if I told you otherwise. I ate it up when I covered a bull and then waved my hat to the cheering crowd."

"You mean you didn't wear a helmet?"

"Are you kidding?" Trace barked out a laugh. "I was too young, stubborn, and cocky. I'd seen some pretty bad wrecks, but never thought it could happen to me. Of course, I was wrong." He shook his head and laughed without humor.

"You don't have to talk about it, Trace."

"I usually don't." He hesitated, looked at her for a measuring moment and then said, "The bull that day was a chute fighter, and I knew I was in trouble from the get-go. He was a damned slinger, and I should have bailed out as soon as I could."

"But you don't have any quit in you."

"I didn't used to," he admitted, more to himself than to her.

"Go on," she encouraged.

"I decided to bear down instead. You know where that landed me."

"In the dirt."

"Yeah." He absently looked up at the blue sky and was surprised it was so easy to talk to her about it.

"What else do you miss?"

"The chance to ride that damned bull again and best him." He looked over at her. "I miss the challenge. The training. The competition. The money. I miss the rush that comes with the danger. There's nothing else quite like it." He reached up and raked his fingers through his wind-tangled hair. "I guess that's why I felt so displaced. Lost. Bull riding was my life, and nothing else could come close to replacing it."

"And when that gets taken away, who are you and what are you worth?"

He looked at her for a long moment. "You get it, don't you?"

Dakota nodded. "Oh yeah." They sat in silence while the boat gently rocked. Then Dakota said, "What do you say we forget about all that serious stuff and just have some fun?"

"Fun?" His dark eyebrows rose above his sunglasses. "Think we can remember how?"

"Surely it's like riding a bike," Dakota answered with a grin.

"Let's hope," Trace answered. "You wanna crank up some music and swim? We can jump in back here in the cove. Wait, you don't have a suit," Trace amended, thinking he might not be able to get past seeing her swim in her transparent clothing.

"Yeah, as a matter of fact, I do. Sierra tossed the one she was wearing in your hot tub in a plastic bag with our lunch. She took it home to wash and thought it might come in handy."

Trace tapped his head. "She was thinkin'."

"And she tossed in some beer too."

"That girl deserves a raise."

"Give her one."

"I was teasing," he said.

"I wasn't. Do we have the money? I realize that the slow economy has hit the marina hard. And I also know that you took over right when things took a nosedive. I'm not an accountant, but I've looked at the bottom line and I'm impressed that you were able to keep the marina afloat, if you will pardon the pun."

Trace hesitated when Dakota looked at him closely, making him wonder if she hadn't guessed that he had secretly funneled in some of his own money early on. She had an uncanny knack for seeing right through him, and so he kept his expression casual. "Yeah, it hasn't been easy, but we do okay," he answered carefully. "Remember, you've got someone smart at the helm."

"Evidently," Dakota agreed slowly, and then looked at him with serious eyes. "Running the marina under those circumstances would have been hard on my father's health. You saved him from that stress and probably added years to his life. Thank you for that."

Trace looked up into the trees while getting his emotions under control, and then turned back to Dakota. "Your father put his trust in me when I felt worthless. I was on a path to self-destruction when I ended up in Tall Rock, and he stopped me in my tracks. There was no way in hell I was gonna let him down."

"Well, anyone who can hang on to a raging bull for eight seconds is nothing but determined."

He angled his head at her. "I never thought of it that way, but I guess you're right. But listen, gas prices have eased up a bit, and Grady and I keep the fishing camp full. I have some ideas to get corporate groups in here, and Grady wants to start a junior fishing club." He wanted to make her aware that even though times were tough, they had plans in place.

"Then do it."

"If you say so, boss lady."

"I say so, Captain." She gave him a sharp salute.

He laughed—really laughed—and it felt damned good. "Okay, no more shop talk. We're playing hooky unless my phone rings, and then I'll have to take care of business."

"I know the perfect place to swim," he added, and started up the boat and eased forward at little more than idle speed. "Just around the bend up here. The cove is shaped like a horseshoe, and if we've had enough rain there will be a waterfall coming up."

"I know where you're talking about," Dakota commented as she looked around. "Wow, I had forgotten how much I loved this lake."

"You've been away for quite some time."

"Nine years."

"You were just a kid," he said with a sideways glance in her direction. "Ever regret it?"

Dakota stood up and looked out over the water. "Sure, sometimes. You know how it happened?"

"No, not exactly. Only that you were a teen beauty queen or something."

"The only reason I entered the pageant was because part of the prize was studio time and a possible record deal. I was all about the music. When I was signed, I was on top of the world, and even though my mother and father tried to stop me, I couldn't give up the chance of a lifetime." Dakota smiled and said, "For a while there, I was America's little sweetheart."

"So what happened?"

Her smile faded. "Pretty simple. I grew up." She shrugged. "Happens to most pop stars."

Trace wanted to know more, but she became quiet and he didn't want to ruin the day.

"Ohmigod, it's beautiful!" Dakota said when they rounded the bend and a small but lovely waterfall came into view. "I remember swimming behind it when I was a kid."

"Sometimes there's fishing boats back here, so we're lucky," Trace informed her as he killed the engine. "We'll drop anchor and jump in if you want to."

Dakota's face brightened. "Yes! And it's getting hot out. This time the water will feel good."

"Last time not so good, huh?"

"Not exactly. Sorry I was such a pain again," she admitted as she stood up.

"Sierra says it's part of your charm."

"Being a pain?"

"Yeah," he answered, and rubbed a hand down his face. "Maybe that didn't come out right. I guess I'm rusty."

"Rusty? Are you flirting with me, cowboy?"

"I'm the *captain*, remember?"

Dakota arched one eyebrow. "You're avoiding the question, Captain Obvious."

"You're right, I am. But I'm the captain so I'm allowed to. Go change, Princess. We don't get to play hooky too often."

"But—"

"But nothing," he said, and put a fingertip to her lips.

"Okay," she drew out the word, and pressed her lips together before turning toward the cabin door.

"Oh, Dakota?"

"Yes?" She paused and turned around.

"You're a cute pain in the butt, if that's any consolation."

She smiled. "Maybe you're not so rusty after all."

Trace grinned when she disappeared behind the closed door. "We'll see," he said, and felt the sweet anticipation that comes with wanting a woman.

17

Playing Hooky

Dakota went into the tiny head, wiggled out of her slightly damp clothes and into the blue tankini. Because she was a bit more full-figured than Sierra, she showed more cleavage and torso, but the swimsuit was still fairly conservative. Of course, Trace had seen every inch of her body so she didn't know why she was worried, but this was in the light of the day instead of the heat of the moment, and she felt butterflies in her stomach.

Deciding she needed to relax, she reached into the small fridge and found a couple of beers. After slipping the cans into Koozie cups, she took a deep breath and headed up to the cockpit. She spotted Trace sitting on the swim platform, dangling his legs in the lake.

"Beer?" she asked, and sat down beside him.

"Thanks," he said. "Like Grady always says, it's five o'clock somewhere, right?"

"I suppose there's really no rules or time frame when you're playing hooky."

Trace took a swig and nodded. "You're right, although you don't seem like you were the hooky-playing kind."

"And you seem like you were."

"Yeah, I was," Trace admitted with a grin. "I used to skip school whenever I could to practice bull riding at my uncle's ranch. He'd cover for me, but my mother always had a way of finding out, and then there was hell to pay. Extra chores on the farm."

"Are your mother and father still farming?"

"No. They sold the farm in Alabama and now have a little cottage by the beach in Gulf Shores."

"Nice."

"They earned it," he said, and took another swallow.

"Do you visit them often?"

Trace looked down at his beer can, then out over the water. "Not as much as I should. My mother hovers. Wrings her hands. Dad doesn't know what to say, so he says very little." He shrugged. "Nothing is the same. It's awkward."

Dakota took a drink of her beer and fell silent, not wanting to seem as if she were prying. She was surprised at how much he had opened up to her already and didn't want to push too far. So instead of asking another question, she pushed up to her feet and said, "Last one in is a rotten egg!" And then she held her nose and jumped in, making sure to create a big splash. When she bobbed to the surface, Trace remained on the swim platform.

"Haven't heard that one in a long time."

"Well, looks like you're the rotten egg."

"Been called worse."

"Are you coming in or not?" she demanded, and sent water flying his way.

"Yes, but I'm gonna find something to float on," he said as he pushed to his feet. A moment later, he returned with a couple of red ski vests and tossed her one, then jumped in without warning. "Lean back against me and slowly slide your legs through the arm holes."

"It keeps floating away."

"I'm holding the vest steady. Just slide right in," he advised next to her ear, and despite the cool lake water, Dakota suddenly felt a flash of heat. "Got it?" he asked. When she nodded, he let her go, making Dakota wish she had fumbled a bit more.

"Works like a charm!" she declared as she bobbed up and down in the water. "Who knew?" She spun around in a circle but then quieted down. "Hey, if I get too over-the-top, let me know."

Trace frowned. "What do you mean?"

"Sierra says I get too perky."

"Just be yourself. Especially today. Promise?"

Dakota trailed her fingertips over the surface of the water and watched the ripples. "Therein lies the problem," she said, and then looked at him. "I'm not sure I know just who I am. Sierra and I were talking about that the other day."

"You're good for her, you know. She acts all big and bad, but I see right through her. In a short period of time, you've given her confidence. She's really starting to . . ." He shrugged, as if trying to find the right word.

"Blossom?"

"Yeah. You know I feel bad that I treated her like one of the guys. She deserved better."

"Not your fault, Trace. She acted like one of the guys. It was safer that way," she said quietly, thinking

Sierra was not unlike him in some ways. But then she smiled. "Grady sure has noticed."

"Tell me about it." Trace leaned back and tilted his face up to the sun. "I told him that if he hurts her, I'll kick his ever-lovin' ass."

"You think he will?"

"Not intentionally. He's a good kid." He hesitated, but then said, "They've been friends for a long time. I'd hate for them to lose that."

"Wow, you've given it some thought," Dakota commented, and then wished she hadn't sounded so surprised.

"Maybe I'm not as heartless as you think I am."

"I know you're not. You don't have me fooled, Trace Coleman," she stated. Not wanting to spoil the moment, she gave him a quick splash. "Race you to the waterfall."

"Wearin' these ski jackets on our butts?"

"I thought you liked a challenge?" she said over her shoulder. It was slow going paddling forward while kicking her legs. "Last one there is a rotten egg!" She tilted sideways in her effort to gain speed and laughed. "I can smell you already!"

"The hell you say," Trace shouted, and easily overtook her.

"Why, you!" she shouted back, and grabbed his feet.

"Let go!"

"No way. This works for me!" She laughed and let him pull her through the water. "You fell for my evil plan," she teased, knowing full well he could kick her off if he wanted to. She laughed all the way to the edge of the waterfall, when he got his revenge and brought her beneath the spray of water. She protested, but he held her there until she laughingly begged for mercy.

Instead of swimming back into the daylight, Trace tugged her behind the cascading spray. The air turned measurably cooler in the shade, and the sound of the water hitting the lake became muted and deeper. Fingers of sunlight reached in to them, causing the water to shimmer and sparkle.

"Wow," she said softly, and took a deep breath of moist air heavily scented with nature. "For some reason, I feel like I should whisper," she said next to his ear. "Like we're intruding into some special place," she explained, and then lowered her gaze. "You must think I'm crazy."

"Right now, or in general?"

Dakota giggled. "Right now."

"In that case, no, I don't. I understand what you're saying."

Dakota nodded with a smile, but then swallowed hard while gazing at him. His hair was slicked back and his wet eyelashes were dark and spiky. The scar that bothered him so much seemed to fade before her eyes, and it was only the masculine beauty that she saw. Lazy droplets of water slid down his face, but it was his mouth that caught and held her attention.

Unable not to, Dakota reached up and traced the outline of his lips with her fingertip—silky soft, wet, and warm. She slid her finger back and forth and then trailed downward and traced the dark stubble shading his jaw before looking back up into his eyes. She held his gaze while she leaned forward, letting him anticipate a kiss, but instead she licked his bottom lip, savoring the taste, the texture, before sliding the tip of her tongue over his chin and up to his jawline, which was lightly abrasive and sent a hot shiver down her spine.

"God, Dakota," Trace said, and with a groan he threaded his fingers through her wet hair and tilted her head back so he could kiss her senseless. He pressed their bodies together, squishing the vests between them in an effort to get as close to her as he possibly could. They kissed on and on, deeply, passionately until they somehow got sucked beneath the waterfall.

And still, they kissed.

When reality set in that they were being pelted non-stop by water, Trace paddled them out into the open. While laughing, he pushed her hair back from her face. "Hungry?" he asked, needing a distraction, or he was going to kiss her all over again and not be able to stop there.

"Mmm, famished. The sun and the water always give me an appetite. You?" she asked in a breathless voice.

"Yeah, let's go dig into Sierra's feast."

They paddled back to the boat, laughing at Dakota's clumsy progress. "Your arms are longer. Not fair!"

"You want some cheese with that whine?"

"No, but a cold beer will do," she said, and chuckled.

"What's so funny?"

"I sounded like I belong here, didn't I?"

Trace grinned. "As a matter of fact, yes. But don't get too cocky at Dewey's," he added with a pointed look. "You know, like standing up and announcing that fights are stupid."

"Well, they are. I was just stating a fact," she protested as she tried to untangle her legs from the ski vest. "Are you going to help me, or just watch me struggle?"

"I think I'll just watch you struggle," he replied, and was rewarded with a splash.

"Whoa!" Dakota said as she finally slid her legs from the armholes. "You must have been drinking when you thought of this idea."

"Mmm, that's a good guess. Of course, I think it might have been a Grady Green suggestion." He took her vest and tossed it into the boat. "After you," he offered, and pointed to the ladder, but then said, "On second thought . . ."

"I won't fall," she promised, but sure enough one of her wet hands slipped on the metal. She ended up catching herself.

Trace chuckled, but secretly wished she had fallen into his arms. Once he was up in the boat, he tossed her a towel.

"Thanks."

"Hey, I'm gonna check my phone to make sure all is well at the marina."

"Okay. I'll get the lunch out on the table below. I feel like I'm getting too much sun on my shoulders and back."

"Let me see." Trace frowned and came over to her. "I should have put some lotion on you. Damn, I'm sorry, Dakota. I wasn't thinking."

"I'll be okay," she said as she showed him her back.

After sweeping her hair out of the way, he said, "You're getting pink. I think there's some sunscreen in the medicine cabinet in the head. If you find it, I'll put some on your back. If not, I want you to put on one of my T-shirts when you come topside. I have a few in the small closet next to the galley."

Dakota turned around and smiled. "Thanks."

"No problem." The thought of her soft, supple skin burning set his teeth on edge. In fact, the thought of any harm coming to her whatsoever bothered him. God, how he wanted to pull her into his arms and kiss her again, but he didn't want her to think he had ulterior motives for asking her out on the lake, and so he refrained.

"Come on down after you check your messages."

"Okay," he answered, and then remembered something. "Hey, that reminds me. Your phone rang earlier. Did you ever check your messages?"

She appeared surprised. "No. I'll look and see who it was. Thanks."

Trace nodded. "Sorry, I should have reminded you. Hope it wasn't anything important."

"Probably not," she commented. "I'm pretty much D list at this point."

"D list?"

"Never mind." She waved a dismissive hand. "Not important."

Trace watched her disappear below and waited for the feeling of unease of getting this close to her wash over him.

But it didn't.

Dakota Dunn, with her contagious laughter, gentle nature, and quirky humor, was slowly drawing Trace out of his shell and making him want to ease back into living. Add a sexy little body and unpretentious sensuality to the mix, and Trace would have to be made of stone to resist. Dakota was doing what Trace thought was impossible, and was healing him from the inside out. If he wasn't careful, he knew he could fall in love with her.

But then again, he once rode bulls for a living. *Careful* wasn't exactly in his vocabulary. "And look where that got you," he murmured as he checked his phone for messages. Oh, but if he were honest with himself, Trace knew he'd do it all over again, even knowing the outcome. Besides, he reasoned, Dakota was a beautiful woman, not a bucking bull. What could she possibly do to hurt him? Risk taking was in his nature, in his blood. Careful, he decided, was overrated, not to mention damned boring.

"Ohmigod!" came from below, followed by a muffled scream and what sounded like a determined growl. "I'll get you, I swear I will!"

18

Rocking the Boat

"What's wrong?" Trace asked after opening the door and stepping down into the cabin. Dakota's back was to him, and she had a spatula raised over her head. "Are you okay?"

"Fine and dandy," she ground out. "Don't you even think about moving!"

"Me?"

"No, him!" She shifted her weight from foot to foot like a prizefighter and pointed at the spider. "I'm just guessing it's a *him*. Maybe not. How do you know?"

Her heart thumped hard and she narrowed her eyes at the ugly black spider from hell. "You already know my phobia, so work with me here."

"Want me to do it?"

"Yes," she readily agreed, but when he took a step closer, she raised the spatula in the air as if it were a stop sign. "I mean, no!"

Trace halted in his tracks. "Okay . . ."

"I'm going to conquer this stupid phobia and kill it myself!"

"Good for you," Trace declared in an encouraging tone. He waited. And waited. With longing, he eyed the lunch sitting on the table. "Um, Dakota?" he whispered.

"Shhh! You'll make it move," she whispered back. Her breath came in shallow gasps, and she raised the spatula an inch or so higher in the air and turned to Trace. "I can't do it. Here."

When she thrust her spider-killing weapon at him in defeat, Trace shook his head. "How about we do it together?"

Dakota looked at him in surprise and gave him a jerky nod. "You must think I'm such a dork. Afraid of something so stupid," she said when he came up beside her. She turned to the spider and glared. "I am not afraid of you," she boasted, but when it scurried an inch to the right, she took a quick step back and bumped into Trace.

He put a hand on her shoulder. "Dakota, lots of people are afraid of spiders. Everyone is afraid of something."

"Really? What are you afraid of?"

"Storms."

"Liar."

"The dark."

"Yeah, right."

"Heights."

"Shut up! I bet you're not afraid of anything. Anything silly at least."

Trace drew in a breath and blew it out. "Okay. Santa."

Dakota spun around and looked at him. "What?"

"I'm afraid of Santa Claus."

"Seriously?"

He nodded slowly. "As a kid, I hated that whole notion of him seeing you when you're sleeping." He wiggled his fingers in the air. "Knowing when you're awake? Damn, I had this awful feeling he was watching, waiting, peeking in my window at night."

"How sad," Dakota said, and patted his arm. "But Santa is a jolly, happy soul."

"I think that was Frosty the Snowman."

Dakota frowned and started humming the "Frosty the Snowman" tune. "Oh, you're right."

"But I have to tell you that I found him to be creepy as well."

"Anything else? Mickey Mouse? Chuck E. Cheese?"

"You're stalling. Come on, now. Let's smash the spider. You and me together."

Dakota closed her eyes and blew out a breath. "Okay," she said, and allowed Trace to put his hand with hers and raise the spatula overhead. The spider was lounging in the small sink, and for a moment she thought he was so innocent and didn't deserve to die just because she found him to be abnormally large and scary.

"Dakota, spiders can be nasty. They bite. Don't feel guilty. On the count of three."

She glanced over her shoulder at him and blinked down at the spider.

"Don't think about *Charlotte's Web*."

"I wasn't, but now I am."

"Then remember that spiders lay lots of eggs."

"Okay! That oughta do it!"

"One. Two. *Three!*"

Dakota resisted, but Trace held her hand firmly and together they swung downward and squished the spider. "Is it dead?"

"You mean your eyes are closed?" he asked from behind her.

"It still counts!"

"Yes, it's history," Trace replied with a grin, as he reached forward and washed the remains down the drain. "You can open your eyes now."

Dakota peeked into the sink and sighed while enjoying the feel of leaning against him way too much. Finally, she turned around, put her hands on his chest and looked up at him. "Step one is conquering my fears. Thank you."

"You're welcome," he answered, and she could feel the steady beat of his heart beneath his warm skin. For a moment she thought he was going to kiss her, and her own heart started beating wildly. "Are you ready to eat?"

"Sure," she said, somewhat disappointed. Dakota could see the longing in his eyes but he glanced away, telling her that he was fighting his attraction to her. She didn't know whether to throw caution to the wind and push forward or do the safe thing and back off. Trace made the decision for her when he turned around and scooted onto the bench seat flanking a round table. Dakota joined him and scooped some potato salad onto her plate. "I guess this folds down into a bed," she commented to make conversation, but then felt her face grow warm.

"Yes," he answered while slathering mustard on his sandwich.

"Ever sleep on it?" she asked, trying to act casual instead of embarrassed.

"Sometimes." He scooped potato salad onto his plate as well. "It's been a while. I do like it, though. The water sort of rocks you to sleep, and it's peaceful

out here on the lake, especially in one of these coves.
Drinking a cup of coffee in the early morning while the
sun rises and the lake is as smooth as glass is a calming
experience."

"Mmm," she said after swallowing a bite of potato
salad. "I bet it is."

"Ever slept on a boat before?"

"No," she answered, really wishing she hadn't
brought up the subject, but in her effort to try to prove
she was perfectly okay talking about beds and sleeping, her mouth just would not close. "But I bet I would
like it a lot."

There's only one way to find out hung in the air between them, but Dakota couldn't bring herself to say
it. Maybe more kick-ass lessons from Sierra would give
her the confidence to say just what was on her mind,
but she wasn't there yet. She crammed a bite of sandwich in her mouth to keep from saying one more word
about beds and sleeping.

And yet she thought about it.

When Trace fell silent, she wondered if his train of
thought was leading him down the same dangerously
delicious direction that included bare skin and silky-
soft kisses. The thought made her so hot that a bead
of sweat rolled down her back despite the welcome
breeze coming in through the cabin door and the small
window propped open directly above their heads. In
an effort to cool off, she reached for her cold beer and
took a long swallow. But just when she thought she
had her wayward thoughts under control, they both
reached for the carrot sticks at the same time. When
their hands brushed together it was as if a hot shot
of electricity started at Dakota's fingers and traveled
downward.

"Sorry," she offered in an embarrassingly breathy voice.

"No problem. You okay? You look kind of flushed."

Dakota waved her hands in front of her face. "It's kind of stuffy down here," she explained. "Think we can cool off in the lake?"

"Sure," Trace answered. "But you need some sunscreen on your back and shoulders. You look for it while I put the leftovers away. Sierra packed enough to feed an army."

Or more for later, Dakota thought to herself. She knew that her friend would like nothing better than to see her and Trace hit it off. "Okay," she answered, and slid from the bench seat. "You said the lotion should be in the head, right?"

"Right. If not, I'll dig out a shirt for a cover-up."

"Okay," Dakota agreed, even though wearing a shirt held little appeal. She located the lotion in the small cabinet beneath the sink, nosed around a bit, and then brought it out to him. "Found it."

"Good," Trace said from where he was bending over while putting leftover food into the fridge.

Dakota angled her head and ogled. The man had an ass you could bounce quarters off. When he straightened and turned around too quickly, Dakota acted as if she were studying a map of the lake that was tacked to the wall, but by his slightly amused expression, she guessed she was busted. "I just bet that map comes in handy." She pointed at it while shaking her head.

"Sometimes. Let's get some of this lotion on you." He reached out for the bottle. "Now turn around." When she complied, he said, "This might feel cold. Hold your hair up for me."

Dakota swept her hair up from her neck and waited

in anticipation of the cold lotion to hit her heated skin. "Oh!" she said, and pressed her shoulder blades together. "You weren't kidding."

"I warned you," Trace said with a low chuckle, but then fell silent while he spread the sunscreen over her shoulders. His hands felt strong and warm, and when he slid the silky lotion over her neck and then down her back she had to bite her bottom lip to keep from moaning. She just bet he would give a masterful massage with slippery hot oil.

"I don't want to miss any spots." Trace tried to maintain his composure, but his body instantly reacted to the erotic sensation of rubbing his hands over her soft skin. One little hook held her bathing suit top in place, and with the flick of his finger . . . an audible groan escaped that he tried to disguise as a cough, but ended up sounding as if he were choking.

"You okay?" Dakota asked.

"I'm fine," Trace answered, not sounding okay at all. He reached for his beer and took a long pull. "Something in my throat," he lied, and thumped his chest and coughed again, sounding so fake that he almost laughed.

"Better?" she asked, and turned around with concern in her eyes.

"Mmm-hmm," he answered, and thumped his chest again.

"Good. Want me to do you?"

"Uh," Trace stammered. "Do me?" The bottle slipped through his fingers and landed on the floor with a thump.

"I meant, do your back," Dakota explained with her face flaming.

"I know," Trace scoffed, which was a big fat lie. For

a heart-stopping minute his imagination had run wild. "I didn't think you meant *do me* like in—aw, hell," he growled, pulled her into his arms, and kissed her. She melted against him and opened her warm, soft lips. She was pliant, yielding and so damned sexy he could hardly stand it.

Threading his fingers through her damp hair, he tilted her head back and explored every inch of her mouth before moving to her neck. She gasped and slid her hands up his back while angling her head to give him better access. Trace took full advantage and kissed a path over her collarbone to the slope of her shoulder. "Maybe we should wait to swim," Trace hotly suggested in her ear. "Let our food digest."

"Mmmm, yeah. To be sure. Oh!" she moaned when he nibbled on her earlobe and then sucked it into his mouth. She reached up and gripped his shoulders while starting her own moist trail of kisses over his chest. When she licked his nipple and lightly nipped it, Trace knew he had to make love to her or regret it forever.

And he was done dealing with regret.

"Dakota?"

"Mmm?"

"Do you want this?"

"Yes."

"Give me a second to put the bed together."

"Okay."

Trace kissed her and then turned to quickly fold down the table and convert the dinette into a bed. He pulled out the middle cushion, located a cover and pillows, and completed the job in record time before lifting Dakota onto the cushions. "Come up to your knees," he requested, and when she did he reached behind her back and unhooked her bathing suit top. "God," he breathed when she tugged it over her head. He gazed at her wearing nothing but blue bikini bottoms, and then reached out and cupped her breasts, circling her nipples with his thumbs. When she sucked in a shaky breath, he leaned in to kiss her deeply. Finally, when he hoped she was wet and ready for him, he said, "Dakota I want to taste you."

"Trace—"

"Please. I want to. Need to." He kneeled down and then scooted her forward and nuzzled her mound while holding her ass in his palms.

"Dear God," she said softly, and threaded her fingers through his hair.

Trace teased and nibbled while kneading her cheeks until she gasped, and he hoped she wouldn't be able to resist what he wanted to do next.

Dakota felt as if she were melting from the inside out. She didn't know it was even possible to be this aroused. Her legs trembled, making it difficult to remain on her knees, but she could not resist the feel of his mouth on her this way and so she grabbed his shoulders, closed her eyes, and held on for dear life.

His tongue felt warm and moist through the fabric, and when he moved higher to nuzzle her navel, she moaned. But then without warning, he tugged her bikini bottom down over her thighs. "Brace your hands on my shoulders and lift up your knees."

Incapable of uttering anything other than breathy noises, Dakota merely nodded and complied. He made quick work of tossing her suit to the side and then bent his head back to the task of driving her wild. His mouth felt shockingly hot on her bare skin, and when his tongue continued to caress her, she all but came undone.

"Trace," her voice was a throaty plea. *This is too much, too intense*, she thought, and when she inhaled a shaky breath, he caressed her gently, lightly, holding back for her to catch her breath before plunging deeply, sucking, licking, loving her intensely. And a moment later, he sent her soaring over the edge.

When her legs became like limp spaghetti, she collapsed and wrapped her arms around him. "Trace." This time his name came out as a long sigh, and while still reeling with tingling aftershocks, she buried her face against his neck. "That was amazing," she managed to whisper in his ear.

"My pleasure," Trace replied, and gently lowered her to the bed and drew her into his arms. When she sighed and snuggled into the crook of his arm, he kissed her on top of the head. It did his masculine pride good to have pleased her so well. Back in his bull riding days, sex with beautiful women had been free and easy, always there for the taking. He thought again about the buckle bunnies who had lined up after PBR events, and when that dried up after his accident, Trace was left feeling bitter and, oddly enough, used. With Dakota, though, it was different. She was with him because she wanted to be, not because of who he was or what he did for a living.

As if somehow reading his thoughts, she tenderly kissed his chest, and it hit Trace hard once again that this was more than sex. He cared about her, and she was giving him every sign that she cared about him as well. He had gone over this ground in his head so many times, but all of the reasons he shouldn't let this happen suddenly failed to matter or even make sense. He felt another piece of his armor fall away and pulled her upward so that he could kiss her again. Trace had never been much for kissing and was more about the main event, but kissing Dakota somehow turned him inside out. He loved it. He kissed her on and on until she arched her back and he knew she was ready for him once again.

After scooting away to shuck his swim trunks, he came back and covered her body with his. She sighed and sensuously rubbed her breasts against his chest. Trace moved with her, rocking gently while kissing her with the same steady motion.

"Trace." His name on her lips was more than he could take, and after threading his fingers with hers, he raised her hands above her head and slowly sank into her silky wet heat. "Oh," she breathed, and wrapped her legs around him.

"God, you feel good." His bum leg, he knew, could give out on him at any moment, but he refused to go faster, wanting to savor each stroke. She was amazingly hot and tight, and her firm, full breasts grazing his chest added to the pleasure that kept building. He went deeper, harder, but when she squeezed her hands tightly to his, his powerful release exploded in a hot rush that seemed to come from his toes.

With a sharp cry, Dakota wrapped her legs around his waist tighter and he could feel her climax with him, first a flutter, and then she clutched him tighter. He was blown away when she arched her back and milked even more from him than he thought possible. He buried himself deep and kissed her with more passion than he knew he was capable of giving. He rolled to the side, fearing he would collapse on top of her, and then held her close. He wasn't a kisser or spooner, but damn it, he felt as if he could stay like this forever.

For a long moment, they were silent, just wildly

beating hearts and deep breathing while being swept up in unexpected emotion.

Finally, Trace rose to one elbow and rested his head in his hand. He looked down at her and trailed a finger down her cheek. "What are you thinking?"

"That I was wrong. This wasn't amazing, Trace."

"What do you mean?" He searched her eyes for clues, and she seemed so serious that his heart lurched.

"You were."

"Hmmm?" he asked, but he was pretty sure he knew exactly what she meant, and his heart thudded harder.

She blushed a deep rose. "I'm totally botching this. Forget it," she pleaded, and turned her face to the side.

"Dakota," Trace coaxed, and with a fingertip gently had her facing him. "Talk to me."

She swallowed hard. "I already assured you what a big girl I am and all that rubbish, and now I'm blathering on like an idiot."

"You're not blathering and you're not an idiot."

"Flattery will get you nowhere. Oh, wait, too late for that." She slapped a hand to her forehead.

Trace laughed.

"Yes!" she exclaimed with a smile.

"What?"

"Nothing."

"Oh no, you don't," he said, and tipped her chin up.

"Okay." She looked at him for a long moment. "I love making you laugh," she confessed. "And you don't sound so rusty anymore."

"So you try to make me laugh?"

She rolled her eyes. "It's not always on purpose."

Trace laughed again and thought she was the most adorable creature he had ever met, hands down. He was falling for her—he knew it—but he could no longer stop his feelings than he could stop a runaway train. And while he knew he shouldn't, he just had to press her further. "Dakota, what did you mean earlier?"

She inhaled a deep breath and let it out slowly. "I might not have lived in the fast lane in L.A., but I do know that sex is just . . ." She shrugged. "Sex. What just happened was amazing, but only because it was with . . ."

"You," he finished for her, and then leaned over and kissed her tenderly. He pulled her against him, spooning. "Let's nap for a while and then go for that swim you were talking about. Sound like a plan?"

"Mmmm, yes," she said, and pulled his arm more tightly around her as she snuggled into the pillow. "A very good plan."

"Thought so," he answered with a yawn, and tugged the sheet up over them.

"Trace?" Dakota asked with a yawn of her own.

"Hmm?" He kissed her bare shoulder and wondered how long he could rest before wanting to make love to her again and again.

"Playing hooky is fun."

Trace laughed. "I totally agree." A moment later, her breathing was soft and steady, letting him know she was fast asleep. He listened for a while, holding her close until his eyes felt too heavy to keep open, and he drifted off with her.

19

Lost and Found

"Grady, I've been trying to call Trace and Dakota for hours, and neither one of them answers. Did you see his boat anchored somewhere while you were out?" Sierra asked while she put away the leftovers from her pulled-pork barbecue supper.

Grady shook his head and rubbed a tired hand over his face. "No, but I was pretty busy trying to find fish. For some reason, they wanted to play hide-and-seek today. Had a couple of arrogant out-of-town bastards who weren't too happy about the lack of action we were getting." He grabbed a potato chip and munched on it. "Acted like it was my fault the fish weren't bitin'."

"I'm sorry you had a rough day." She reached in the fridge and slid a beer his way. "Maybe this will help."

"You're an angel," he told her as he twisted off the cap. After taking a long swig, he said, "Yeah, I wanted nothin' more than to toss their asses overboard."

Sierra laughed. "That wouldn't have been a good idea."

"No, trust me, it was a great idea." He took off his

ball cap and scratched his head. "Ah, then later I gotta go over to my folks' house and help clean out the barn."

"Tonight?" Sierra frowned when she noticed dark circles beneath his eyes. "Tell them you already put in a hard day's work," she said as she wiped down the island.

"Wish I could. My sister is gettin' married Saturday in a big ole redneck barn wedding. I've been helpin' out most every night. Normally, I don't care so much, even though it's been cuttin' into my pool playing time, but tonight I'm beat."

"Want me to come over and help?" Sierra found herself asking.

"Like you haven't put in a hard day? I couldn't ask you to do that, Sierra."

She shrugged. "You didn't ask. I offered."

He reached for a handful of chips before she dumped the leftovers back into a big can. "Good point. Still . . ."

"Look, if you don't want me to, that's fine," Sierra said a bit stiffly. She was beginning to feel as if she were throwing herself at him.

Grady twirled the bottle in a circle and gave her a curious look. "Now, why wouldn't I want you there?"

"I don't know." She shrugged, feeling a bit silly at her outburst. She needed more lessons in tact from Dakota. "I haven't heard a thing about Miranda's wedding, not even in town. Is this sudden?"

He took a swallow from his bottle and set it down with a thump. "Hell, no. I'm sure there's been more planning put into this thing than Princess Diana's," he complained with a shake of his head. "She's marrying this fancy-pants guy from up East. Met him at Vanderbilt, where he was going to law school."

"And he agreed to a barn wedding?"

Grady chuckled. "Yeah, that boy is whipped. It's funny, because his mother wanted a clubhouse deal with all the trimmings. My mama wanted a lawn wedding at our farm."

"What did Miranda and her fiancé want?"

"His name is Jason Dean McAllister the Third. Can you believe that?"

"What did he want to do?"

"A destination wedding on the beach in Mexico, or some such bullshit."

Sierra leaned her elbows on the kitchen island. "And your mama won out?"

"You ever met my mama?" His voice rose an octave.

"Sure have, at church. She's a little bitty thing."

"Don't let that soft-spoken Southern charm fool ya. She's a steel magnolia through and through. Actually, though, the deciding factor was when Miranda got wind of Jason Dean McAllister the Third's mother's complaining that she did not want one of those big, fat redneck weddings for her precious son."

Sierra wrinkled her nose. "Well."

"That's not exactly how Miranda put it, but yeah. Suddenly, the wedding was being held in our backyard."

"And Jason Dean McAllister the Third didn't protest?"

"I told you, he's whipped."

"Or maybe he loves your sister so much that he wants to please her."

"Well, that's another way of puttin' it."

"This isn't really going to be a redneck wedding, is it?"

Grady groaned. "Hell, no. When it's all said and done this could be on the cover of *Southern Living* magazine. My backyard—perfect for corn hole, horseshoes, and volleyball—is now home to a damned gazebo, a fancy-ass fishpond and a brick-paved patio. All in place of my poured-concrete basketball court."

"Are you serious? That must have cost a fortune."

Grady shrugged. "It cost some, but you know how it goes out here in the country."

"The barter system."

"Exactly. A favor for a favor. The actual wedding, though, has been hush-hush. My mother didn't want half the town crashing the thing, and the invitations pretty much said so."

Sierra pushed up from the island. "Guess my invitation got lost in the mail."

"I want you to come to the wedding with me."

Sierra felt her cheeks grow warm. "I was joking, Grady, not fishing for an invite."

"Well, I'm inviting you, and I'm not joking."

"You do not want the likes of me mixing with your blue-blooded in-laws."

"Yes, I do."

"Grady . . ."

"Dammit, Sierra, just say yes!"

"Well, since you put it so nicely," she joked, but her heart was beating fast.

"Good, I'll take that as a yes."

She opened her mouth to protest, but he interrupted with, "You all done here?"

"Yeah."

"Then come on."

"What?"

"You did offer to come over and help, right?"

"Yeah, when I thought it was a big-ass redneck affair. I can't do any froufrou kind of stuff."

"You can help me in the barn. Believe me, you want to stay as far away from my mother and sister as possible. I'll have a cooler of cold beer and music blasting. You don't really even have to do a thing. Just keep me company."

"But—"

"I'm gonna go round up Gil. I'll meet you out front in my truck in five or ten minutes," he said, and hurried out the back door.

For a moment, Sierra just stood there. "Now, how in the hell did that just happen?" she mumbled, but her train of thought was interrupted when her cell phone rang. When Dakota's name appeared on the small screen, she pounced on it and flipped it open. "Where the hell are you?"

"With Trace. We fell asleep and just woke up a few minutes ago. I saw your missed calls. All ten of them."

"Well, excuse me for carin'."

"I'm just teasing."

"Yeah, everybody wants to mess with me today."

"Who put a burr up your butt?"

Sierra drew in a long breath. "Too long of a story to tell now. I've got to meet Grady in a minute."

"Ooooh!"

"Shut up! I'm not the one out for a day*long* lunch. I was worried."

"Sierra, Trace knows this lake like the back of his hand."

"Yeah, but you were with him, and I seem to recall that unforeseen disasters tend to follow you around."

"I'd argue, but it would be pointless, and, well, I suppose somewhat true," Dakota confessed with a laugh. "But anyway, we're fine."

"Well, thanks for telling me! I was about to come out lookin' and slap you silly when I found your sorry ass. Listen, I have to go. Call me later. I have news."

"You can't leave me hanging!" Dakota pleaded.

"Catch ya later," she said, and flipped her phone shut while Dakota was sputtering another protest. She had to smile, though, thinking that some shenanigans must have gone on for them to be out so long. She locked the back door and hurried down the sidewalk leading around to the front of the building. When she spotted Grady's truck, a shiver of excitement slid down her spine. As she approached the passenger's side, Gil barked a greeting.

"Get in the back seat, Gil," Grady ordered as he leaned over to open the door for Sierra. Gil obeyed, but poked his head through the seats and rested his paws on the center console.

"Don't you dare lick me, you mangy dog. You smell."

"Don't blame Gil. It might be me."

"Could be," Sierra agreed, and made a show of sniffing the air. He smelled like coconut sunscreen and looked damned sexy in his board shorts and orange tank that molded to his chest. When Sierra leaned her elbow on the console, Gil snuck in a lick. "Ew!"

"Gil!" Grady snapped. "No. Down!"

Gil whined and laid his head down on the console, looking guilty and forlorn at the reprimand. He did the pathetic doggy thing where one eyebrow goes up and then the other, as if he didn't really understand what he did that was so wrong. Feeling bad that she got him in trouble, Sierra said, "It's okay, Gil. I know I smell good enough to eat."

Grady gave her a low chuckle. "Now, just how do you seriously expect me not to comment on that?"

Sierra felt her face heat up. "Do and I'll kick your ass. I meant that I smell like the barbecue I slow cooked all day. Will ya get your mind outta the gutter?"

"Now, just what fun would that be?" Grady glanced her way and had to smile when he witnessed her pink cheeks. "You do smell good enough to eat, because your barbecue was excellent. Do you ever think you're wasting your talents by working at the marina?"

Sierra hesitated but then answered, "Sometimes. But the pay's not bad, and Trace pretty much lets me be my own boss. It's crossed my mind, though. I think I'd like to do take-out meals for families. You know, not a sit-down restaurant per se, but home-cooked meals for workin' families, like the big chains do but with more comfort-food dinners, just like they would cook at home if anyone really did that anymore."

"That's a great idea," he said, and looked over at her with respect in his eyes. "You've been researching this?"

She toyed with the hem of her T-shirt. "Yes, as a matter of fact, I have. How about you, Grady?"

"Trace is well aware that I've been saving my tournament winnings toward that little bait shop that's been for sale forever just on the outskirts of town. I'd still be the resident fishing guide, but he'd have to get someone else to do the maintenance work that I do," Grady explained as he headed down the road.

"How close are you to your goal?"

"Mmm, I'm gettin' there. Someday I'll make them

an offer they can't refuse." He frowned over at Sierra when a sudden thought crossed his mind.

"What?"

As if feeling something was up, Gil lifted his head, and both he and Sierra looked at Grady with anticipation. "The bait shop has a full-service kitchen. They used to serve take-out lunches—you know, soups and sandwiches—but with a little updating it could be used for the kind of business you just explained."

"Really?"

"If you want to go over and take a look at it sometime, let me know. I head over there at least once a month and dream. Come to think of it, a drive-through window wouldn't be out of the question," he added with the arch of one eyebrow. "Think you might be interested?"

"Oh, Grady, I'm just pipe-dreamin'. My daddy found out it's too hard to compete with the chains."

"But what you're proposing could work. Especially if you added delivery service. Dinner at your doorstep . . ." He pursed his lips and thought about it for a moment, and then nodded. "I like the idea, Sierra." He looked over at her when he stopped at a red light. "It could really fly."

"It would be helpful to people with special diets. I would have vegetarian, no-sugar, no-wheat, low-calorie. High-protein. Stuff that the chains have but in limited variety. I would even do favorite family recipes." She shrugged. "I don't know. It would be a risk."

"But maybe worth taking," he said, warming even more to the idea. He nodded again. "This is exciting," he said, and reached over and patted her leg. "Hey, what's wrong?" he asked when Sierra swallowed hard and swiped at her face.

"Nothin'." She shook her head hard, but Grady would have none of it and pulled the truck over to the side of the road and killed the engine.

"Grady, just what are you doin'?" She was trying to sound badass, but her voice shook.

"I'm not startin' her back up until you tell me what's botherin' you. Did I say somethin' to hurt your feelings? I can be such a dumb ass."

Sierra sniffed loudly and shook her head again. "No. Can we just go?"

"Not a chance."

"Okay." Sierra inhaled a deep breath that lifted her shoulders, and then let it out slowly. "No one," she began, and swallowed hard, "has ever taken me seriously. When I proposed trying this at Daddy's diner, everyone, especially my brothers, scoffed at me."

"All the more reason to give it a try."

"Yeah," she said with a ghost of a grin, and turned to look out the window. "I've always been sort of invisible. Or even worse, in the way."

Grady thought about how she had been treated as one of the guys at the marina and felt a stab of guilt. He reached over and tilted her chin back around to face him.

"When you became so interested, talked to me like I mattered and had a brain in my head—well, it sort of choked me up." Her eyes swam with unshed tears. "Oh, damn it all to hell and back," she said when a fat tear finally escaped. "Why am I tellin' you this?"

"Maybe because you can tell I care." Grady reached over and brushed the teardrop away with the pad of his thumb.

"I oughta kick your ass for makin' me cry, Grady Green," she said, but it came out soft and sexy.

Something shifted inside of Grady in that very moment and he knew what it was. He was falling in love with Sierra. All this time, he had been going after long and leggy when what really turned him inside out was this little spitfire who was hard to handle but easy to love.

"I could do it, you know."

Grady grinned. "You already have." He looked into her eyes, and when his gaze dropped to her mouth he had to kiss her. When he leaned across the console, Gil moved out of the way as if knowing what was on his master's mind. "Come here." He pulled Sierra closer and kissed her gently, softly, but took his sweet time, until his cell phone rang.

After reluctantly pulling his mouth away from hers, he looked down at the screen. "It's my mother. Probably wondering where I am." With a sigh, he picked up. "I'm on my way, Mom. I know I said six o'clock, but I got tied up at work." He winked at Sierra. "I'll be there in ten minutes, tops. No, I won't speed. Yes, I've had dinner. Okay, me too." He hung up and shook his head. "No, you can't back out now," he joked to Sierra, and then pushed the automatic locks to prove his point.

Sierra laughed and looked so happy that it touched his heart. It didn't dawn on him until now that she always looked a little sad. And perhaps lost. Well, if she were lost, he had just found her, and he wasn't about to let her go. *God*, he thought to himself. *Talk about whipped.* Now he understood what happened to other guys; he just never thought it would happen to him.

"Wait, why are you looking at me like that?"

"Like what?"

"I don't know."

Grady put the truck in gear. "If we don't get to my house in five minutes, my mother will be calling again."

Sierra opened her eyes wide. "Ohmigod, they don't know I'm coming, do they?"

"No. And guess what?"

She blinked at him.

"I've never brought a girl home with me before."

"You're lying."

"Nope."

"Well, this isn't a date and I'm not your girlfriend, so it doesn't count as bringing a girl home."

"You think so?" Grady smiled as he rounded the bend in the road and turned down the one-lane gravel road leading to his family farm. A moment later, he parked in a paved driveway and pointed to an old Victorian farmhouse. "There's my family home." He pointed at her. "You're a girl. It counts."

"But I'm not your girlfriend," Sierra protested as he scooted from behind the wheel.

Gil bounded out the door as soon as he opened it and ran like hell to play with the hound dogs his father always kept. Grady hurried over to the passenger's side and reached for the door handle just as she was opening the door, causing her to tumble into his arms, which was the scenario he was hoping for.

"Put me down, Grady! People are lookin'!"

"I know." He kissed her.

"What are you doin'? People are going to get the impression that you're my—that we're together."

"I know. We are together."

"But we're not dating."

He waved at his sister, who was heading their way. "You're coming to the wedding with me, right?"

"Yeah."

"Well, that's a date. So we are dating."

"But," she said, tugging on his arm. "I'm confused, Grady. What are you saying? Don't mess with me."

"I'm not," he said, and looked down at her with serious eyes. "I want you to be my girlfriend."

"Just like that?" She snapped her fingers.

"No, not just like that, but yes. I'm going to introduce you as my girlfriend."

"You are not!"

"Watch me," he said, just as his sister reached them. "Hey, Miranda, how are things going?"

"Better after my third beer."

"I'd like you to meet my girlfriend, Sierra Miller. Sierra, this is my sister and the bride-to-be."

"Nice to meet you, Miranda." Sierra said with a shy smile.

"Girlfriend?" Miranda asked with a big smile. "And you were snapping your fingers at my baby brother?" Miranda looked up to the sky. "Thank you, God. My prayers have been answered."

"She wasn't really snapping her fingers at me."

Miranda raised her eyebrows at Sierra. "Were you?"

Sierra pointed at Grady. "There he is." She snapped her fingers. "I do believe I was."

"Do it again!" she said, and took a picture when Sierra complied. "I don't really know you yet, but I already love you," she said, and gave Sierra a squeeze.

"You holdin' up all right?" Grady asked Miranda with a measure of concern.

Miranda groaned. "I just keep out of Mother's way.

Look, here comes the drill sergeant now. See ya! Nice to meet you, Sierra."

Grady could tell Sierra was nervous at the prospect of meeting his mother, so he took her hand in his. "Hey, Mom," he said when his mother reached them. She was in a yellow sundress and sandals and as always looked as cool as a cucumber.

"Hello there, Grady. Now, who do we have here?"

"This is my girlfriend, Sierra Miller. We work together at the marina. Sierra, this is my mother, Tara."

"Mrs. Green," Sierra said, and extended her hand.

"Oh, do call me Tara," she offered in a polite tone, and turned to Grady. "When were you going to tell me you had a girlfriend? Why am I always the last to know everything?" She raised her palms in the air, but gave Sierra another polite smile and a brief hug. "I must be off. There is so much to do!" Her fingers flitted in the air. "Your father is hiding from me somewhere. If you find him, send him my way; would you, dear?"

"Sure, Mom," he said with a serious nod, as his mom left to tend to the flowers.

"Are you gonna rat out your daddy?"

"Not a chance."

Sierra laughed, but then said, "Why are you doing this, Grady? Introducing me as your girlfriend this way?"

"Sierra, we've been friends and worked together for such a long time. I don't know why I was so blind to how I felt about you."

"Maybe because I'm not a leggy blonde with big breasts."

"I don't want a leggy blonde with big breasts. I want you. Or at least a chance with you. Look, I know we have a ways to go, but I want to give a relationship a shot, if you're willing."

"Shouldn't we have had this conversation first?"

Grady gave her a sheepish look. "I wasn't sure you'd give me a chance."

"Oh, come on. You have to have known I've had a crush on you for a long time."

Grady drew her behind a big oak tree, away from prying eyes. "Yeah, but I also knew you thought I was a player who couldn't commit."

"I was right."

Grady cupped her chin in his hand. "But it's different with you," he confessed, but he felt her resistance and knew she would have looked away if he hadn't been holding her firmly. "Look, I'm sorry," he said, and dropped his hand. "I went about this ass-backwards and didn't play fair. I was just afraid that if I didn't force your hand you might not ever trust me or give me a chance." He took a step back and ran his fingers through his hair. "When you and Dakota were all jacked up at Dewey's and those guys were hitting on you, I was so damned jealous I couldn't see straight."

"That was the plan."

He looked at her in surprise. "Well, it worked."

Sierra reached out and tugged him closer. "You're right. Grady, I've known you for a long time. Seen you in action. My biggest fear is that you can't stay committed to one girl."

"There's more, isn't there?"

She nodded. "And taking this step means we can never go back to being just friends. That loss would be hard to handle."

"Tell me about it."

She looked up at him with earnest eyes. "So let's give this our best shot, okay?"

"Not a problem."

"And one more thing."

"What?"

"If you know it's not going to work out, tell me. I would rather that you be honest."

"I promise to be honest with you, Sierra. You can count on it."

She smiled. "Thank you. That's all I can ask for. Now, we'd better get into that barn and get to work before your mama hunts you down like a hound on a rabbit."

"Sierra, really, you don't have to lift a finger."

She gave him a shove. "You know me better than that. I'm not a sit-back-and-watch kind of girl."

"And it's one of the many things I like about you," he said, and took her by the hand. "Let's go, girlfriend."

20

In the Still of the Night

"I think we took playing hooky to a whole new level," Dakota commented after Trace walked her up to her cabin door. "I'm a crazy combination of totally tired and well rested."

Trace followed her inside and pulled her into his arms. "I know what you mean."

"You were right. Sleeping on the boat was the best."

He grinned down at her. "The sleeping part came in second-best for me."

Dakota tilted her head to the side and gave him a shy smile. "Mmm, I must say, I have to agree with you there, Captain." She loved this playful side that was coming out in him.

"That's good to know, or my male pride would have taken quite a hit."

"No chance of that," Dakota assured him, but she felt a sense of loss that the day was over and she didn't want him to go just yet. "Would you like something to drink? I have some sweet tea."

"I would like that, but I really should head over to the office and do some paperwork and check up on things."

"Oh." She longed to put her cheek to his chest, hug him tightly and entice him to stay, but she stepped back. "Well, thank you again for the lovely day, Trace. I can't remember when I had so much fun and felt so relaxed."

He tucked a lock of hair behind her ear and smiled. "Me too." He hesitated as if wanting to say more, but then walked toward the door. Dakota followed, hoping for one last kiss before he left, but he pushed open the screen door and walked out. On the first step of the porch, however, he paused and said, "Hey, did you ever check your messages?"

Dakota nodded. "All but one was from Sierra wondering where the hell I was at, as she put it, and I called her back while you were bringing up the anchor. The other one was from my manager."

Trace's eyebrows shot up. "Really? Anything important?"

"I'm not exactly a hot commodity, so I'm guessing no, but I'll give her a call back. I am eager to dust off my guitar. The local inspiration is jump-starting my creativity."

"Well, I should let you go, then."

Dakota nodded and gave him a smile, but she felt him pulling away, retreating into his shell, and it bothered her. "Don't work too late," she said, as he walked down the steps.

He glanced back at her. "I won't," he promised, but kept on going as if he were somehow anxious to get away from her.

Dakota stood there, and as she watched him walk

away, she had the urge to run after him, grab his arm and tell him not to retreat but to move forward and to learn to trust again. But she didn't. Instead, she headed back inside and tried to remain upbeat. The day had been amazing. Surely he would want more of the same?

She knew she certainly did.

And yet as he left—when she had been craving one last kiss to make the magic last just a little bit longer— he had simply walked away.

The cabin seemed so quiet that a sense of loneliness washed over her. Dakota suddenly felt restless, out of sorts, and headed to the kitchen for a glass of tea. If she hadn't had sun on her shoulders and a pink-tipped nose as evidence, the day could have been just a dream.

With a sigh, she poured the tea and leaned against the counter. After all the cheerful sunshine, the waning light made her moody. She flicked on lights, sipped her cold beverage, and made mental notes of things she needed to make the cabin feel more like an extension of her personality instead of the constant reminders of the childhood memories that for some reason made her feel melancholy. She had cut her childhood short, missed so much, and for what?

Closing her eyes, she pinched the bridge of her nose with her thumb and index finger. "Don't do this," she said firmly, and took a deep breath, reaching for the inner strength that had always come to her rescue. She didn't allow her shoulders to slump or tears to fall, and instead went in search of her guitar.

After flipping the light on in her bedroom, she spotted her guitar case leaning against the wall in the corner, looking as lonely as she felt. "I've neglected you too long," she said, and, while she unsnapped the buckles and opened the lid, tried not to think about the fact that she was talking to an inanimate object. "Okay, so I'm a little crazy. Sanity is overrated, right?"

Thankfully, the guitar did not answer, so she wasn't too far gone. With a fond smile, she lifted it from the velvet casing and gave it a quick strum. She started to sit down on the bed, but the room felt stuffy after the warm day, and so she paused to turn on the paddle fan and open the windows wide, knowing that the room would soon cool off enough to sleep in.

She decided, however, to grab her tea and head out onto the front porch, where she could watch the stars pop out and enjoy the light breeze on her sun-kissed skin. She sat down on the top step and leaned against a wooden post and played a few chords while allowing her mind to wander. When she closed her eyes, her body felt the rocking motion of the water as if she were still on Trace's boat. Oddly, the motion felt soothing, calming, and her imagination brought music to her fingers and lyrics to her head, and she began to sing.

Trace locked his office door and headed over to his cabin. After grabbing a bottle of water from the fridge, he went out onto his deck, sat down, and tried to think of anything other than Dakota. Since his lounge chair was on the far left of the deck, all he had to do was turn around and he could see her cabin. It took everything in his being not to do so. He was falling for her too hard, too fast, and setting himself up for getting hurt. They needed to go back to plan A instead of this plan B thing they suddenly had going on. While he knew he was being fickle, unfair, and above all damned stupid, he couldn't help it. He took a long swig of cold water, stretched out his legs, and felt a sharp stab of pain.

"Well, hell." Gritting his teeth, he massaged the sudden tension bunching up his thigh muscle. Funny, after thinking about it for a minute, he realized that his leg hadn't tightened up on him like this for a few days. Ah, damn, but it suddenly ached now. He guessed he would soon need a long soak in the hot tub, or he would suffer all night long. With a sigh, Trace lifted the arms to tilt the chair back and then gazed up at the inky blue sky dotted with glittering stars. He tried to relax, but he felt odd. He supposed he felt a bit off-kilter after sharing a picture-perfect day with a woman he had vowed to stay the hell away from. With that gloomy thought, his leg tightened up even more and he glanced over at the tub that he hadn't been in since the night with Dakota, Sierra, and Grady.

With a groan born of frustration, Trace ran his hand over his face, pausing at the slightly puckered skin at the corner of his eye that bisected his cheekbone. "She never seems to notice," he whispered into the night. He inhaled another deep breath and looked back up into the sky just in time to see a star shoot across the heavens, and *Make a wish* filtered through his brain.

"I wish I could get Dakota Dunn out of my head," he grumbled, and ironically, a mere moment later, Dakota's voice softly came to him as if floating on the night breeze. "Oh, that worked," he grumbled again with a glare up at the heavens, but he supposed there must be some sort of rule that if you really didn't mean it, your wish would not be granted. "Like I believe in that crap anyway," he said. But in the sudden silence that followed, he wondered if he had simply imagined the sound of her voice, and so he sat very still and cocked his head to the side, waiting. There it was again.

She was singing.

In the still of the night, her song drifted across the road to him, causing every other nocturnal noise to fade into the background. Trace leaned back, closed his eyes, and simply listened. Her voice was deeper, stronger, much more lyrical than he expected, and he felt inexplicably drawn to the haunting quality that seemed to reach out and grab him.

At first, he paid little attention to the words, but when she stopped and started, repeated and changed, he realized she was composing a song. He recalled her comment about getting local inspiration, and smiled in spite of his inner turmoil. The process went on for a while, punctuated by what sounded like frustrated strumming and an occasional curse that coming from her sounded more amusing than angry.

From his angle almost directly across the road, he could hear her pretty clearly and was disappointed with sudden silence and the slamming of her screen door. If he raised his head above the lounge chair, she might realize he was listening, so he sat there and waited, wanting more. But just when he thought the impromptu performance was over, he heard the door shut again, and after a few minutes she began strumming and singing once more.

Trace had no idea how much time elapsed, but he was held captivated by the soothing sound of her voice and the tender yet sometimes amusing lyrics about finding love in a small town. It wasn't until he finally heard her go inside for the night that he realized he had forgotten all about soaking in the hot tub, and, in truth, his leg had stopped aching. Trace shook his head and wondered why he continued to back away from something that could be so good.

He sat there for a little while longer, reliving the day up until the moment when he had wanted to kiss her one last time but had walked away, knowing full well that a kiss would lead to another and he would likely be in bed with her right now.

God, how he wanted to be. But what silly thing was he truly scared of? The answer was cute, little, could-not-kill-a-spider Dakota Dunn. "Why?" he asked, grinding his teeth together, but he knew the answer. The only thing he had ever truly committed to one hundred percent had been bull riding. He had given his heart, his soul, even his well-being, and he didn't know if he had the strength left in him to ever give of himself in that total way again. And he also knew that Dakota was an all-or-nothing kind of girl. Her brave I'm-a-big-girl, no-strings-attached speech was a crock, and she had already pretty much admitted it, and she deserved much more.

With another long sigh, Trace pushed up from the chair and went inside. He started to turn toward his bedroom, but instead he walked into his living room and looked out the window over to Dakota's cabin, wondering like a lovesick fool if she was thinking about him or fast asleep.

Her cabin was dark, making him think she was doing the sensible thing and getting some rest, which is precisely what he should be doing. Playing hooky had its price, and tomorrow he would have a full day's work ahead of him. When he passed the kitchen on his way to the bathroom, the digital clock read well after midnight. With that in mind, he brushed his teeth, shucked his clothes, and slid beneath the covers.

And thought about Dakota.

With a groan, he punched the pillow so hard that several fluffy feathers escaped, but he did not care and punched it again. "Damn!" He closed his eyes and then realized he was squeezing them shut like a little kid. If he wasn't so frustrated he would have laughed, but instead he punched the pillow again, thinking all the while that Dakota was most likely sleeping like a baby.

Dakota flopped onto her right side for a minute, couldn't get situated with her pillow, and then rolled to her back, but knew she would never sleep on her back, so she rolled to her left side and blinked into the darkness. Boy, it was dark. She pulled the extra pillow to her body, closed her eyes, but remained completely awake.

"Well, hell's bells," she grumbled, borrowing one of Sierra's many curse-word combinations. She had Trace Coleman on the brain, a man who was probably sawing logs while he had the nerve to keep her awake. While he walked away without so much as "I'll see ya later" or even a little bitty kiss on the cheek, she had spent the night writing a song inspired by his sorry ass.

His sorry ass. Now there was a country song title. After all, she was supposed to be doing kick-ass, not sappy-ass, songs with happy endings, and if she thought of the word *ass* one more time, she was going to scream!

She punched the pillow so hard that she felt she might have broken her wrist. She lifted her arm and rotated her hand in a circle. "Ouch!" Well, at least sprained her wrist anyway. She turned over, tossed and turned, pushed the pillow away when it made her too hot, and then felt bare, so she pulled it to her again. But then she was reminded she was in bed alone, hugging a pillow instead of a body, and with a little squeal, she tossed it to the floor.

"I don't need you!" she growled at the innocent pillow, when of course she was really referring to one Trace Coleman, who she was sure was absolutely not tossing and turning or thinking nonstop about her or reliving the waterfall kiss over and over and over like a crazy person.

The jerk.

Dakota glared down at the pillow, really wanting it back in bed with her, but she'd be damned if she'd give it the satisfaction. "No way," she said, and then realized she was once again speaking to an inanimate object. She punched the bed this time, totally forgetting about her almost-broken wrist, and let out a very loud yelp, not from pain but from frustration. It wasn't one of her movie-worthy screams, but it rang out loud and clear in the dead of the night.

Oh, crap.

The windows were open wide, and she just bet Trace heard her. "No way. He's sleeping like a log." And even if he did, she had cried wolf so many times that he surely would ignore it anyway, right?

21

Pillow Talk

"What the hell?" Trace frowned into the darkness, wondering if he had just heard Dakota scream. Surely he had imagined it. He lay very still and strained his ears. An owl hooted. A coyote howled. He sighed, thinking he had mistaken an animal for Dakota, and closed his eyes once again.

But what if she had screamed?

Trace opened his eyes. His heart thumped at the prospect that something could have happened to her. The reasonable part of his brain reminded him that it was the middle of the night and not too many disasters could befall someone sleeping in a cozy cabin. But then again, he thought, he was talking about Dakota, who could probably find a way to hurt herself in a padded room.

"I need to be put in a damned padded room," Trace grumbled as he pushed back the covers and stood up, knowing full well if there was any chance at all for him to get some much-needed sleep he had to know she was safe and snuggled in her bed. But how? Walk over there? Call her? He paced back and forth and finally picked up his phone and decided to send a text message.

He typed: *Did you just scream?* While shaking his head, he pushed the SEND button and then waited, but not for long. A few seconds later, his phone beeped and his heart lurched when her name appeared on the screen. He opened the message that read: *No.* Trace, feeling silly, frowned at the phone glowing in the dark. Perhaps he was imagining things after all. With his cell phone still in his hand, he slid back beneath the covers and like an idiot wondered what he could ask simply to keep the contact with her coming. *God, I am pathetic.*

A moment later it beeped again. He eagerly opened the message and it read: *Okay, yes, I did.*

Feeling vindicated, Trace quickly typed back: *Are you okay?*

She sent: *Yes. Sorry. Don't tell Sierra I screamed again.*

In spite of his mixed-up feelings, Trace smiled, relieved, and typed back: *Why did you scream? A spider?*

No.

What then?

There was a pause before she answered: *Nothing.*

Which, of course, meant something. Although his reasonable brain urged him to type *Good night*, he persisted: *Tell me.*

After another pause, she answered: *I hurt my wrist a little.*

Trace frowned, not liking her response, and sent: *Are you sure you are okay?*

She answered quickly this time: *Yes.*

Trace typed back: *Okay.* He waited, anxious for more contact from her, but the phone remained silent. But just as he was giving up hope, it beeped again and his heart pumped harder when her name popped onto the screen. He opened the message: *Don't worry, and go to sleep.* Trace smiled, thinking that it was uncanny how they were beginning to know each other so well in such a short period of time.

And he suddenly wanted her next to him, right now. This minute. He really should go over and check her wrist to make sure that she wasn't playing it down, even though he knew he was grasping for straws. He typed: *I'm coming over to check your wrist.* He put his thumb on the SEND button, but then hit DELETE. Instead he typed: *Good night.* Trace hit SEND but then felt a stab of disappointment. He waited, hoping for the phone to beep again, but when it stayed silent this time, he placed it on the nightstand and then laid his head on the pillow. "You're acting like a damned girl," he muttered, and peeked beneath the sheet. "Oh, thank God. My balls are still there."

Trace tucked an arm behind his head, and for a long time lay there thinking about everything and about nothing, but mostly about Dakota. If anyone had ever told him they thought he would become a loner, almost a recluse, he would have laughed in their face. And he couldn't imagine a time when a beautiful, sexy woman was a stone's throw away and had made it clear that she would welcome him with open arms, but he remained alone in his bed. Had anyone even suggested such a notion, he would have laughed even harder.

And yet here he was. "Unbelievable," he muttered.

He supposed he had such a difficult time accepting his fate because even though he had worked his ever-living butt off to become a champion, he had never really been challenged by the prospect of failure. Everything from girls to school had come easily, and except for an occasional injury, as an adult he had cruised along without a care. And while he had loved his friends and family in an abstract way, he had never really dedicated himself to anything other than bull riding.

Trace stared up at the ceiling and thought, *How sad is that?*

After the bull riding injury, he had worked pretty damned hard to destroy his life. And if it hadn't been for Charley Dunn, he might have succeeded. After that, he had been going through the motions, not really thinking about anything more than getting through the day, but little by little he realized how his attitude had been changing without him even knowing it. He cared not only about the day-to-day production, but the Willow Creek employees as well, especially Grady and Sierra. While there were no guts, no glory, Trace took satisfaction in a job well done. The realization suddenly came to him that he truly was dedicated to running this marina. But it went beyond obligation.

In the quiet darkness, Trace had a lightbulb moment and acknowledged to himself how much he really did enjoy Willow Creek Marina and Fishing Camp. And while watching shadows dancing on the wall, another unexpected thought hit him: For perhaps the first time in his life, he was focused on others rather than himself.

And damn, it felt good.

With a smile, Trace thought about Dakota facing her fear and trying to kill the spider. She couldn't do it herself, but together they had gotten the task done. Perhaps this whole loner thing he had going on wasn't the way to go after all. He recalled how Dakota had mentioned that she had felt like a fish out of water in

L.A., and he hoped Willow Creek would be her healing place as well. With that thought, his muscles relaxed and his eyelids felt heavy. As he started to drift off, a feeling of peace washed over him and he thought it was about damned time to stop hiding and start living.

As his breathing became deep and even, he could almost hear Dakota's voice coming to him soft and sweetly. He smiled, sighed, fell fast asleep.

The song Dakota had been writing grabbed hold of her brain and would not let go. The perfect lyrics started coming to her, and she knew from painful past experience that if she didn't get up and write them down, all would be lost come morning or even a few minutes from now. Even though she was dead-dog tired, with that in mind, she turned on the small bedside lamp and leaned over to pick up her guitar. Anticipating this would happen, Dakota also had her pen and notebook within reach. Rubbing her eyes, she yawned and propped up the pillows behind her back. She started strumming the strings while singing the refrain, frowned, and then made changes.

The music poured from her heart and she sang from her soul, forgetting that it was the middle of the night and that her windows remained wide open. An hour later, she had a Carrie Underwood–worthy country love song that would surely bring tears to the eyes of even the most cynical of listeners. "Forever and ever and always . . ." Dakota sang, letting the last word trail off softly. Again, not kick-ass as requested, but Dakota loved the lyrics and couldn't wait to get the chance to record it.

She sighed as she finally put her guitar to rest and then slid back beneath the covers, but her brain was still buzzing too much for sleep to overtake her. She thought about the news from her manager again and felt a shiver of excitement. When she had finally spoken to Ruth Jackson, Dakota had been shocked to learn that not only did the country music division of Sundial Records want new material from her, but also that her old pop music songs apparently had some Taylor Swift elements that they were interested in. They actually wanted her to polish up and turn some of her old tunes into country versions! So, according to her manager, they wanted to go more of the Carrie Underwood route and have her do some sweet songs, tapping into her old image while mixing it up with unexpected sexy songs to get the best bang for their buck.

Vince Marruso, a respected producer at Sundial Records, was interested big time, but wanted her in the studio as soon as she was ready so they could, as he put it, strike while the iron was hot. They had changed the game plan from kick-ass to pretty and perky with a sexy edge, and Vince was convinced that Dakota was a perfect fit. Add that to the fact that her old fans were of the right demographic, and, he said, she had all the qualities to shoot to the top in record time.

Dakota had been floored by the conversation, and it had been like striking a match to her creative flame. She was well aware of being at the right place at the right time and didn't want to miss the opportunity to resurrect her career. Trace had put a positive spin on Willow Creek finances, but Dakota knew it was always a constant struggle. Breathing life back into her career meant easing the financial strain on the marina, and even though she couldn't begin to wrap her brain around leaving, she knew what she had to do. Too many people were depending on her. For the next week, she vowed to write like crazy and then head to Nashville for some studio time.

Dakota closed her eyes and felt another shiver of excitement slide down her spine. While she had been out of the loop for a few years, she instinctively knew that the two songs she had just written were good, and she was itching to write more. She did, however, decide to keep the information to herself, not wanting to jinx this golden opportunity by blabbing about it to her friends. She would tell them if an offer was made, but keep it under her hat until then.

With a sigh, Dakota tucked her hand beneath the pillow, and with just a few hours left until sunrise, she fell into an exhausted sleep.

22

Voices Carry

Trace couldn't stand it any longer. By midafternoon, after not seeing the cute hide nor blond hair of Dakota, he decided to come up with a reason to knock on her cabin door. He figured that taking her a leftover lunch was as good an excuse as any, so he headed over to the kitchen to round something up.

When he opened the screen door, Trace stopped in his tracks and stared. "Wow," he said while shaking his head.

"Hey there." Sierra said. She had her arms elbow deep in a huge metal bowl, mixing together what Trace knew would soon be some of her famous meatballs. He sometimes thought that she wasted her culinary talents on this fishing camp. But it was Grady over at the fridge that drew his attention. Was he wearing an apron?

"How many eggs you need?" Grady asked with his back to them.

"Just bring the whole carton over here," Sierra answered, and gave Trace a wink. "I'll need the milk too and maybe more breadcrumbs."

"Gotcha," Grady said, and turned around.

"What the hell?" Trace shook his head at Grady, who was wearing, along with the apron, a backward ball cap. "You don't really expect me to kiss you, I hope?"

"Not unless you want an ass whuppin'," Grady answered. "What the hell kind of question is that?"

Trace shrugged and pointed at Grady's chest. "Says KISS THE COOK on your cute little outfit," he answered with a grin.

Grady looked at his chest. "Oh yeah, damned if it doesn't. I had forgotten. Well, come on over here, big boy, and lay one on me."

"When pigs fly," Trace answered. "Sweet, though."

Grady, who was almost impossible to embarrass, laughed. "Yeah, I kinda like this look," he answered with a wiggle of his butt, and then turned his attention to Sierra. "How many eggs you want in there?"

"About four or so," she answered while adding breadcrumbs.

Trace folded his arms across his chest. "Since when did you become sous chef instead of a fishing guide?"

"A who *what*?" Grady asked.

Sierra grinned and explained, "A sous chef is second in command behind the head chef."

"Oh. Learned somethin' new. Guess I'm not a fancy pants like Trace over there."

"Hey, dude, I'm not the one wearing the apron."

"Um, Grady, he's got a point," Sierra teased, and nodded for him to crack another egg and add it to the ground beef mixture. "Shake a little garlic salt in there, will ya?"

"Hey, you know why I put this on," Grady told her. "And it wasn't to get a kiss from Trace."

"I'm hurt," Trace complained with his hands to his cheeks, getting a laugh from them both. He remembered a time when he was always cracking jokes, and it felt good to bring smiles to the faces of his friends. He vowed to do it more often, until it became second nature again. He remembered when Dakota said she had wanted to make him laugh, and he suddenly understood. Making those he cared about happy felt damned good. "So, why aren't you out on the water, Grady?"

While shaking the garlic salt into the big bowl, he answered, "The boys were up late playing poker and getting their drunk on. They were pretty hungover and wanted to come in early from fishing, so I came over to help out Sierra here in the kitchen."

"Didn't you play with the boys last night?" Trace asked.

Grady reached for another egg and cracked it when Sierra gave him a nod. "No, we went over to my parents' farm to help get ready for my sister's God-almighty wedding that has taken on a monster life of its own."

Trace raised his eyebrows. "We?" When Sierra blushed, he felt a warm rush of happiness for them. "So you two are . . . do the kids still call it dating these days?"

Sierra glanced at Grady, who answered, "I had to talk her into it, but yeah. She's coming to the wedding with me. But it's a big ole secret, so don't say anything or my ass will be in a sling."

"It's a secret that you're going with Sierra?"

"No, the damned wedding from hell is hush-hush.

Mom doesn't want wedding crashers from all over Tall Rock dropping in, turning Miranda's fancy affair into a big-ass redneck wedding. Personally, I think it's inevitable, but I haven't divulged that little bit of information to them." He paused and then added, "Hey, you and Dakota oughta come."

"Then we'd be crashing. Isn't that what you're trying to avoid?"

"I can fix that," Grady promised, and picked up his phone. "I'll call Miranda right now. You two are both celebrities. She'll be thrilled. Be right back."

Trace opened his mouth to protest, but then clamped it shut, reminding himself that he was going to break out of his seclusion and start living again. Going to this wedding would be jumping in with both feet. But then again, he was never a wading-into-the-shallow-end kind of guy—at least he never used to be.

He was aware that although Sierra continued squishing her hands through the meatball mix, she was also watching him carefully. "Okay, what?" he asked.

"The little pop princess sure has shook things up around here, hasn't she?"

Trace leaned a hip against the kitchen island. "You got that right."

"You have to admit it's been fun, Trace. It was pretty damned boring around here before she arrived."

Trace pursed his lips but nodded, not sure how much of his feelings he wanted to share when he was still getting used to the idea himself.

"So what brings you over here to the kitchen?"

Trace shoved his fingers through his hair, feeling a little foolish. "Dakota was up late last night writing songs. I thought I'd run a late lunch over to her, in case she's hungry."

Sierra started forming generous-sized meatballs. "That's sweet of you."

"Yeah, sweet. That's me all right. Damn it, Sierra, what the hell am I doing? Dakota Dunn doesn't belong with the likes of me."

"Why don't you let her decide that?"

Trace closed his eyes and inhaled deeply.

"Look, for what it's worth, I know how you're feeling. It's scary but . . . exhilarating."

Trace arched one eyebrow. "Exhilarating?"

Sierra's cheeks turned pink. "I'm tryin' to expand my vocabulary, okay? Work with me here, or you'll get a meatball in your face."

Trace laughed and raised his palms in the air. "Please don't aim and fire."

"I won't, but only if you march over there to the fridge and pack that lunch you were talkin' about. There's leftover barbecue and slaw in plastic containers. Then over in the pantry you'll find buns and chips. Pack it up and hightail it over to Dakota. You know you want to, and she will appreciate the kindness."

When he hesitated, she raised a meatball in the air as if she were shot-putting. "Don't make me do it. You know I will," she said, even though they both knew she wouldn't.

"No, do it," Grady said after he entered the kitchen. "I dare ya."

Trace shot him a look.

"Maybe I don't dare ya. Hey, Trace, Miranda said that you and Dakota have to come. She even ran it by the drill sergeant."

"Drill sergeant?"

"My mother," Grady explained. "So are you really gonna ask Dakota to go?"

When he hesitated again, Sierra picked up another meatball. "I'm ready to lock and load."

"I think so," Trace answered quietly.

Sierra lowered her ammunition. "Hey, I shouldn't be joking about this or pushing. You do whatever is right for you, Trace."

"Thanks," he said, and then turned to pack a shopping bag with food and soft drinks. "See y'all later," he said as he walked toward the door.

"Say hey to Dakota for us," Grady called over to him. "No pressure, but it would be fun if you came to the wedding, and Miranda is really excited about the prospect of you two attending."

"Thanks," Trace answered as he pushed open the screen door. He was reminded that going out in such a public place would likely cause some attention that he didn't want, but then again he needed to just get the hell over himself once and for all. With that thought in mind, he walked across the street and knocked on Dakota's door before he could talk himself out of it.

He waited for a moment and then knocked again. With a frown, he noticed her car was in the driveway, and then knocked a little louder. "Dakota?" he called through the open window. After no response, he tried the door. To his annoyance, it was open, and so he walked inside. "Dakota?" he called, and put the bag in the refrigerator. When he straightened up and turned around she was standing in the doorway, rubbing her eyes.

"Trace?" Her voice was heavy with a just-woke-up huskiness that made him want to groan. She wore a big pink T-shirt that hit her midthigh, and God help him when he noticed she wasn't wearing a bra. "Whadaya doin' here?"

"Bringing you lunch. And for the record, I knocked and called your name several times. But you really should keep your door locked," he told her firmly.

"Evidently," she said with a sleepy smile, but then frowned and tried to smooth her messy hair without any luck. "What time is it anyway?"

Trace reached into the pocket of his cargo shorts and glanced down at his phone. "Two thirty."

"What?" She pushed her hair back from her eyes. "Nuh-uh."

"Are you just waking up, Princess?"

Frowning, she blinked and then yawned. How she could make yawning sexy was beyond him, but she somehow managed. "I was up till almost dawn writing songs. Um, yeah, I just woke up. Well, I woke up around ten, groaned, but then fell back asleep. Wow, I'm rambling, aren't I?"

"You need caffeine, don't you?"

"Yes." She gave him another sleepy smile. "You're an angel."

"Yeah, I get that all the time."

"I bet you do," she commented with a low, husky laugh.

"Coffee or Mountain Dew?"

"Mountain Dew, if you have it."

He nodded and opened the fridge.

She peeked over his shoulder. "Wow, you brought me stuff? You truly are an angel of mercy."

Trace nodded. "I could hear you singing, so I knew you were up late." He cleared his throat as he popped the top and handed her the soft drink. "I thought you might be hungry, so I brought leftovers from the kitchen."

Dakota took a sip of the sweet fizzy drink and tried

to hide the sudden unexpected emotion clogging her throat, but Trace seemed to sense her discomfort.

"Hey, are you okay?"

"Sure." She waved a dismissive hand in the air, but he was having none of it and took a step closer.

"Seriously, what's wrong? Did it have something to do with your phone call?"

"No."

"What, then?"

Dakota licked her lips and then looked up at him. "I know you understand that when you're on top of the world, everyone wants to be your friend. When I was no longer the It Girl, that all dried up." She gave him a small shrug. "No one has done anything thoughtful like this for a long time."

"Yeah, but there is a big difference." Trace put his hands on her shoulders. "I don't have any ulterior motives here. I hope you know that."

"I do. And it makes your thoughtful gesture even better," she said, and then put the heel of her hand to her forehead. "Wait, I just realized you said I kept you up with my singing! I'm so sorry! I should have known my voice would carry, but I guess I just got caught up in the process and didn't think. You should have yelled at me to stop."

"I didn't want you to stop," Trace admitted, and gently pulled her hand from her forehead. "You kept me up for a while, but I found your voice relaxing. Soothing. Believe me, I didn't mind."

"You're just being nice."

"Nice?" Trace chuckled. "Yeah, I get that all the time too. Seriously, you have an amazing voice, Dakota. Pop princess, my ass. You're very talented," he said, and laughed softly. "I guess I could have put that differently. . . ."

"Thank you," she acknowledged shyly. "No, you got it right. Teen pop stars don't get much respect and should be allowed to grow up and mature, but very few are allowed to make that transition."

"You deserve nothing but respect," he said firmly. "And the song you were writing? I couldn't get it out of my head."

"I worked on it a little more, but thanks. That's the best compliment you could give me about a song," she responded with a sincere smile. "I really appreciate your saying so. After so many years of being kicked around, it's hard not to doubt myself."

"I understand," Trace said, and drew her into his embrace as if it were the most natural thing in the world for him to do.

"Are you going to stay and eat with me?"

He pulled back and took a step away so he could look at her. "Unfortunately, I have to pay for playing hooky. Too much work to do, but I'm going to take some of Sierra's spaghetti and meatballs over to my place for later. Would you like to join me for a late supper? If you're not too wrapped up in your songwriting, that is."

"Sounds nice."

"Oh, and Dakota?"

"Yes?"

Trace cleared his throat and felt a little uneasy about asking her to Miranda's wedding, but then told himself he was being a big-ass wimp and forged ahead. "Grady's sister, Miranda, is getting married this Saturday. Would you like to go with me?"

She seemed surprised, but smiled and nodded. "I'd love to! Is Grady taking Sierra?"

"Yes."

Dakota clapped her hands together. "Wonderful! It will be fun. Just let me know the details."

"Good. I'll call you later when I get finished with work," he said, and turned to go. At the doorway, however, he paused and pivoted to face her. "By the way, your song wasn't the only thing I couldn't get out of my head," he said quietly.

Dakota's eyes widened a fraction, and she put one hand to her chest. Then she gave him a smile that shot straight to his heart, and for a moment he was rooted to the spot, unable to take his eyes off of her. She stood there with her messy hair, bare feet, and without a stitch of makeup, and Trace didn't think he had ever seen a sexier sight. He smiled back, something that was becoming second nature once again, and then turned to go before he simply had to stay.

With a thudding heart and butterflies in her stomach, Dakota watched Trace walk away. Emotion, warm and velvety, washed over her, and she knew in that moment that she was falling in love with Trace Coleman. Of course, she realized she didn't exactly have a lot of experience, having dated only sporadically, but even still, her heart seemed to have been waiting for this very moment, and somehow she just knew. She also knew—at least she thought she knew—that Trace felt the same way, even though she was sure he was fighting it.

"Go ahead and fight it, Trace Coleman," Dakota said to herself. "Give it your best shot, but you won't win," she added with a determined smile.

Dakota stood there for a minute longer, savoring the soft yet giddy feeling that made her want to twirl in a circle. And so she did, but then lost her balance and had to grab hold of the kitchen counter. She laughed out loud, loving this silly, happy, and yet slightly frightening blend of emotions that made her want to do something loud and crazy.

Love. The word swirled around in her brain and oozed downward, and she thought about twirling around again but didn't risk it. Instead, she grabbed her Mountain Dew and headed to her bedroom for her guitar, knowing that creativity was going to go straight from her heart to her fingers.

Evidently, falling in love with a big, bad, broody cowboy was quite an inspiration, because she didn't stop to take a break until the pads of her fingertips became tender and raw. By the end of the week, Dakota wanted to have a half dozen songs to send to Vince Marruso, and at the rate she was going, it shouldn't be a problem.

Life, she decided, was finally looking up.

23

Hand in Hand

The rest of the week flew by with Trace and Dakota developing a routine where she would write all day and he would bring dinner to her cabin, or she would join him at his. After dinner they would make long and lazy love, and then start the process over again the next day. She felt so relaxed and happy that the music just poured from her heart. The only exception was the evening when Dakota and Sierra went shopping for the wedding. They had chosen spaghetti-strapped sundresses, high-heeled sandals, and clutch purses to match.

"Do you think my hair looks silly like this?" Sierra asked while scrutinizing her updo in the mirror. "Tell me the truth."

"No," Dakota assured her. "It makes your neck appear longer and looks very sophisticated."

Sierra rolled her eyes. "That's just it. I'm not sophisticated. What if Grady laughs?"

"Then I'll punch him in the nose."

"Yeah, right. You don't even know how to punch."

"Then I'll kick him in the shin," Dakota said.

"You'd break a toe in those silly-ass shoes."

"Sierra, you look amazing. Grady isn't going to laugh. If anything, he's going to trip over his own tongue."

Sierra inhaled a deep breath and looked down at her high-heeled shoes. "He'll laugh when I fall and put another crack in my ass. How'd you talk me into these anyway?" she asked.

"It was hours into our shopping excursion and you were so ready to leave that I could have talked you into combat boots. You were coming up with ways to kill me that would have stumped *CSI*."

"Oh, right. I had blocked it from my brain."

Dakota looked down at Sierra's white sling-back sandals and her shiny red toenails, which they had painted earlier. "You aren't going to fall. Look, we're both short and we're both with tall men. We had to have heels in order to dance."

Sierra leaned against the vanity and groaned. "I can't dance! I'm going to be a total walking disaster. Just watch me fall into the cake! Or that pond they dug that's full of big goldfish."

"Come on. Cowgirl up. Now take a good, hard look at yourself."

Sierra looked at her reflection in the mirror. Her smile trembled at the corners, but she nodded. "Not too shabby, I guess." Then she swallowed hard. "If you make me cry, I'm gonna slap you silly," she said, and dabbed at the corner of her eyes with some toilet paper. "Dakota, I know I suck at being nice and everything, but I have to tell you that I'm sure glad you moved here. It's not far-fetched to say that you've changed my life."

Dakota felt tears well up in her own eyes. "And you've changed mine," she said, but then felt a little flash of fear when the thought suddenly occurred to her that if all went well, she would most likely be moving to Nashville. She had been so wrapped up in her songwriting that she hadn't really thought past getting it done. Wow, her heart thumped hard at the thought.

Sierra put a hand on Dakota's shoulder. "Hey, you okay? You look like you've seen a spider."

"I am so over the whole spider thing."

"Really?"

"Not really, but I'm fine." She gave her a short, swift nod and then reached for her lip gloss. Not wanting to spoil the evening, she pushed the possibility of moving away from her mind, telling herself that she would cross that bridge if and when it happened. She glanced at her thin gold watch. "Trace should be here soon. You're still meeting Grady at the wedding, right?"

"Yes. He wanted to come over and pick me up, but I know he's needed at the farm. He said Miranda was doing fine, but his mother was wigging out."

Dakota gave her a little nudge with her elbow. "You are going to knock Grady's socks off," she said.

Sierra snorted. "More like step on his feet, but whatever."

Dakota looked at Sierra in the mirror and shook her head slowly. "He is so into you."

"Shut up."

"He is, and you know it."

She turned and looked at Dakota. "It's hard for me to believe."

"Believe it."

Sierra smiled. "I'm trying," she said, and then her eyes widened. "Ohmigod, but Dakota, you and Trace?

That is such a love story. If anyone had said he would be going to a big wedding, I wouldn't have believed it. Have you noticed that he doesn't limp so much or try to hide his scar with his hair? Amazing. It's like he's been transformed. You are so good for him. Oh, crap. I'm about to cry again!"

"Let's stop this mushy stuff and get our drink on," Dakota said in her best Sierra imitation.

"Now, that's what I'm talkin' about. Woo hoo, girl, you are really starting to fit in here," she said, and put her hand over her mouth when there was a knock at the door.

Sierra peeked out the small bathroom window and turned to Dakota. "Grady is with Trace after all. Ohmigod, he looks amazing in his tux. And holy crap, Trace cut his hair! And shaved! Here, squeeze next to me."

"Wow, he sure did." Dakota blinked at him in amazement. His hair was still on the long side, but trimmed up nicely. The five-o'clock shadow was gone, and the scar that always stood out before seemed to fade into his skin. The light blue summer suit brought out his eyes, accentuated his deep tan and made his shoulders appear even wider. "Hot damn," Dakota whispered, drawing a low but decidedly nervous chuckle from Sierra as they ducked their heads so as not to be seen.

Sierra took Dakota's hand as they walked toward the front door, then suddenly stopped. "If I fall in these *Sex and the City* shoes, I'm gonna toss you into the pond with those big, ugly spotted fish."

"You won't fall," Dakota promised her. "Just don't drink too much."

"Like that's gonna happen," she scoffed in her best kick-ass tone, but she gripped Dakota's hand like a lifeline.

Dakota gave Sierra's hand a reassuring pat before opening the door. "Hi, guys. Come on in."

Trace stepped inside first, followed by Grady, who said, "You ladies look amazing."

"I sure hope so," Sierra said. "Took all doggone day! I mean, really, this process started at the crack of dawn. We're buffed, puffed, exfoliated, and tweezed literally starting from our toes to the hair on our head. Every inch on me is as smooth as a baby's bottom. And dear lord, I'm givin' y'all way too much information, aren't I?"

Trace and Grady stood there and blinked, but Dakota angled her head and said, "Yes, you are." She made a motion like she was zipping her mouth shut.

"I told you I'm a teensy bit nervous," Sierra said, and turned back to Trace and Grady. "Well, you boys look good enough to eat."

"Sierra!" Dakota whispered, and widened her eyes in a stop-it look.

"You know you were thinkin' the same thing. Admit it," Sierra challenged.

When all eyes were on her, Dakota felt her cheeks grow warm. Trace arched one dark eyebrow and Grady struck a pose, and suddenly they were all laughing.

When Grady offered his arm, Sierra asked, "Why are you here? Shouldn't you be helpin'?"

Grady groaned. "I had to escape the madness. You were my excuse."

"Oh, nice—put it on my shoulders!"

Trace and Dakota laughed, drawing a fake glare from Sierra.

Grady grinned. "Yeah, I thought it was a good plan."

Sierra slid her arm through his. "Well, I just hope I

don't embarrass you in front of the fancy-ass Yankees.
I'll try to pipe it down."

Grady looked down at her. "Sierra, don't you dare
change a thing. I love you just the way you are."

Dakota's hand went to her chest and she exchanged
a quick look with Sierra, whose eyes rounded.

Grady remained unruffled and gave Sierra a light
kiss on the lips. "I meant to say that. Maybe not in front
of people the first time," he joked, but then turned serious, "but I meant it."

Sierra gave him a smile that trembled at the corners.
"If you make my mascara run, I'll kick your ass," she
said in a husky voice full of emotion.

"You and what army?" he replied, but looked down
at her with adoring eyes. "We'd better go, or my mother
will send the police after me." He turned to Trace and
Dakota. "See y'all there."

After they left, Dakota turned to Trace. "You're aw-
fully quiet."

He shrugged those impossibly wide shoulders.
"Who could get a word in edgewise with those two?"

Dakota nodded. "I get the feeling that Grady has
finally met his match," she commented with a laugh.
But then she said, "Trace, I know this is a big step for
you."

He shrugged again. "Yeah, and I teased you for
being afraid of a spider. Here I am getting intimidated
by a backyard wedding." He ran a hand down his face
and sighed.

"We don't have to go," she softly assured him.
"We're sort of crashers anyway."

He put his hands around her waist and pulled her
closer. "I need to do this," he told her, and then shook
his head. "No, I want to do this."

"Then we will do it together. And by the way, you look so very dashingly handsome. I'll be the envy of every girl there."

Something flashed in his eyes, as if he might dispute the fact, but then he said, "Thank you. Dashing, huh?"

"Yes."

"Of course, you're beautiful, Dakota." He smiled at her. "Hey, you know what?"

"What?"

"You're good for me."

She put her palms on his chest and looked up at him. "We're good for each other," she amended, and pulled his head down for a soft kiss. Finally, she stepped back and slipped her hand in his. "Come on, let's go."

24

A Big Fat Redneck Wedding

"Wow, this is unexpected," Dakota commented when Trace pulled his truck between a silver Mercedes SUV and a red BMW convertible. Fancy foreign cars gleamed between mud-spattered pickup trucks in a grass field that had been converted into a parking lot.

Trace turned to her and arched an eyebrow. "This wedding is going to be interesting."

"Mmm, I think you could be right."

Trace put his hand over hers and gave it a quick squeeze. "Stay there so I can come around to get your door."

"Okay. It might be slow going in these sandals." She tilted her toes up and winced. "Sierra is going to kill me."

"You'll be all right once we get to the backyard. Just hold on to my arm."

Trace took a deep breath as he rounded the bed of the truck, trying to calm a sudden flash of nerves that twisted in his gut. He couldn't remember the last time he had been in a suit or with a beautiful woman on his arm, and now here he was doing both in a big crowd of people. It was widely known that he had retreated from society, and his appearance with Dakota Dunn, no less, was sure to cause quite a stir.

"What the hell am I doing?" he muttered beneath his breath, but when he opened the door and Dakota smiled, his trepidation vanished and was replaced with a hot rush of something that he suddenly realized was happiness. He smiled back as his hands spanned her waist and he helped her down to the soft grass. All the while, he thought that this wasn't a fleeting feeling of elation that came from covering a bull or winning an event, but rather a deep sense of contentment that Trace knew could be long and lasting if he would allow his heart to open up and accept it.

With her hands braced on his shoulders, Dakota looked in his eyes, and although no words were spoken it was as if she understood what he was thinking. "Dakota," he said, about to lean down and kiss her, when a loud, booming voice startled them both.

"Hey there, y'all better watch out for cow pies!" yelled a portly man dressed in a suit a good two sizes too small. His white hair stuck out at odd angles and his equally white beard grew clear to his chest, making him look like Santa Claus gone wild.

Dakota gave Trace a little nudge and whispered, "Don't worry, I don't think he's the real Santa."

Trace chuckled. "But now you can see why I was afraid."

While hobbling their way, Santa Gone Wild yelled, "We tried our best to clean 'em up, but I'd be on the lookout jest the same. One of them fancy-pants ladies stepped in one and was as mad as a hornet. Miranda's daddy sent me out here to warn everybody else to be careful. I suggested a sign, but Tara would have none of it." He extended his hand, making his sleeve go halfway up his forearm. "Sam Dickens. Guessin' from your truck y'all are friends of the bride. Miranda's my godchild." He puffed his chest out with pride, making Trace wonder if the one button fastened over his belly was going to pop off like a slingshot.

Trace shook Sam's hand. "Trace Coleman. And this is my, um, friend Dakota Dunn." He glanced uncertainly at Dakota, but he wasn't sure how to introduce her.

"Well, I'll be—I thought it was you!" He pumped Trace's hand hard. "It's an honor. Truly. You are a legend. Nobody's ever gonna be better'n you."

"Thanks," Trace said quietly.

"You know there's been many a time when I was gonna head on over to Willow Creek Marina just to get the chance to shake your hand, but I knew you were keepin' to yerself and I wanted to respect yer privacy."

Trace inclined his head. "I appreciate that, sir."

"Oh, dang it—call me Sam!" he protested, and finally realized he was still pumping Trace's hand and abruptly stopped. "Sorry, got carried away," he apologized, and then focused his attention on Dakota. "Nice to meet you too," he said, and shook her hand politely. "I know your mama and daddy. Real good folks, and they are proud as peacocks of you." He leaned in closer. "It's not common knowledge, but I know you saved Willow Creek Marina from development. Woulda ruined Pine Hollow Lake for us folks here in Tall Rock. I wanna thank you for that," he said in a low, serious tone.

"I was happy to do it," Dakota replied. "I have fond memories of the lake."

"Good to have you back, Miss Dunn. And tell Rita Mae and Charley I said hi." He took a step back and did a sweeping motion toward the big farmhouse. "I've taken up too much of yer time. You two better git on over there and find yerselves a seat. Remember to watch yer step."

"Thanks." Trace nodded. "Will do." He cupped his hand around Dakota's elbow. "Ready?"

"Yes, I am." Realizing that his question probably had more than one meaning, Dakota nodded. She knew that they were at a crossroads in so many ways, and even though the future was uncertain, Dakota felt stronger and more focused than she had felt in a long time. Trace held on to her firmly, guiding her and yet allowing her to make her way carefully and slowly across the cow pasture. She had to all but tiptoe in her heels, but with his help she made it to the edge of the backyard.

Sierra immediately spotted them and waved from a seat close to the front, and while Dakota would have rather stayed in the back row, she couldn't disappoint her friend, and waved back. Heads turned their way, many of them in recognition of either her or Trace, and when a murmur rippled through the crowd, Dakota gripped Trace's hand a bit harder. She had never really been comfortable with her celebrity status, and felt a trickle of sweat roll down her back.

Stage fright.

She remembered it vividly even though she had kept it a secret from everyone and even denied it herself. That same frightening feeling washed over her like cold water on her warm skin, but she smiled as if she were completely at ease with all eyes upon her.

As if sensing her sudden discomfort, Trace gave her hand a reassuring squeeze. She felt angry with herself that he was making this huge step back out into society, but she was the one wigging out, so she stiffened her backbone and didn't let anyone see that she was afraid.

"Hey there," Grady said, drawing Dakota's attention away from her terror. He held out his arm to Dakota. "I was given strict orders to seat you two next to Sierra, or there would be hell to pay. And by the way, Miranda is stoked that you're here, and I'm supposed to thank you."

"Is she nervous?"

Grady shook his head. "She's fine. It's the mothers of the bride and groom that have their panties in a wad. I swear, when I get married it will be in Vegas with a preacher that looks like Elvis."

"When?" Trace asked with a grin.

"I meant if I ever."

"Right," Trace commented with a slow nod. "Just a little slip of the tongue."

"Quit talkin' dirty to me," Grady said in a stage whisper, then turned to Dakota. "Come on, gorgeous, let's get you up by Sierra before she comes marching back here and seats you herself."

Knowing eyes were still upon her, Dakota tucked her arm through Grady's and walked down a white linen path between rows of white chairs leading up to a gazebo. The fishpond Sierra had talked about was to the right, gurgling peacefully, and wildflowers of every color adorned the gazebo and flowed from pots lining the path between the chairs. A huge tent had been erected near the big red barn, which she knew had been cleared out for dancing the night away. *Country chic*, Dakota thought; it was the perfect blending of both worlds.

As she walked down the aisle, Dakota had to smile at the difference between the groom's and the bride's family and friends. On the right, a colorful array of designer dresses and suits accented with gold and silver glinted in the late-day sunshine. On the left, Sunday-best dresses and suits in shades of tan and gray that only came out of the closet for weddings and funerals seemed calm and muted in contrast. The heady scent of flowers mingled with earthy farm, while a sense of anticipation filled the air.

"Isn't this exciting?" Sierra asked when Dakota sat down next to her.

"It would be a lot more exciting if I had a cold beer in my hand," Grady grumbled before heading off to do his groomsman duties.

"Hey there, Trace," Sierra said. "Took y'all long enough to get here."

Trace leaned over. "We were sidetracked in the parking lot," he explained.

"Oh," Sierra said and nodded. "Did Sam corner ya? He is a huge fan and was so excited to meet you. Others are looking your way."

Trace nodded and was about to elaborate, but when the music started playing, a hush fell over the crowd and they all sat up straight and waited.

Since Dakota could never seem to control her tears at weddings, she folded her hands tightly in her lap and bit her bottom lip. Still, she found it difficult to maintain her composure when a sweet little flower girl in a beautiful beaded dress tossed red rose petals onto the white carpet. A wreath of rosebuds and baby's breath sat slightly askew on her blond curls, adding to her shy charm. Two lovely bridesmaids wearing frothy green gowns walked slowly with the groomsmen.

"Grady looks so handsome," Dakota whispered to Sierra, whose eyes were misting over as well.

The maid of honor was next, and then the congregation stood when the wedding march began. Miranda appeared looking radiant as she took her father's arm. Dakota had a sudden vision of her father doing the same thing, and felt a stab of longing for her parents. She vowed to call them if this country singing career took flight, and to come clean with them if it didn't.

The ceremony was simple but lovely, with personal vows that had many a hanky dabbing at eyes. Dakota thought that Grady was wrong and the entire evening would move forward without a single hitch. But right after the preacher pronounced Miranda and Jason man and wife, someone yelled, "Woo hoo, let's party!" Jaws dropped on the right side, while whoops and applause of agreement rang out on the left, including Grady's, garnering a dual glare from Miranda and his mother. He quickly sobered and offered his arm to his bridesmaid, who appeared to be the sister of the groom and was not amused.

And the festivities began.

As the night wore on, the beer and wine flowed and the lines between the haves and the have-nots blurred. After music started playing in the big red barn, hair literally came down. Pins from elaborate updos went flying, and Prada shoes were kicked off as easily as Payless. When someone spiked the punch, all bets were off.

The women dominated the dance floor while the men sat back with longneck bottles and shook their heads. When the band took a break, Dakota and Sierra came back to the table, breathless from kicking up their heels to "Cotton Eye Joe," but when the speakers started blasting old-school disco, Dakota tugged Sierra to her bare feet and they were once again up on the floor. A circle of women formed with Miranda in the middle while they collectively belted out "It's Raining Men."

Someone, and Dakota thought it was Jason Dean McAllister III's mother, shouted, " 'Dancing Queen'!" A shout of approval went up, and suddenly, in a red-neck *Mamma Mia!* way, everyone was doing the Electric Slide to ABBA's famous song. Cameras were rolling, and Dakota shouted to Sierra, "You just know we're going to end up on YouTube!"

"I wish I knew how to do this stupid dance!" Sierra complained, and turned the wrong way. "Day-um!"

"Just follow everyone else," Dakota shouted back, and sure enough Sierra easily caught on. After a hilarious attempt at "Booty Call," the band returned for the next set, starting with the crowd pleasing "Friends in Low Places."

"Whew!" Dakota said as she approached the table. "That was fun!" She picked up a napkin and dabbed at her forehead.

"Sure was!" Sierra yelped when Grady pulled her down onto his lap, almost tipping over the folding chair. She didn't protest, though, when he kissed her soundly.

Dakota sat down next to Trace and smiled while fanning her face. "I haven't had this much fun dancing in a long time!"

"Me neither," Trace said with a grin.

"You weren't dancing!"

"No, but I had fun watching you," he said.

"I'm not so good, but I've always loved to dance," Dakota said with a smile.

"The next very special song, 'Listen to Your Heartbeat,' made it to number three on the *Billboard* charts," the DJ suddenly announced, and then shaded his hand over his eyes as he gazed around the tables. "Dakota Dunn, are you in the house? Stand up and take a bow!"

Dakota's eyes widened when an all-too-familiar song started playing. "Listen to your heartbeat," her sixteen-year-old voice sang loud and clear through the speakers. "Yeah, yeah! Listen to your heartbeat, yeah, yeah!" Dakota put her hands to her cheeks and shook her head when the crowd started to cheer.

Sierra looked across the table at her. "Ohmigod, is that you?"

Dakota nodded slowly.

"Well, you heard the man! Stand up!" Sierra said, and wiggled her fingertips in a shooing motion.

"Do it!" Grady encouraged with a big grin.

Dakota glanced at Trace, who had an unreadable expression on his face. But he gave her a gentle nudge and leaned over next to her ear. "Go on, Dakota. Give the crowd what they want. You deserve the recognition."

After giving him a small smile, Dakota scooted back her folding chair and stood up. When the crowd cheered louder, she waved. She sat back down and took a long swallow of beer.

"You have a great voice," Trace said in her ear, and gave her a squeeze on her leg. "And a lot of talent."

"Thanks," she said. "This song has a lot of energy. It's fun to dance to."

"Then let's do it."

"You mean dance?"

Trace nodded. "Hey, I've got some moves," he said in a mock-hurt tone, as he stood up and tugged her to her feet.

"You have to come with me," Dakota said to Sierra and Grady.

Miranda rushed over and gave Dakota a big hug when she and Trace reached the dance floor. "This is so exciting! Thanks for coming!"

"My pleasure! Your wedding is lovely, and you look stunning!" Dakota hugged her back, and then started dancing with Trace, who seemed uncomfortable, which made his dancing with her all the more endearing. While his movements were a little stiff, he did have some rhythm. Sierra wasn't faring much better with Grady, who was giving it all he had with a goofy booty shake that even made Trace laugh. Dakota suddenly realized how lucky she was to have these friends in her life.

When the DJ played "Can't Help Falling in Love," Dakota sighed. "I love this song," she commented, and swayed her shoulders back and forth.

"Would you like to slow dance?" Trace asked.

"Was I that obvious?"

Trace chuckled. "Yes."

"We don't have to."

"I want to," he said into her ear. "It's been a while, so I might be a little rusty."

"Come on," Dakota said to Grady, and grabbed him as he started to leave the dance floor. "Get Sierra in your arms. Don't be a party pooper."

Grady turned to Sierra, "Let's dance, baby doll. *Party pooper* and my name are never linked together."

"Now, that I believe," Dakota said with a laugh. "Come on, Sierra," she said when Sierra shook her head. "It's easier than fast dancing."

"But I don't know how to slow dance," she admitted with a blush.

"As you just witnessed, I'm not much of a dancer either but not bein' much of something has never stopped me from doin' it, so why start now?" Grady tugged her closer to him and gave her a quick kiss. "We can wing it, believe me."

"I might step on your toes," Sierra warned him.

"Like that would hurt," he countered with a grin.

"Aren't they cute?" Dakota asked when Trace pulled her back into his arms.

"I do think they are made for each other. It just took them a while to figure it out. I never would have guessed that Grady would fall so hard," Trace said, and chuckled when Grady dipped Sierra and then spun her around, bringing her bare feet off of the floor.

"Yeah, I'm loving it." Dakota put her head on Trace's shoulder and swayed with the music. It felt good to be in his arms, and he was a surprisingly skillful dancer despite his injured leg. If it bothered him, he didn't let it show.

At the end of the song, Trace whispered in her ear, "Do you want to head back and enjoy a nice, long soak in the hot tub?"

"Mmm, sounds nice," Dakota agreed. "Just let me find my shoes and we can say our good-byes. Are you okay to drive?"

He nodded. "Yeah, I stopped drinking a while ago. But I do have a bottle of wine chilling in the fridge."

"Thinking ahead, were you?"

"Only all day long," he admitted, and gave her a kiss.

They made their good-byes quick, and when they got to the edge of the cow pasture, Trace picked up Dakota and carried her to his truck.

"Trace, what are you doing?"

"Getting you home as fast as I can," he admitted. "I wasn't kidding when I said I've been thinking about having you in my arms all day long."

Dakota gave him a sassy arch of one eyebrow. "Well, then, put the pedal to the metal, cowboy."

Trace tilted his head back and laughed.

"What? Did that sound silly coming from me?"

"Not at all. You're definitely finding your inner redneck, Dakota. And damn if it isn't sexy as hell."

Dakota laughed with him and then reached over and cranked up the radio. She harmonized with Toby Keith and then sang along with Sugarland while the sultry night breeze blew in the open windows and lifted her hair from the back of her neck. She looked over at Trace and smiled, thinking she had never in her life felt more happy and alive.

Once they were at his cabin, they headed around to the back deck. When Trace pulled her into his arms from behind, Dakota leaned against him and said, "It's so beautiful here." She gazed up into the inky blue sky dotted with glittering stars. "Peaceful."

Trace kissed the top of her head. "It's been a healing place for me," he said, surprising her with his admission. "I hope it will be for you too," he continued, and then paused as if he wanted to say more but was refraining. Finally, he said, "Let's get out of these clothes and relax." Releasing her, Trace walked over, cranked up the heat and said, "I'll be back in a minute with the wine, and then we'll slip into the tub."

"I don't have a swimsuit," Dakota suddenly remembered.

"Good," Trace answered with a grin. "I'll be right back."

He returned shortly with the bottle and two glasses.

He poured the wine and clinked his glass to hers. "To new beginnings," he said, and then took a swallow.

Dakota smiled and then took a sip of the cold Chardonnay. "Nice," she said. "The wedding was fun, but this is even better."

"I agree," Trace answered, and started unbuttoning his shirt. When Dakota glanced left and right, he said, "Don't worry. We're secluded back here," then pulled her into his arms.

Dakota slid her hands up over his bare chest, loving the feeling of his warm skin and hard muscle beneath her palms. She pushed the shirt over his shoulders and reached for his silver belt buckle. His muscles tightened and then quivered when her fingers lightly brushed over his abdomen, and when she unzipped his fly he drew in a quick breath. Feeling bold, sexy, powerful, she pushed his dress pants past his hips and palmed his very nice butt, drawing him closer. She kissed his chest and toyed with the elastic of his boxer briefs until he moaned his protest.

"Touch me," he said, low and husky in her ear.

"Gladly." While she continued to kiss his chest, she reached between their bodies and caressed the hot, hard length of his erection.

"God, Dakota." He reached behind her back and unzipped her dress. The soft material slid from her shoulders and pooled at her feet, leaving her in a skimpy beige push-up bra and matching bikini panties. Trace looked his fill and then pulled her close, rubbing his steely hardness against the silky material before bending his dark head to capture her lips.

They stood in the moonlight and kissed with the confidence of two people finding each other and falling deeply in love. The night air felt warm, sultry, but edged with coolness blowing through the trees on the night breeze, while the sounds of nature hummed in the distance, creating an earthy backdrop for lovers.

"Forget the hot tub. I want to make love to you beneath the stars," Trace said, and tenderly kissed her bare shoulder.

"That would be perfect."

"Wait here," he instructed. Mere moments later, he returned with a thick comforter and two pillows. He spread the makeshift bed out on the deck and took her hand and pulled her into his embrace. He kissed her deeply, soundly, and with a passion that went straight to her heart.

They sank down onto the comforter. While on their knees, they kissed and caressed, savoring the reality of what had been fantasized about all day long. Finally, Trace slid his hands up and unhooked her bra, allowing her breasts to tumble free. When he bent his head and took one nipple into his mouth, Dakota's breath caught in her throat. His mouth felt so warm and his tongue so soft that she let out a sigh. "Trace," she said, arching her back, wanting more and more, and he gave it to her until her thigh muscles trembled and her knees gave out.

By the time he gently eased her to the comforter, Dakota felt as if she were melting from the inside out. Trace slid her panties down and off and then removed his boxers, but before he came to her, he remained on his knees and gazed down at her. "You look stunning in the moonlight," he told her, and then lovingly trailed his fingertips over her body. Her skin was so achingly sensitive that his feather-light touch sent an erotic tingle racing throughout her body. "Trace," she said, and reached up with her arms, "come to me."

"Dakota." He covered her body with his and kissed her softly, tenderly, until passion took over. When Dakota wrapped her legs around him, Trace threaded his fingers with hers and made sweet love to her beneath the moon and the stars.

Afterward, he pulled her into his arms and held her close for a long time. Neither of them spoke. After a while, he tucked the comforter around them. While her eyes fluttered shut, Dakota thought that there was no other place on earth that she would rather be than with her head on Trace Coleman's chest and his arms wrapped around her.

Just as she was about to doze off, her cell phone beeped. She frowned, realizing it was in her purse, which was lying on the chaise longue and was within reach, and yet she didn't want the outside world to intrude. It beeped again.

"You need to get that?" Trace mumbled, half-asleep but sounding sexy as hell.

"Mmmm, no, it just means I missed a call. I had my phone on silent earlier," Dakota mumbled back, but then wondered who would have been trying to contact her. "I guess I should check to make sure it's nothing important." Thinking it could be her parents, her heart pounded, and with a concerned frown she leaned over and reached up for her purse.

25

Fly Me to the Moon

"Everything okay?" Trace came up on one elbow and put his hand on Dakota's waist.

"Yes." Dakota flipped the phone shut. "Everything is fine."

"Are you sure?" He eased her hair over her shoulder and kissed her neck.

"Nothing that can't keep until morning," she assured him with a small smile, and then snuggled back into his arms with the phone still in her hand.

"All right," Trace replied, but didn't sound convinced. "But if you need to talk, let me know. I'm right here."

"Thank you. Just hold me close, okay?"

"Gladly," Trace said, and wrapped his strong arms around her. But instead of falling asleep, Dakota stared off into the darkness and thought about the message. Ruth Jackson, her manager, said that Vince Marruso of Sundial Records wanted her in the studio in Nashville tomorrow afternoon. Vince loved the songs she had sent to him thus far and wanted to go full speed ahead and possibly talk contracts. He went on to say that her sweet Southern style was hot right now and he didn't want to waste any time, hoping to have a single release ready as soon as possible, with the hopes of sending her on the road with a headliner for a fall concert series.

Dakota blinked and inhaled a deep breath. It was enough to make her head spin. By rights, she should be over the moon. And yet joy failed to come, and she knew why. She was coming to love it here at the marina. She loved her new friends.

But most of all, she loved Trace Coleman.

While she craved the feel of her guitar in her hands and knew her new songs were spot-on, the thought of performing on stage and going on the road for weeks on end held no appeal. And yet how could she let everyone down? Or pass up an opportunity that many musicians only dream about and never get the shot at once, much less twice? She thought of Sam Dickens, who earlier that night said her parents were proud of her. She considered Ruth Jackson, who worked hard to make this happen, and then sighed deeply. Her financial success would mean more cash flow to the marina. People were counting on her and believing in her.

She had to do it.

Her throat closed up at the realization, and then a hot tear slid down her cheek.

"Hey, are you okay?" Trace asked, and kissed the top of her head.

Unable to speak, Dakota nodded.

"So you're not going to tell me what's bothering you?" While his question was casual, his tone held a measure of hurt.

"Let's talk in the morning," Dakota answered, trying to stay calm, but the husky tremble in her voice gave her away. Realizing she was still clutching the phone in her hand, she placed it on the chaise longue and snuggled against his warm body with her head on his chest.

"If that's what you want, but I don't think either of us will sleep unless we talk about the phone call."

She nodded but remained silent, and swallowed hot moisture that gathered in her throat.

"I'm not trying to pry, but you can talk to me about anything. You know that, right?"

Dakota nodded again and said hesitantly, "The call was from my manager. She said that Vince Marruso of Sundial Records loves my new songs and wants me in the studio."

"That's good news," he said, but Dakota felt the slight tightening of his muscles in his arms. "When?"

"Tomorrow."

"Oh."

"I was supposed to come here to find an edgy, kick-ass style, but apparently they want a more mature country version of my pop days—an older Taylor Swift kind of sound that's really hot right at the moment."

"It all makes sense now," he said quietly. "You never truly planned on moving back here, did you?"

Dakota's heart pumped hard at his sudden distant tone. "I wasn't sure what I wanted, Trace."

"Yes, you did. We were just the inspiration for your new material, nothing more."

"How can you say that? This marina—Grady, Sierra, especially *you*—all played a part, but that's not just who you are to me, Trace."

"Right," he said in a short, clipped tone.

Dakota pushed up to her elbow. "You're not being fair."

"And you think using all of us is fair? We were just a means to an end for you," he said darkly, and then laughed without humor. "When will I ever learn?"

"Learn what?" Dakota asked, and swallowed hard. This was not happening.

"Women are users. You're no different. And I was stupid enough to think that I was . . ." He shook his head and looked away.

"That you were what?"

"Nothing," he answered tersely, but then sighed. "Good luck, Dakota." He pushed up to a sitting position and rested his forearms on his knees. "Look, I don't blame you. If I could go back to bull riding, I'd get the hell out of here and do it in a heartbeat."

"Really?" Dakota asked softly. "Would you?"

"Sure." He angled his head toward her cabin and then looked away. "Go on and get a good night's sleep. You've got a big day ahead of you. So just go."

While Trace's harsh words cut deeply, Dakota wasn't sure she believed him. "Do you really want me to leave, Trace? Say the word and I won't."

His head snapped up and his heart beat like a jackhammer. He suddenly knew that she wasn't talking about just tonight.

"Give me a reason to stay," she said in a calm, even tone, and waited.

Trace knew that she wanted him to say that he loved her, and God help him, he did. He knew she wanted him to tell her not to go, and she wouldn't. He knew it. But how could he? Music was her dream, in her blood, and she was talented. He fully understood how she felt and would not, could not take that away from her.

He loved her way too much, and even though it killed him, he forced his tone to be cold, harsh, and said, "Go on back to your music, Dakota. It's the reason you came here in the first place. It would have been nice if you had been honest from the start, but whatever." He shrugged. "You got what you wanted and then some. Now go. Let me get back to my peaceful life before you barged into it."

"Come with me."

For a moment, her request stunned him. "And carry your bags?" he asked, even though part of him wanted to throw his stuff in a duffle bag and follow her to the ends of the earth. "I know I'm the hired help, but no thank you," he added, and looked away.

"I didn't mean it like that," she answered.

The tremble in Dakota's voice made Trace want to take her into his arms and hold her close. He also worried about her heading out on her own. She was too giving, too trusting, and he wished he could be by her side to protect her and watch over her, but he forced himself not to think that way. The rigors of the road would be tough, and seriously, what would he do all day? Plus, the fact that he worked his ass off here at the marina and she seemed to think he was replaceable hurt as well.

"You might not realize it, Princess, but your investment is in my hands. Willow Creek Marina makes a tidy profit because I work hard. I even . . ." he said, and then stopped himself.

"You what?"

"Nothing."

She looked at him sharply. "You put some of your own cash up, didn't you?"

"Hell, no. I blew all my money. I was down to my last twenty bucks when your father found me."

Dakota gazed at him for a long, measuring moment. "Then you got some money from somewhere," she said, almost more to herself than to him, and then her eyes widened. "What did you sell?"

"Nothing!" he said, but made the mistake of glancing at his hand.

"Oh, my God." She put her fingertips to her lips. "Your Ring of Honor?"

Trace would have denied it, but she pinned him with her gaze. "It meant nothing, and this marina means a lot to this community and the people who work here."

"But your ring? Trace, that ring is only given to bull riding legends. It represents strength and courage."

"Dakota, your father rescued me from the path I was heading down. I was like a snowball heading straight to hell. The least I could do was save this marina. It was the right thing to do."

"The honorable thing." She shook her head slowly and reached out to him, but he ignored her trembling hand.

"You're giving me more credit than I deserve."

"But—"

"It was a piece of jewelry. Forget about it. Look, Princess, if your little trip to Nashville doesn't pan out, you need me running this place. I know it's just a fishing camp and small marina, but the livelihood of many depends on me. I don't like to let people down."

"Believe me, I fully understand. And I didn't mean to make light of what you do here. I'm sorry. For everything." She put a hand on his knee. "And yes, you're right. I came here to get my act together and resurrect my career. I didn't intend to stay." She gripped his knee tighter. "But, Trace, I didn't know that I would—"

"Stop it, Dakota," Trace harshly interrupted. If she said that she loved him, he would ask her to stay and that would simply be wrong. He could see in her eyes that she wanted him to, but how would she feel a month from now? A year from now? He could not let her pass up this amazing opportunity. He knew how it felt to be on top of the world, and Dakota was lucky enough to be getting the second chance of a lifetime. He would not ruin it for her, and so again he forced his tone to be hard. "Go back to the bright lights where you belong, Dakota."

"This is my home," she protested hotly.

"Really? You might have been born in Tall Rock, but you'll never fit in here. You're a city chick through and through," he said, knowing he was hitting close to the bone, but he pressed on even harder. "Besides, what we had here was fleeting, and what you are being offered is the chance to fulfill your dreams for the rest of your life. Don't screw it up because of this." He swung his hand in an arc.

"This?" Her eyes widened. "What exactly was this, Trace?"

"Sex, Princess."

"Don't call me that."

He shrugged, and even though it was tearing him up, said, "Sierra said once I was no Prince Charming."

"Apparently, she was right." She blinked at him and swallowed hard. Then, as if just realizing she was still naked, she scooted back and scrambled for her clothes. Unable to find her underwear, she cursed and slipped her dress over her head.

Trace had to fist his hands so he wouldn't reach out to her. He wanted to grab her, hold her close, and tell her not to go, and yet he couldn't. "Good luck, Dakota," he finally said in a more civil tone. "And take care of yourself."

"Go to hell," she said in a broken tone, and turned and walked away.

"Believe me, I'm already there," Trace whispered into the dark.

26

Butter My Butt and Call Me a Biscuit

The pen in Dakota's hand felt as if it weighed twenty pounds, and as she put the tip to the signature line, a cold bead of sweat rolled down her back. Her breath came in short gasps, and for a sickening moment she thought she might actually pass out.

"Are you okay?" Ruth Jackson asked with a frown on her face. "You don't look so good, Dakota."

"I'm fine," she lied, but the words on the page blurred and the pen slipped from her cold, clammy hand. "Could I have a bottle of water, please?"

"Sure," Ruth answered, and scooted back from the table. "I'll be right back."

"Thanks." Dakota tried to smile, but failed. The past two weeks had gone well in the studio. She loved the creative process, loved the music. But the rest? "Terrifies me," she whispered. "I cannot do this." She put a hand to her chest and swallowed hard.

Ruth breezed back through the door and handed the cold bottle to Dakota. "Here you go."

"Thank you," Dakota replied as she unscrewed the plastic cap. She took a long swig and set the bottle down on the shiny surface of the table. Everything at Sundial Records appeared bright, reflective, and modern—even the pen. Outside the huge picture window were tall buildings casting long shadows.

"Talk to me, Dakota," Ruth encouraged in her no-nonsense tone.

"I miss the lake."

"Excuse me? You mean that fishing camp?"

Dakota nodded. "Yes. I miss my cabin. My front porch. Friends. The sounds of nature and the smell of the water." *Trace.*

"What are you saying?"

"I'm saying that I can't do this."

"Dakota, the songs are phenomenal. Everyone is buzzing with excitement. You could be the next big thing. What is holding you back from stardom? A fishing camp?" Ruth reached over and patted Dakota's hand. "Look, I know you've been down this road before. It can be a roller coaster ride. But this is your shot at something lasting instead of fleeting. Take it, for goodness' sake. If you don't, you'll regret it the rest of your life."

Dakota thought about that for a long moment. "No, what I'll regret for the rest of my life is giving up the peace that I found for the terror of performing live. Tour buses and hotel rooms. Lack of privacy. Losing myself."

"Sure, there is a price to pay, but it will be well worth it. Believe me."

Dakota shook her head slowly. "No, Ruth. For the

first time ever, I'm going to believe and trust in myself." She tapped a finger to her chest. "What I want and not what others want of me."

Ruth leaned forward in her black leather swivel chair. "Tell me what you want and I'll get it for you."

Dakota looked Ruth straight in the eye and said, "Sell my songs."

"What?"

"I've come to realize that I'm a songwriter. A creator. That's what I've always loved." She tapped her chest again. "The music lives in my heart, my soul, but I'm not a performer."

"There's not nearly as much money or fame."

"Neither money nor fame make you happy. I'm living proof. Look, I know there are plenty of musicians who live for the road and performing live. Thank God, because they bring so much joy to the audience." Dakota shrugged. "But it's just not in me. I want to create, compose songs that people will sing along with—that they'll remember and love, that maybe even make a difference in their lives, bring back memories or help ease them through a difficult time. But that's where it ends." She handed Ruth the pen. "Sorry."

Ruth pursed her lips and blew out a long breath.

"You think I'm crazy, don't you?"

Ruth reached over and squeezed Dakota's hand. "I admire you for turning down what most could not. There are a lot of people who do something they hate for a living simply for fame and fortune or ego. You are obviously made of stronger stuff." She patted her hand once more. "I commend you for that." Ruth shook her head again. "Having said that, I can't talk you out of this, can I?"

"Not on your life."

"In this business, you have to be in for all or nothing. It's life consuming. There's no reason to move forward if you're not in one hundred percent. Hey, I represent songwriters too. Believe me, the wheels are already turning."

Dakota smiled and felt as if a huge burden had been lifted. "Thanks so much for understanding." She stood up and walked around the big desk.

"While you were totally professional, just like you used to be, I could tell that something was wrong. I should have approached you sooner, but I chalked it up to nerves." She stood up and gave Dakota a hug. "Head back to your happy place where this inspiration came from and keep the material coming, okay?"

"Will do."

"I have to ask. Is there a guy involved in this decision of yours?"

Dakota pulled back and asked, "Why do you say that?"

Ruth shrugged. "There were many times when you had this faraway, dreamy look on your face. Are you missing more than the lake, Dakota?"

Dakota felt a heaviness grab hold of her heart. "There was someone. It didn't work out."

"Maybe now it can."

"No." She shook her head sadly, but smiled. "Sell those songs for me, okay?"

"Will do. Are you heading back to Willow Creek tonight?"

"It's my home now. So yes." She gave Ruth another hug and then hurried to her hotel room, packed, and headed down the road in the direction of Tall Rock. She needed grass beneath her feet and a front porch to sit on. She needed to hear Sierra's laughter, Grady's jokes, and Gil's happy bark.

What she needed most were Trace's strong arms around her.

But she would not let that happen. *Fool me once, and all that*, she thought with a sad shake of her head. She decided for a while, until her heart healed, she would have to avoid him at all costs, which wouldn't be an easy task, since he lived right across the street. She would do as she once promised and stay out of his way. If she found herself stuck in a bathtub or tossed overboard, she would call 911, not Trace Coleman.

Dakota looked at her watch and decided if she only stopped once she could make it home to see the sun set over the lake and maybe grab some leftover supper from the kitchen. She considered calling Sierra to let her know she was on her way, but because she hadn't talked to her friend since she left, Dakota wasn't sure what kind of reception she would receive, so she decided to keep her arrival a surprise.

As she drove, she wondered if Trace had thought about her at all over the past two weeks while she had been in Nashville. It ticked her off that her thoughts kept centering on a man who had made it clear that she meant nothing more than casual sex, and every time her phone rang she wanted it to be him. "No more," she said firmly. "I'm going to head to Dewey's Pub and find me a hot young cowboy," she stated with fervor.

To make Trace jealous?

"No, to move on," she answered her pesky brain. With a groan, she turned on the radio to take her mind off of Trace Coleman once and for all. He probably hadn't given her a thought and would be annoyed that she was back at the marina, messing up his orderly life once more. "Well, too bad," she muttered, and started signing along with Taylor Swift's song "Love Story," but then wrinkled her nose. "Yeah, right. Happily ever after is a crock," she mumbled darkly, and then smiled, thinking that "He's No Prince Charming" would be the title to her next song and she'd sing it very loudly as she wrote the scathing words. Yeah, she'd sing it loud and proud and hope it became the song of the year, and when she accepted her award she'd tell the whole world that the song was about a broody, jackass cowboy who wouldn't recognize love if it slapped him upside the head.

"There, I feel much better now," Dakota said with a brisk nod, but of course she really didn't feel better in the least. Then she had to go and think of the other songs she had written with Trace in mind, and a lump formed in her throat. "Damn it all to hell," she cursed, and smacked the steering wheel. She swerved so hard that a tractor trailer truck honked its horn at her. "Damn you, Trace Coleman. I hope your ears are burning!"

After nearly clipping the truck, Dakota cranked the music up loudly and sang at the top of her lungs. She stopped at a red light, and while tapping her fingers on the steering wheel to Kenny Chesney's "She Thinks My Tractor's Sexy," she saw a Ford dealership out of the corner of her eye and smiled slowly, knowing exactly what she needed to do.

An hour later, Dakota rolled down the highway in a mean-looking jet-black Ford F-150. She should have been intimidated by the big truck, but in the mood she was in, Dakota drove like she owned the road. She stopped only once to gas up, use the ladies' room, and to purchase a giant cherry ICEE that froze her brain and turned her tongue bright red. Just as she was taking the last slurp, she pulled into her driveway. She tried really hard not to look over at Trace's cabin and almost did it, but at the last minute glanced his way. Lights were on, so she assumed he was home, which meant she could head over to the kitchen and grab some dinner without running into him.

Thank God for small favors.

After she dragged her luggage inside, she opened the windows. "It feels good to be home," she whispered, and then headed out the door to the kitchen.

"Well, butter my butt and call me a biscuit," Sierra said when Dakota opened the back screen door. "You're back?"

"Yes," Dakota answered in a rather small voice.

"But what about Nashville?"

"Done."

Sierra wiped her hands on a dish towel and tossed it onto the kitchen island. "So you mean to tell me we've all been moping around here thinking you're gone for good, and all for nothing? Trace has been wound tighter than an eight-day clock and even Gil had been sulking around." She tapped her cheek and paused as if in thought. She put her hands on her hips for a moment while giving her a measuring look. "Need a beer?"

"Definitely."

Sierra turned and grabbed a couple of bottles from the fridge. She slid one over to Dakota, who took a long swig.

"Are you back because it didn't pan out?"

"No, I'm back because I want to be. I discovered that songwriting is my passion. Not going on the road to perform."

Sierra's eyes widened. "Does Trace know?"

"No," she said crisply.

Sierra rolled her eyes. "Please don't tell me y'all are gonna play that stupid stubborn game? The man has been miserable without you."

"He was miserable before I came here, Sierra."

"Yeah. But not while you were here."

"Look, Trace made it clear that he didn't give a fig if I left forever."

"Oh, give me a break."

Dakota put her hands on the island and leaned forward. "It's true!"

"And you believed him?" Sierra raised her palms in the air.

"Why wouldn't I?"

Sierra gave her a stare. "Dakota Dunn, if your brain were made of dirt, you wouldn't have enough for a garden."

Dakota mulled that one over and said, "Oh. Well, that wasn't very nice."

"No, but damned true!"

"So what are you saying?"

Sierra took a slug of beer and then thumped down the bottle. "Did you ever think that he pushed you away so that you would chase your dream rather than stay with him? That he didn't want to hold you back from something you wanted—from a chance of a lifetime, no less? It tears him apart he had to give up what he loves, and he certainly wouldn't want you to. Come on, Dakota. Think about it. The man was being as unselfish as it gets!"

"He was so mean about it. He said I didn't fit in here."

"Of course. How else could he push you away? He knew exactly what he was doing."

"Oh, God. What if you're right?"

"Trust me. I'm right." She came around to Dakota's side of the island and put her hands on Dakota's shoulders. "It happened the way it should. You went to Nashville and made the decision for all the right reasons. You shouldn't have had to give up your dream, Dakota."

"I would have."

"Yeah, but now you can tell him that for sure and really mean it. Now you know what you really want. What you need. This is perfect. Go to him."

She put her hand to her chest. "I don't know if I'm brave enough to risk giving my heart to him a second time."

Sierra gave her shoulders a little shake. "Oh, quit with the sappy song lyrics and get your ass over to his cabin. He's probably in the hot tub."

"His leg has been bothering him?"

"Since you left. It's all about stress, tension. He needs you, Dakota. I really, truly believe he let you go because he loved you and not the other way around."

Dakota felt tears well up in her eyes. "If you're wrong, I'll kick your ass into next week."

Sierra half laughed, half sobbed, and then squeezed her hard. "Good one. Now go!"

27

Coming Home

Trace eased into the hot, bubbling water and sighed. His damned leg had been as tight as a drum all day. He stared down into the swirling water and thought about Dakota for what seemed like the millionth time that day, and slapped the surface. "Damn." Now here he was, sitting all alone once again in his hot tub, wishing she were with him. After a few minutes the jets ceased, and he leaned against the edge with another long sigh. He wanted to call Dakota and see if she was okay and ask how things were going.

But he didn't.

He actually tried a couple of times just that day to think of marina-related issues as an excuse to contact her, simply to hear the sound of her voice. Once he even picked up the phone and dialed her number. "God, how lame is that?" he voiced out loud, and then sat up straight and frowned. "What?" He cocked his head to the side, thinking he was hearing things when Dakota's voice seemed to softly float to him on the evening breeze.

She was singing.

Trace closed his eyes and listened to the love song and pictured her on her front porch, strumming her guitar. The tightness in his leg ceased and he relaxed. A smile spread across his face.

And then the music stopped. He sat up and waited, straining his ears, but heard nothing but the buzz of insects and the howl of a coyote.

Okay, he was officially losing his mind. He settled back into the water, closed his eyes, and sighed once more.

"Care if I join you?"

Trace's eyes opened wide and he shifted, slipped, and flopped around like a duck taking a bath.

"I'll take that as a yes." She arched one eyebrow and smiled.

Trace opened his mouth to say something but could only swallow hard when she started unbuttoning a western-cut plaid shirt tucked into frayed cutoffs. His heart hammered when she reached the last button, but instead of slipping out of the shirt, she stopped. Well, damn.

"You got any more longnecks in that cooler?"

"Yeah," he finally croaked. The shorts barely covered her butt, and when she bent over and fished around in the ice, he about swallowed his tongue. She used the tail of her shirt to twist off the cap and then tilted the brown bottle up and took a long pull from the beer.

"That hit the spot," she said, and licked her lips. She set the bottle down on the edge of the tub and slipped out of her shirt, revealing a shiny blue bikini bra. She took another drink of her beer, letting him look his fill before she shimmied out of her frayed cutoffs and kicked them to the side. "Here I come, cowboy."

When Trace watched Dakota, wearing a tiny blue bikini, ease into the tub, he went from his duck impression to a fish opening and closing his mouth as if gasping for air. Deciding he needed to appear calm, cool, and collected, he closed his mouth and cleared his throat. He rested his arms on the edge of the tub and struck what he hoped was a nonchalant it's-no-big-deal-that-you're-here pose, but one elbow slipped on the slick surface and he slid sideways into the water. He came up sputtering. "I meant to do that."

Dakota laughed softly. "Are we switching roles?"

Trace threaded his fingers through his wet hair, shoving it out of his eyes. "Just what's going on here, Dakota?"

"I'll cut to the chase. I love music. It is in my blood."

"I know."

"And you sent me away, thinking you would keep me from fulfilling my dreams if you asked me not to go."

Trace remained silent, not sure if he was ready to put his heart out there yet again.

"But it's songwriting that's my passion, not performing."

His heart beat harder, but he said, calmly, he hoped, "Okay."

"Trace, I realize now that you let me go chasing my dreams instead of holding me back when you knew I would have stayed had you asked me to."

Trace looked down at the water.

"Am I right?"

Trace hesitated, and then slowly lifted his head and looked at her across the shimmering surface. "Yes. And it was the single most difficult thing I have ever done. Bar none. And I've done some tough stuff in my day."

"You love me that much?" she asked softly.

"Yes," he answered quietly, firmly, and with conviction. "You know, when I was PBR World Champion, earning big purses and adored by fans, I thought that life was good. But you know what?"

"What?"

"It took me a while, but I figured it out. Fame is fleeting, Dakota. What we have here isn't. The money was fun but meaningless. But what I have with you . . ." he began, but then pulled her into his arms and kissed her the way he had been dreaming about for two solid weeks. When he finally pulled back, he repeated, "What I have with you . . ."

"Will last forever," she finished for him.

"Yes." He gently brushed her wet hair from her face. "Dakota, you've healed me from the inside out. You make me relax, laugh, and sooth away my aches and pains." He hesitated and then added, "And when I look in the mirror, my scar seems to fade—almost disappear."

"You know, I never really did see it when I looked at you." Dakota reached up and traced the scar with her fingertip. "I thought about you constantly while I was gone."

"Good," he said, and brought her fingertip to his mouth.

"And it ticked me off so much, on the way home I started writing a song called 'He's No Prince Charming.' "

"A song of revenge about me, huh?" Trace chuckled. "So you did find your inner kick-ass redneck."

She gave him a little splash. "Yes, and I like it," she teased, but then sobered. "Actually, what I've found is the confidence to live my life on my own terms. Do what's right for me. When I won the Miss Teen beauty pageant, I allowed others to tell me the songs I should sing, what I should wear, how much I should weigh, for goodness' sake! I hid my fears, my loneliness, and my sadness while doing what I was told to do instead of what I wanted to do. I pleased everyone else and never myself." She cupped his cheeks in her hands. "But, Trace, you gave me my wings, let me go when you could have told me what to do too. You gave me the power to decide for myself."

"I should have done it differently."

She shook her head. "You knew me well enough to realize that any other way, I would have stayed. You allowed me to find myself. But you know what else? The day that we smashed the spider together, you made me realize that it's okay to need someone too. I've wanted to stand on my own two feet for such a long time that I had to learn that it's okay to reach out to others for help. I want you, Trace, but I need you too."

"It feels good to be wanted, needed, loved."

Dakota nodded and tapped his chest. "For who we are and not what we do."

"I really do love you," he said quietly, and then kissed her softly.

"And I love you, Trace. This is where I belong."

"Me too," he said, and leaned in to kiss her again, but pulled back when he heard footsteps and frantic yelling. "What in the world?"

"Gil, get your mangy-ass sorry self back here!" Sierra shouted. "Grady, call your dog!"

"Gil!" Grady yelled, but a moment later the Australian shepherd bounded around the corner to the back deck. Upon seeing Dakota, he ran over to the hot tub, skidded to a furry stop, put his paws up on the edge, and licked Dakota's cheek.

"Gil!" Sierra rounded the bend in hot pursuit, followed closely by Grady.

"Sorry," Grady said. "Gil saw you earlier and went nuts. His little stub of a tail wagged, and he was off like a rocket. I think he heard your voice too and just had to find you."

"Hey, is that your kick-ass F-150 in your driveway?" Sierra asked, and jammed her thumb over her shoulder.

"Damn straight," Dakota replied, and gave Sierra a high five.

"You traded your bimmer for a pickup truck?" Trace asked with a shake of his head.

"Sure did, and I love it," she answered with a laugh. "I felt like I was queen of the road!"

"Nothin' sexier than a hot little number behind the wheel of a truck," Grady commented, and pulled Sierra to his side.

Trace leaned in closer to Dakota and said in her ear, "I agree."

"If you're lucky, maybe I'll take you for a ride," she whispered back, and then bent over and scratched behind Gil's ears. "So you missed me, Gil?"

Gil answered with another tongue licking.

"Gil! Down!" Grady snapped his fingers and sighed. "Yeah, Dakota, thanks a lot. Everything went to hell in a handbasket after you left. Sierra has been on the warpath, Gil's moped around lookin' for ya, and Trace bit everybody's head off that even came close to trying to talk to him. I tried to be the voice of reason, and you have to know that I wasn't too good in that role. I gotta tell ya, it sucked."

"Sorry, everybody." Dakota looped an arm around Trace's neck and gave him a kiss on the cheek.

"You should be," Trace said. "And you've got a lot of making up to do."

Grady raised his hands in question. "So you're back for good?"

"Yes."

Grady raised his hands higher and looked up at the sky. "Thank you, God!"

Dakota laughed. "You say that now, but wait until I find myself in another pickle. You might just eat those words."

Grady shook his head. "Never," he said to Dakota, and hugged Sierra close. "We all missed you."

"Thank you. It's good to be here. Group hug?" Dakota asked with a smile, and got a groan from everyone.

"Hell, no," Grady said. "Group splash!" He and Sierra kicked off their shoes and plopped into the hot tub, clothes and all. "Woo hoo!" Grady yelled, and the splashing began.

Dakota laughed until her sides hurt, and then hugged Trace. Yeah, it was good to finally be home.

"I'll get it, Daddy," I shout from where I'm washing the supper dishes.

"Okay, Jolie," he calls back from his workshop just off the kitchen. He's busy whittling Christmas ornaments for a craft show and I don't want to interrupt him. This year's drought hurt our tobacco crop, so what started out as a therapeutic hobby now brings in much-needed income. Another sharp rap at the front door has me grabbing a towel and hurrying through the living room to see who might be coming our way on such a cold night.

"Hold your horses," I grumble. Our farm is miles from town, so it's not as if we often have visitors just dropping in for social calls. After wiping my wet hands, I toss the dish towel over my shoulder and open the door. *Oh wow* rings in my head but doesn't reach my mouth. Now, I'm not usually one to be rendered speechless, but when I see who is on our doorstep, I get tongue-tied and flustered.

"Jolie Russell?" our visitor asks.

"Ughaaaa." Forgetting about my tongue-tied situation, I then try to respond but manage only this weird noise, which I then disguise as a sneeze. "Chu." Sometimes you just have to think on your feet.

"God bless you."

This time I'm smart enough to merely nod while rubbing my finger beneath my nose as if I really did sneeze.

"You are Jolie and your daddy is Wyatt Russell, correct?"

"Last time I checked."

He gives me a half grin. "Good. The name and address on your mailbox were faded and I wanted to be sure I hadn't taken a wrong turn in the dark. Cody Dean." He extends his hand and I give him a firm handshake just like my daddy taught me.

"H-hey there," I manage to sputter. Of course, like everybody else in Cottonwood, Kentucky, I'm already well aware of who he is. Cody, the elder son of Carl Dean, is back from his fancy Ivy League education to take over his daddy's company. The Dean family is like royalty here in Cottonwood, with Cody being the prince. I also know that Dean Development has been buying up farmland for subdivisions all over Cottonwood, and I suddenly get light-headed at the prospect of why Cody is paying us a visit, because I'm pretty sure it isn't to ask me on a date.

"Sorry to have stopped by unannounced, but may I come in?"

"Oh . . . why sure—where the hell are my manners?" I blurt out, and then wish my tongue had remained tied. "I mean, um, please, come on in," I amend softly, since I tend to shout when I get jittery, even when it's not necessary. With a smile that goes wobbly on me, I step aside for him to enter. As he passes me I get a whiff of expensive-smelling aftershave that makes me want to pant after him like a lovesick puppy. "Pop a squat," I offer, and gesture toward the sofa. "Um, I mean, have a seat." God, I suck at this.

"Thank you." Cody's tone is refined, but the hint of amusement in his blue eyes has my chin coming up a notch. Admittedly, I'm a bit lacking in social graces, having lost my mama at the tender age of ten. I'm more at home fishing and four-wheeling with guys than dressing up for dinner dates, not that shaking Cody's hand didn't give me a hot little tingle that traveled all the way to my toes. I might be a little rough around the edges, but I still have all my girl parts, and Cody Dean is making all of those particular areas stand up and take notice. But I remind myself that Cody Dean is here for a reason, but it sure isn't to romance me.

When his gaze sweeps the room, pride stiffens my backbone. Unlike him, we might not have much, but although everything is old and outdated, it's clean and as neat as a pin. I'm starting to get a little out of sorts as I watch him look around our humble home with what seems like open curiosity.

"What brings you here?" My blunt question carries slightly more bite than intended.

Cody's dark eyebrows shoot up at my tone. "A business proposition," he answers smoothly. "Is your father home, Jolie?"

Oh, holy crap. I tamp down the don't-mess-with-me attitude that tends to land me in hot water, putting a smile back on my face. "Why yes, he is. I'll get him. Um, make yourself at home."

"Thanks." He inclines his neatly cropped head and sits down on the sofa. I hope he thinks it's an expensive antique instead of an ancient hand-me-down, but then beat myself up for caring. Cottonwood is a fairly small town, but it has a large social gap between old Southern money and dirt-poor farmers. Carl Dean has been known to be hard-nosed in his business dealings, but it's been rumored that Cody is trying to soften the family reputation for ruthlessness.

My knees are a little shaky as I walk toward the doorway, but I suddenly remember my manners. "Would you like something to drink? Sweet tea?" I'm about to add crumpets just for fun, but I'm not sure what a crumpet is and I'm quite sure we don't have any. About the best I could do is Oreos, and that's if Daddy hasn't eaten them all. Well, okay, I might have had one or two, starting with the icing first. The finer points of Southern hospitality must be in me somewhere, but because we so rarely have visitors, except for those who come for outdoor activities like four-wheeling, fishing, and such, I have few opportunities to practice those finer points. Still, I'm trying. "Anything?"

"No, thank you," he says, but then adds, "On second thought, a bottle of water would be nice."

Well, la-di-da. "Um, all I have is plain old water from the cistern." My daddy thinks that buying bottled water is the dumbest damned thing ever imposed upon the American public, and I'm pretty much with him on that one. When Cody hesitates I add, "We're fresh out of Perrier, but the tank is clean."

His mouth twitches as if he isn't sure if he should smile or not, but then he waves a hand at me. "That's okay. I'm fine. Don't go to any trouble."

"Oh, it's no bother." Of course I'm going to bring him a glass of water just to be ornery. I'm bad that way, "I'll go find Daddy."

I walk slowly out of the room, wishing I were wearing something better than worn jeans and a George Strait T-shirt, but when I get to the kitchen I scurry into the workshop. "Daddy!" I say in what is a whisper for me but what is a normal tone for most folks. "Guess who's sittin' on our very own sofa?" Daddy blows sawdust off an angel, but when he opens his mouth to make a guess I blurt, "Cody Dean!" *Dean* comes out so high-pitched that our old mutt, Rufus, lifts his head and whines.

"Ya don't say." Daddy frowns and looks down at the angel with a critical eye.

"He wants to talk to you!" I tell him.

When Daddy doesn't move, I reach over and tug him by his flannel shirt. "Hurry," I urge, and all but drag him from the room. Although I love the farmhouse, I hate raising tobacco, the very crop that's responsible for the death of my mama. "Just a second." I pause to draw a glass of water from the faucet and make a mental bet with myself as to whether Cody will drink it.

When we enter the living room, Cody politely stands up and shakes my daddy's hand. "Nice to meet you, Mr. Russell. May I have a few minutes of your time?"

Daddy nods, but I see the stubborn set of his jaw and my hope plummets. He eases down into the overstuffed chair while I march over and hand Cody the glass of water.

"Thank you," he says, and while looking at me drains half the contents before setting it on the scarred coffee table. He gives me an I'm-on-to-you smile, and I can't help but grin back at him. His smile deepens, causing a little dimple in his left cheek, and I have to grab the back of Daddy's chair for support. I hang out with guys all the time, and while I've been sweet on one or two of them, none have ever turned me inside out with a mere smile.

"So, what brings you here?" Daddy asks, even though we suspect the reason. Rufus, who must sense the excitement in the air, sits back on his haunches and we all three look expectantly at Cody.

After clearing his throat, Cody leans forward and rests his elbows on his knees. "There's no reason to beat around the bush, Mr. Russell. I'd like to make you an offer for your land."

"I'm not interested," Daddy tells him.

What? "Daddy, hear him out," I say.

Cody shoots me a grateful glance. "I'm prepared to offer three million."

When my knees give way I grab on to the back of the chair so hard that my fingernails dig into the nubby fabric.

"Sorry, Cody," Daddy says.

Oh no! A little whimper escapes me.

"Three and a half million," Cody counters, and I breathe a sigh of relief. Who knew that Daddy could bargain like this? I arch an eyebrow in an expression that says, *See, we're not as stupid as we look.*

"Money isn't the issue, son. This here land is where I lived with my dear wife, Rosie. I'll never leave it."

Oh . . . emotion suddenly clogs my throat. I can't argue with his reasoning, but I also have to think that Mama somehow has a hand in this sudden windfall. Color me crazy, but I tend to feel her presence now and then.

Cody steeples his fingers and for a long moment remains silent, but then says, "You don't have to leave your land. I'll set aside your plot and you can keep several of the wooded acres as well. Now, you *would* have to rebuild. Mr. Russell, this isn't going to be your average subdivision. I'm proposing a gated community with upscale homes. I might add that this would bring in much-needed tax dollars to Cottonwood."

Daddy shakes his head. "Who could afford homes like that around these parts?"

"Kentucky horse money. I've done my homework. There are plenty of wealthy Kentuckians. These homes will sell quickly. Of course, we would build your house first."

Daddy slowly runs a hand down his face and then looks back at me. "Jolie? What do you think?"

I kneel down beside the chair and put a hand on his arm. "Daddy, I know that Mama would want this for you. It seems like a good thing all around." I squeeze his arm. "It's okay to do this," I assure him, and then hold my breath.

My daddy's eyebrows draw together and he gazes down at me for a moment before looking over at Cody. "Son, do we have a few days to think this through?"

"I'm sorry, Mr. Russell. I have other property in mind as well and time is of the essence."

Daddy sighs. "Well then, would you give us a minute or two?"

"Yes, sir, of course," Cody answers with a little less determination and a bit more understanding.

"All righty then." After standing up, Daddy takes my hand gives my arm a tug. "We'll be back in a bit."

"Take your time," Cody says.

"Thank you," Daddy responds. I'm suddenly very proud of my father. He might not run in the same circles as Carl Dean, but my daddy is a hardworking man of honor and conviction, and they don't come any better. I'm irritated that Cody is forcing us into a decision this quickly and I wonder if this is a business tactic to put the hat on us and seal the deal. But when I toss a questioning glance his way, his dark head is bent toward the floor and he seems to be deep in thought.

Reaching the doorway, I look over my shoulder. As if Cody feels my gaze upon him, he suddenly looks up. When our eyes meet I feel an unexpected jolt of heat. His own eyes widen a fraction and I wonder if he feels it too. But then I tell myself I'm crazier than a June bug in May and quickly turn my head.

My tummy is doing flip-flops as I follow Daddy and Rufus into the workshop. What had begun as an ordinary winter night suddenly feels surreal. Trying to clear my head, I inhale a sharp breath that smells of sawdust and paint and then turn my attention to my father.

"Jolie-girl, what should we do?" He sits down in his whittling chair and rests his elbows on his knees.

"Oh, Daddy, don't get me wrong. I love this farm. But I hate the constant struggle and worry on your shoulders." I hesitate and then add, "And you know how I feel about the tobacco." Lung cancer from smoking took my mother's life. She was so beautiful and vibrant. Watching her suffer haunts me to this day.

He closes his blue eyes and swallows hard while absently scratching Rufus behind the ears. "Daddy." I put my hand on his shoulder. "You deserve this."

After a long sigh my father looks up as if he's asking my mama for guidance and then, as if getting his answer, nods slowly. "Let's do this, baby girl."

My smile trembles a bit when he stands up and pulls me into his arms.

"You're sure?"

"Yes," he answers gruffly, and then kisses the top of

my head. "Now let's go tell Mr. Cody Dean the good news."

Entering the living room, Daddy looks Cody Dean straight in the eye, extends his hand, and says, "Son, you have a deal."

Cody smiles and grasps Daddy's hand. "Congratulations, Mr. Russell." He glances at me and inclines his head. "And you too, Jolie. I'll have the paperwork drawn up tomorrow, but I trust your handshake is binding."

And just like that, we're millionaires.

Also Available from
LUANN MCLANE

"An author to watch."
—*New York Times* bestselling author
Lori Foster

A Little Less Talk and a Lot More Action

Macy's chance for love is slipping from her fingers. College football coach Luke Carter has a penchant for hot-bodied babes, not curvy hairdressers like Macy. And some big-time schools may be luring him away. Then a country singing star's hair emergency turns into a big break for Macy.

Making it in Nashville boosts Macy's confidence, but when Luke interviews for a job at a local university, she'll have to put up or shut up—or lose him forever.

Available wherever books are sold or at penguin.com